Storm Chaser

Ariel
Dominelli

CITY OWL
PRESS

STORM CHASER

CITY OWL PRESS
www.cityowlpress.com

Cover Design by Ariel Dominelli. All stock photos licensed appropriately.

Edited by Lisa Green.

For information on subsidiary rights, please contact the publisher at info@cityowlpress.com.

Print Edition ISBN: 978-1-64898-379-5

Digital Edition ISBN: 978-1-64898-380-1

Printed in the United States of America

For everyone who ever let me talk their ear off when I could only get words out that way.

Especially Scott, MK, Maya, Katie, Dylan, Nick, and Amber (way back when). I promise to keep putting my stories into books and save 4 am chats for other people's novels or swords.

CHAPTER 1
THE SHOT
"I WAS BORN AS AN ACT OF
JUSTICE."

XÓCHITL RAMIREZ | JULY 14

"The National Powered Protection Department has issued a severe warning for this area. Please shelter in place."

A discordant chime played over the truck's speakers before the message looped.

"They blockaded most of the roads, but I think I can cut through this alley to get close enough." I tapped the GPS display with my finger where the unmarked alley might get me past the roadblocks. The PPD's automated warning continued to urge us to turn back. The department's angry, birdlike screeches rang on all our devices. Leo's face was grim. I geared up for the upcoming conflict, tightening straps on my protective vest and taking inventory of the contents of my pockets; my medical card, press ID, extra lens, and phone were all accounted for. Once I had on enough layers to broil under the sun, I looped my camera around my neck.

"One photo only, through the fence, you can prop it between the chain-link. Take the long zoom," Leo demanded.

The long zoom would be too difficult to get lined up. However, I nodded in false agreement and attached the wide-angle lens.

"I need at least ten shots to get one worth money," I said laughing.

"Through the fence," he said, sounding like our dad as he scolded me and eyed the camera.

"I'll jump the fence and get one good one, then pop back real quick."

I could feel my grin bubbling to the surface, a tell I was lying. I'm sure he caught it.

This was Apex, the big one, *the* hero of the world, a god among men. Even a half-decent photo of him not produced by his agency was worth a month's rent. I had never caught him prior, not for lack of trying a dozen times that year. I missed him by seconds last time, only to see the wreckage left behind in his wake. All I captured were craters and scorch marks; never had I laid eyes or lens on him. I needed to look at his face and find what "goodness" was there. For fifty years, he had been celebrated almost universally. I had to see why, even though I knew it wasn't true. I thought of Mom and balled my hands into fists.

The truck stopped suddenly, enough to jolt me from my thoughts. Leo had his hand over his face under his glasses, brow furrowed.

"Welp, you're gonna die," he decided as I opened my door. Poor choice of words if he thought it might be true.

"Probably," I said, still delighted. I stepped out of the passenger seat of the cab and onto the ground.

As I went to leave, he called out, "JUST ONE PHOTO!"

"Yes, *Dad*, a good photo."

I waved my hand over my shoulder, looking back for a last time. The truck, decorated with a bright peach and mint logo of a smiling cactus, seemed at odds with the dingy backstreets it was currently inhabiting.

In the cab, Leo had pulled his mustard-yellow beanie over his eyes, hiding his face and hair. The sound of an explosion grabbed my attention, and I turned to see smoke on the opposite side of the alleyway. I ran toward the excitement and climbed to the top of the fence, my foot finding purchase on the chain and padlock, which were doing a terrible job of keeping me out. I set my viewfinder to my face while mounted on top of the fence, but still nothing was clear. The passage must have been two hundred feet long or more, but only ten feet wide, like a canyon between two large apartments that typically gathers dumpsters and trash bags.

Maybe I can get a good photo. Good but not great.

Another explosion blasted through the air, causing a ringing in my ears and nearly toppling me from my perch. I jumped blindly into the obscured alley.

A concussive blast tore through the area just as my feet hit the pavement. When the smoke cleared, a man came into view, floating ten feet over me. His cape glowed from the light outside this narrow alley, its aura silhouetting his broad form. The white outfit always read as cheap and cheesy in the movies or comics, but now, in person, it was pristine and ethereal against the smog around him. My camera made whirring sounds as I raised it, trying to focus on the figure overhead.

I got two, maybe three clicks of the shutter before I even saw the robot charging me. The copper-toned metal man was topped with a large CRT TV screen where his head should be; it flashed an exclamation point in orange text followed by a simple message: "Run!"

Fear jabbed at me. I should have told Leo I loved him before I left. I snapped another photo of the robot, my camera raised in the reflection of his metallic frame. I clicked as seconds dragged into ages. A blinding white triangle at the center of Apex's chest started to glow. The air hummed with power as debris floated around me, weightlessly as though we were deep below water. A blast of light hit the robot's back. Then, gravity returned with a wave of heat and shrapnel, and I was flung backward.

I hit the ground. My elbow moved in a way it wasn't meant to, my hand still clasping the camera. I saw the last shot displayed in a cracked preview before the LED screen went black, and I smiled. Everything became heavy. I could've been a pincushion filled with a million tiny pieces of robot and concrete. The pain was almost enough to keep me awake as I murmured what might have been my last words.

"Got it."

CHAPTER 2
ROBOT RUN

"PEOPLE CANNOT TAKE WHAT
BELONGS TO THE GODS."

XÓCHITL RAMIREZ | JULY 17

"Hello and good morning, New York! I'm sitting here with Xóchitl Ramirez."

The talk show host said my name correctly; maybe she had practiced. I felt confident that this would go well.

"Hello!" I said a bit too loudly.

I waved with my uninjured arm; the attempt at casual and natural movement had become increasingly stiff and forced.

"It's being called a once-in-a-lifetime photograph defining the age of the heroes. Rarely do we ever get a glimpse of a real Powered altercation. How did you do it?"

She was trying to put me at ease, but flattery and casual posture couldn't help me feel less out of depth. I was not typically the face in photographs.

"By getting too close," I answered.

A pre-recorded laugh track played over the speakers behind me as I lifted my cast and sling to emphasize my point. A cameraman yawned. I often wondered if that was the job I should have been doing, shooting the same few angles of the same painted faces day in and day out.

.

At least my camera wouldn't get crushed regularly.

"This isn't your first venture into the glamorous life of superheroes, is it?" she asked. "Your blog, *Storm Chaser*, has been gaining notoriety as of late." As she gestured to a blank screen between us, I looked and wondered what photo they would put over the green rectangle. I hoped it wasn't the one of Artemis that was being used in PSAs around the city like a propaganda painting.

"Your exposés on Powered individuals always have such clever insights. Should we expect a story linked to this photo as well?"

"Unfortunately, the only two who really know what happened there were the ones in the shot," I answered. "That's why I do this. We don't often know what Powered people are actually up to. Guesses and lies flood every part of our day, from action movies to comics to the news... I just try to sift through the bullshit for everyone."

The cameraman jumped up as if shocked and panned away from my face to the reporters. Apparently, the term "bullshit" wasn't allowed. *Whoops.*

"We will be back after this short commercial break." Her face froze in a perfect plastic smile that lasted too long to be authentic. "We try to keep it light on this program and family-appropriate, and we support our caped heroes on this network," she snapped at me in a whisper, though it was loud enough to be picked up by her mic. She adjusted her dress and hair. I looked down at my lap. A pencil skirt and a nice blouse were supposed to make me feel professional, but even after a stylist took over my hair and makeup, I looked like my head had been edited onto the body of someone else. I never felt cut out for interviews; someone with people skills probably wouldn't do what I do. It was part of the job though. If I promoted my blog more, I sold more photos and maybe folks actually read the articles if I was lucky. I tapped my heel against the ground in front of the chair as we were counted back in from break.

"And we are back with the wonderful Xóchitl," she exclaimed

with rehearsed enthusiasm. "What's your next story? What do you have in store for us?"

I knew I should have made an effort not to offend her. She was just trying to do her job. "I mean, of course, I'd love to know the origin of these powers," I said. "For sixty years now, some people have randomly gained these amazing abilities. Last week, Artemis had a building dropped on her and came out without a scratch! With figurative gods walking around me, I can't help but wonder…why her? Why Apex? Why any of them? Half of them aren't even good people, let alone heroes."

"I want to know how she hasn't aged in twenty years," the host spoke in a rush, trying to cut me off. "Artemis, if you're watching, please share your skin care routine."

She smiled and waved her hand in a familiar gesture.

Right, I was supposed to keep it light.

The canned laughter returned, and I watched that same exhausted cameraman pick his nose. The rest of the interview passed in a haze. I gave up speaking honestly and let the woman with the perfect smile take the lead on every bit of witless dialogue. I fought mild frustration with gritted teeth. She signed off the interview by saying she looked forward to speaking to me again.

Once the cameras were off, she left the studio without a word. I sat in the too-big chair for a moment, wondering if I looked like a child or just felt like one.

A few hours later, I returned to the food truck with Leo. "Why even have me on your stupid show if you don't want to hear what I have to say?" I kicked the truck's tire, almost losing balance in the heels I wore for the interview.

"Your photo of Apex is on the cover of every newspaper in the city—she had to interview you. It's her job," he said, leaning out the service window of the café truck to hand me a too-sweet iced latte.

I plopped onto the concrete next to the truck, carefully staying in the wheel's shadow where it was reasonably cool. If my puncture-proof vest was too hot for summer, wearing pantyhose was hell. I pulled my laptop out of my backpack.

"This is why I self-publish," I said, opening the device and loading up my camera roll from my SD card.

"I thought you hated money and wanted to live in protest without making a cent," he remarked, before turning his attention to a guest in a red shirt waiting patiently. He took the order and disappeared into the truck; the sound of espresso and milk steaming followed as my brother made his money. I clicked through the roll of photos until it reached the winning shot.

"I sold the photo, didn't I?" I said, holding the laptop screen toward my brother with a giant smile. He didn't look up from his work. I could hear a metal scoop cracking through an ice bin, followed by the sputtering of a nitro tank. I held the pose for a while until my one working arm got tired.

"That was barely enough to cover your medical debt and get you a new camera," he responded a full minute later. This was how we talked most days—stilted, partial phrases passed between orders and picked up with no missed beats. Inevitably, someone in line cleared their throat, and Leo apologized for the delay in an alien version of his voice.

He slung coffee at strangers for the next few hours while I watched people and worked.

I had even worse trouble focusing than usual. I cycled through the photos while playing thought experiments.

Why was Apex chasing the robot? Why was the robot telling me to run? Did the robot mean to defend me from the blast, or was it a careful touch of Apex's that kept me alive? I mean, he shoots lasers—they are known for precision. He must have carefully aimed around me. Hell, I'll never find out. I should be looking for a new story, not obsessing over old ones.

I looked through the photos again and again, as though they could provide any kind of answer. When they didn't, I closed my laptop and stared at the sidewalk.

I'd always been good at pattern recognition—it was probably a byproduct of my mind being in twenty places at once. As I lost focus again, I entertained myself by finding the fashion and food trends of people walking around me.

There was a rise in the popularity of brick-red shirts. They might have been from a local designer. My stomach also noticed the soft-serve ice cream in some kind of fish-shaped waffle cone from a neighboring food truck, tempting me to spend money I didn't really have. I sipped my now room-temperature drink as a poor consolation.

Around one o'clock, Leo's cold brew ran out. As he plopped a small cactus magnet that said "Sorry, Sold Out" over the price, nearly everyone in line left. I went back to the computer, searching for used and discounted cameras. Fortunately, I still had most of my lenses, so I didn't have to replace my kit completely. I was about to hit "Order" when Leo tapped my shoulder. Looking around, I realized the café was buttoned up, the shutters of the service windows were closed, and the menu board had already been hauled inside.

"Off the truck. I need to shift."

Leo offered me his hand, and I stood up, then took a significant step away. I drank my now-warm, once-iced latte and watched him. He held his hands out in front of him as if solving a Rubik's Cube only he could see.

As he did this, I noticed how much older he looked. Only a few years senior to me, the long days of work and maybe the use of his gift had added a hollowness to his cheeks and bags below his eyes. His once-trendy haircut had grown out and was haphazardly hidden under a hat. There was a sound of paper tearing and a soft click as something unseen fell into place. The food truck stayed the same on the outside: the cactus smiled, and the phone number and website remained printed, but the inside was now replaced with a functional tiny home.

Our truck's inside was cool, cozy, and dim. It was permeated with a soft amber light as if it was always the golden hour. The necessary pieces of furniture were all neatly stacked and tucked away to leave as much floor space as possible. This whole place was Leo'ss engineering and building. His powers couldn't create objects. He could only tuck them away and pull them out again. Pockets, he called them. We built desks and lofts for months and made this new home for ourselves with our hands.

There were three different interiors Leo created. The food truck was always bright and cool in tone as though it was midday, even in the middle of the night. Home was the warm orange glow of dusk, while a version we kept for storing supplies glowed a sickly green. Two summers had passed since we sold the hatchback and moved into the food truck. This was a place for us to be ourselves, living in peaceful honesty without the judgment of our family.

Leo was my brother, but not by blood. When my mother passed, we thought my dad would return from his work, but he never did. Leo's family took me in after that. I spent the end of high school at their table, in their home, learning to speak Tagalog and how to be part of a new family. I moved out when I was seventeen after I had gotten into college. It was too much to ask for any more of their time.

Leo used to visit me in my dorm, and we constantly argued about our family and how they loved us or about how they were good people. I told him he should just be himself, and they would love him...after all, they always wanted a son. I argued with him for months to come out to them, but I was wrong. They disowned him. He said it wasn't my fault, but I had hounded him for months about it. I may not have caused the rift, but I had quickened the tempo.

It was never a conversation. If he lost his family, so did I. A simple fact. I now had a smaller family and a smaller home—built by amateurs, sure, but perfect in every way.

"You drive, I'm done," he said, half-asleep already as he fell onto his pillow. Space transition seemed to have gotten easier on him, but food service in the hot, sticky summer had not. I buckled up in the back of the truck and set my laptop on the desk.

"In a bit, I'm still scrounging for money. How'd the café do today?"

"Enough to buy milk tomorrow," he said, rolling over and kicking off his worn Chucks into the narrow space behind my chair.

I scrolled through the photos, again hoping maybe there'd be another good one…or at least, something middling.

Click, a blurry mess from hopping the fence.

Click, the ground.

Click, a cape corner.

Click, the automaton running, his face a scramble of code and an exclamation point. Studying the image, the robot was quite the feat of engineering, showing off a retro-futuristic build with copper panels hammered into place over unique and complex features I could only make out while the explosion happened and in the debris.

Click, just his hand. Three metal fingers wrapped around a tube of some kind with a label on it.

Click, nothing.

I leaned back in my chair, staring at the van's ceiling. My body suddenly felt heavy, as though the literal weight of our bills was stacked on me.

Breathe, I reminded myself.

I sat back up and examined my cracked and destroyed camera. It looked like it had been run over by the truck. The display screen had fractured in a deep spiderweb pattern with little slivers of glass missing. The top was caved in. It was more like a crumpled soda can than a camera at this point.

Luckily, the SD card still worked or this would have been for nothing. I sighed and turned my attention back to the laptop.

Click, the shot: the good one, the 10k-that-mostly-went-to-the-local-hospital shot.

Apex loomed over the robot, light shooting from the center of his chest in a beam, an explosion to backlight the robot's remains.

Click, a blurry image of him looking down at the broken

camera. He was not merciful, at least not in this frame. At this single indignant moment, he was no longer the pinnacle of mankind but a beast on the hunt. His jaw was clenched, his brows were furrowed, and even his perfectly slicked-back hair now had loose strands falling onto his forehead. I knew he brought me to the hospital and saved me, but the camera captured a moment of disgust when he first saw I was there in the alley with him. It felt like he was seeing me *through* this photo, inconveniently in danger.

There was a pain in my chest, and I realized I'd been holding my breath.

Click, and I shut the laptop. I rolled back on the chair and walked over to the cab. Sitting in the driver's seat, Leo was snoring. The low, rhythmic, grumbling breaths reminded me I was where I belonged, safe and sound. It was at that moment the question I had been circling all day dawned on me.

"How *did* my camera get broken?" I asked out loud. It had been damaged. Sure, the screen had been cracked, but it was now nearly flat, as though put through a mechanical press.

That last shot was taken when I was only half-conscious after the blast.

Why? Why would he ruin my camera?

I didn't realize where I was going at first as I started driving, and then I found myself back in that alley, rolling to a gentle stop. Some haphazard remnants of police tape hung off the fence, illuminated by a security light from a few paces away. The bright yellow was a small reminder of what had happened here, a Band-Aid over the scorched remains of a fight.

I got out of the truck. Even though the sun was down, it was still unbearably hot and muggy. I walked through the thick fog to the fence and put my good arm up to grab some of the chain-links over my head. I shrugged out of my sling and put my hand on the chain despite my cast. I might have been able to hop the fence again, but it would be a struggle. While I was working up the courage, a heavy sigh came from behind me.

"Please don't hurt yourself," my brother said, still groggy with exhaustion.

"I think I'm missing something," I said, still bracing for the climb.

"Walk around, dumbass."

"I thought you were asleep," I shot back, embarrassed at how easy the solution was.

I would have thought of walking around...eventually. I shrugged the sling back on and circled the building. As I did, a strange movement caught the corner of my eye. There must have been some kind of infestation.

"Glad I got a head injury where there's a freaking rat problem."

"I did warn you."

I rolled my eyes at him and continued scanning my surroundings, running my hand over the brick. The rough bits of metal sticking out of the grout were cool for such a hot day.

The alley looked different now. Maybe this was what our hero saw the night he defeated the metal man. I examined the soot marks all around the area. Leo had his hands in his pockets as he rolled a metal pipe with his foot. His face scrunched up in repulsion at the smell of the dumpster.

"Why are we digging through trash again?" he asked.

"I thought I saw something, going through the photos, but I'm not sure."

I pulled out my phone and squatted down to look in the dark below the dumpster where I had seen the movement of something earlier. The rough debris from the fight bit into the bruises on my legs as I lay down to peer deeper. My breath caught as I spotted a glittering silver cylinder in the light of my flashlight app. I pressed my face against the concrete before reaching as far as my good arm could go. I was barely able to graze it with my fingertips. My shoulder strained as I stretched out flat on the pavement. Finally, I was able to inch the thing toward me.

I knelt up to examine it. It appeared to be a small metal capsule with etched lettering that read, "Sample 0021, McCalister, Maxwell 07/14/1926."

"That's Apex's old civilian name," I said, turning the capsule over in my hand.

I sat up and unscrewed the lid. A small vial of blood fell out into my palm. Leo leaned over me, and I handed him the metal outer shell. As he turned it over in his hand, studied it, and then reattached the lid, a faint orange light started blinking from one end.

"Is it gonna explode?" he asked, panic seeping into his voice as it began to beep in time with the orange blinks.

"It doesn't seem likely. If it had explosives, they probably would have gone off when the whole bot detonated." As I spoke, something shot out of the wall, shaking free of the crumbling mortar between bricks before flying at Leo's hand. I jumped, startled by the movement. Leo screamed and tossed the metal casing into the air, covering his head with his arms. I stretched out my good arm to barely catch the vial, stumbling and nearly falling back to the ground in the process.

Something rolled from the underside of the dumpster: two metal bolts, each with an orange C on the top. I watched transfixed as they bounced toward the center of the alley, defying gravity as they began assembling themselves into an improbable machine. A few bits and bobs shuffled over and attached, arranging themselves in a quick and unnatural manner. All the pieces joined to form a fragmented robotic hand with two fingers and a thumb. After the bits clicked into place, the thing launched itself toward the case.

Leo tried to stomp on the robotic hand, to no avail, before sprinting out of the alley toward the street. The robotic hand magnetically snatched the metal cylinder from mine as it scurried off down the alley on two fingers. More glass and metal shards oozed from the nooks and crannies of the buildings around us and moved to rejoin the rest of the machine. Soon, a complete hand had formed, and the wrist was sprinting away at an impossible pace; even some of its familiar-looking copper shell returned. I started to pursue it but stumbled, bouncing my shoulder off the wall before clumsily chasing the hand. Leo yelled something as I chased after it from the alley, but the context of the scream was too hard to decipher as I chased around the next corner.

I pocketed the fragile glass blood sample and prayed I could remain on my feet well enough to protect it. Ahead of me, a robotic forearm attached itself to the metal wrist, and the once-nimble hand started to drag the rest of its arm behind it. My run slowed to a walk to match its pace, yelling at the few sidewalk pedestrians to clear the way. After a few blocks, Leo caught up with the truck. I climbed in just as the arm gained an elbow.

Some integral pieces of the robot zipped in from another direction. Eventually, a shining torso assembled and began crawling with the two newly repaired arms. People shuffled out of the way as it dragged itself across the concrete. We followed with our hazard lights on for miles, creeping along behind it.

"Where do you think it's going?" Leo asked.

"Wish I knew. We could meet it there, stop and get breakfast, take a nap maybe." I sighed as a person blared their horn and swerved to the wrong side of the street to get around us.

At a quarter to two in the morning, we left the city as the robot crawled its way through the midtown tunnel. People were far more upset about the traffic disruption than the slowly reassembling wonder of technology. It had legs at this point, but it still shambled more than walked. Because the knees were still forming, the left foot dangled at an odd, limp angle below the rest of it. Wires jutted out in various directions, forming lumps and nests around its no-longer-smooth joints. We stayed alongside it with our hazards clicking, getting honked at and flipped off. "This can't be good for business," Leo said, waving apologetically and nodding.

A little sports car zipped around us so fast, it looked like they were going to hit the robot in front of the car. I reached over to beep the horn in front of Leo.

"We have to be the most hated people in the city," he said, shoulders dropping.

It was another grueling hour until the robot could run, but once it started, it was faster than any man. Its heavy footsteps left cracks in the pavement as it sprinted down the highway.

At four-thirty, we arrived at a broken-down brick building with severe burn damage and a large, foreboding iron gate. The robot ran through the gate, making gaps in itself to slide effortlessly through, then reassembled on the other side. The shiny copper plates scattered our headlights through the front yard, illuminating the gnarled overgrown garden.

"That looks bad," Leo said, squinting behind his glasses into the darkness.

I tied my hair up; it was an ordeal because of the stupid cast.

"Can't be that bad. The robot wasn't even scared," I retorted, trying to steady my hands. If I showed hesitation now, I knew Leo would spiral out.

"I don't know if robots can feel fear, Xóchi," Leo started. "Wait, what are you doing? Are you kidding me? You're going to blindly charge in there? It's probably private property! Sun's up in an hour or two. Please, let's just wait!"

"But he forgot this."

I flashed the vial, and Leo's hand slipped between his glasses and his face to pinch the bridge of his nose.

"You're still all beat up from the last stupid thing you did. Do you need to try a new one so fast? You won't be able to sell any photos you take—you don't even have a camera!"

I flashed my phone in response.

He continued to protest as I put on my coat and tightened my boots. He backed the truck around so that the top of the box was parallel to the gate.

Leo pulled out his phone and quickly swiped at it for a few seconds.

"Google says this is Nikola Čapek's old lab. An explosion

closed it down after it killed the owner and fifteen other employees in 1979."

"Ooh, ghost scientists, that's a new one," I laughed.

I grabbed a flashlight as I got out of the cab.

"I am more worried this place won't be structurally sound than I am of ghost scientists... I'm also worried about whether the robot has guns," he said.

"If I die, tell Dad I love him."

I rolled my lousy shoulder and closed the door.

"Which dad? Mine or yours?" he shouted after me.

"The good one!"

I circled the truck, awkwardly climbing the ladder with one arm still slung up. I squinted at the building, and now, with the headlights turned away, I was barely making out the silhouette of the collapse. I could scarcely see the ground below as the morning fog started rolling in. I walked to the opposite side of the truck, ran two steps, then jumped over the gate into the dark of the garden below.

I stood on wobbly legs and checked my pocket where the glass vial was. There was no broken glass, and thankfully, no new broken bones either. I checked behind me to see the truck glowing slightly against the woods on the other side of the gate.

No turning back now.

Flashlight on and flickering, I walked forward toward the decrepit building. I caught a glimpse of an old security camera following me and wondered if it was linked to the robot or not. The front door was open, but it creaked as I walked through. The hairs on my neck stood on end as my footsteps echoed around me in a hallway that no longer had a ceiling. Broken photos lay scattered over the floor, and ivy trailed down the wall, mixed with mold. I followed the breadcrumbs of loose, rolling robot debris to a security room with a wall of CRT TVs. In front of them sat an ancient man in a wheelchair. Standing next to him was the robot, presently completely assembled. The man's skin and hair were an uncomfortable shade of green in the light of the old screens. A voice croaked out to me as I stood in the doorway.

"Hello, Ms. Ramirez. You must have questions."

"It's what I do. Ask questions, that is," I stammered as I circled around. If this is where the robot was going, then it must work for him. Or his partner? Or just remote-controlled like a two-legged indestructible drone meets a phlebotomist.

My eyes scanned the room but kept wandering back to the recently reassembled robot. it now had the big screen for a face like before, this time displaying a reflection of the room from an alternative perspective.

"Then ask," he said.

He reached beside him for a brittle, antique teacup with the ease of a man much younger.

"Why do you want Apex's blood?"

"Maxwell has been a patient of mine for over seventy years."

"He didn't seem to want you to have his blood, or work with your, erm, colleague? Does he know he's a patient of yours?" The lab around us hardly looked functional. I didn't know the net worth of Apex, but I could safely assume he could afford a doctor who didn't operate out of a ruin.

"His illness took his mind many years ago, and he stopped willingly participating in treatment. But a cure must be found. No one so mad should be so powerful," he said as he sipped his tea. "He was a good man, once."

I doubted that this was true, that an old man cracked a secret that top minds had surely been working on for years, though I still held on to a bit of hope.

"A...cure? F-for...powers?"

The man nodded at me calmly, as if he hadn't just threatened the most powerful being in existence out loud.

"I'm very close, child, so very close."

"Why not go through legitimate channels? Surely, there are thousands of people who would pay good money. Then you could work in a real lab with less of a...Scooby Doo atmosphere," I said.

The man's laugh sounded more like a wheeze.

"It would fall into the wrong hands or be destroyed, just like last time."

The robot's screen flashed a newspaper article about this building exploding forty years ago, and I realized this was all intentional. I had stumbled on the lab hidden behind a fake death.

"You're Nikola Čapek? That would make you...well over one hundred years old. Wouldn't curing your powers...kill you? Strange you treat it as an illness. It seems to have saved your life."

What a strange, slow suicide.

"There are worse things than dying. My daughter deserved a cure; she was so little, and she lost control. She deserved a full life," he said. "I'm so close to a cure now. I nearly have it. I just need the blood."

The man held his withered palm toward me, pleading eyes warped behind thick, round glasses.

"I'm sorry for your loss, sir," I whispered to him, knowing how useless and limp that phrase was, how it had always been sung in rounds after grief in a hundred voices. For a moment, I hated myself for adding to the chorus. In my pocket, I held the small vial tight.

"I lost people too. I get it, I do. I also dedicate my life to that loss, but experimenting on others...there has to be a better way."

I caught my reflection in the lenses. My eyes watered a little. Some of the makeup from the interview was still present; the foundation they used was too light for me. Tears left dark trails in their wake.

Is this right? People die from uncontrolled powers. If they could be cured, how many lives would be saved? Mom might still be here...

My nails dug into my palm around the vial.

Could such a small thing really change so much?

I started to pull it out of my pocket when, suddenly, the robot charged at me. The blow knocked me back, and I lost my grip on the vial. I didn't even hear it hit the ground. Weightlessness came over the lab; litter flitted around me, papers and ivy leaves fluttering like birds. I recognized that humming sound; I knew what was coming. The roof crashed as it gave way to a laser. There was an explosion, and I felt metal pressing around me on all sides.

Not this again.

I couldn't believe condolences were my last words.

A blast of heat overwhelmed me. The world turned black.

CHAPTER 3
CULTIVATED CURIOSITY

"AS A REWARD FOR MY TRANSGRESSION, I WAS GIVEN A PUNISHMENT WRAPPED IN A GIFT."

MARLIES

When I was young, my world was small, and so was I. On my father's tiny farm, the cycle of seasons year after year looped like a familiar song. I knew some others lived differently. I saw cars drive down the main road sometimes, and the older kids would sneak magazines or music around. Tradition stated that we would be offered the outside world at sixteen and we should journey back only if we felt we belonged in our community.

I cried when I left, unsure what the world would look like. My father hugged me tightly, then turned me toward the other teens leaving. All of us went to New York City. One of the boys knew a song that was sung of it, and we were all curious. It was one of less than ten times I had been in a car. I watched my world shrink into the distance from the back window. The drive was so long, I thought we would run out of land. The whole day was blurry with fear and tears; yet even all these years later, I remember the city coming into view. It had stolen the stars right from the sky. I was angry. People hadn't lied to me. I knew the world was out there. But I hadn't realized how small my part was until that moment.

As soon as I could, I ran. I was too hurt to be afraid. I had my black hair tied up in a braid I once found beautiful, hidden under a cap for modesty. I couldn't wait to be free, so I ripped the cap off and threw it, letting my hair that had been nested up in the cap fall in awkward unpinned braids and clumps around my shoulders.

I stopped at a place with people gathered around, screaming and lining up to see something. Velvet rope lined a red carpet, a barrier everyone seemed to respect. I peered over the crowd to find out what the fuss was about and saw a woman made of stone standing a head taller than me, carved perfectly; she looked as though she was breathing. It took me moments to realize she was alive.

People yelled, "Artemis!" and this was a name I knew, a god from old stories in Greece. At the time, I thought it had been a costume or something for a holiday.

I watched for a while, standing in my ankle-length, indigo-dyed dress in the hot sun. She was, in fact, living and yet also made of stone—it was a duality I couldn't wrap my head around. She moved her hands strangely, and a woman off to the side spoke. She talked about love, acceptance, and a charity school for deaf children. After her brief speech, she walked by and signed books and took photos with people. I had nothing for her to write in and no phone for photos, so I simply stuck out my hand to shake hers. She smiled and shook. The stone was cold and smooth. She was marble, just like she appeared.

Awe-struck, I stammered out, "Are you a god?"

She laughed silently and shook her head no. She made a hand gesture.

Years later, I would learn the meaning of her signs.

"No, I am like you."

At the time, all I knew was that she was pointing at me. After she spoke, she flew off. Floating serenely for a moment before jumping off the air as though an impossible platform was below her, she gracefully skipped through the sky until she was hidden behind one of the towering buildings.

Standing in the dispersing crowd, I realized I had no idea how to return to the van and my old friends. I approached a policeman and said as much. I gave him the name of my hotel, and though he gave clear directions, the whole time he gawked at me as though I was some kind of freak.

It was late when I arrived in the lobby of the hotel. The woman at the desk said my friends were in the rooms upstairs, and when I looked lost, she was kind enough to walk me there. I shared my room with a girl from another town like mine. I wish I could remember her name now. I remember that she was scared and bookish and didn't want to leave the room except to go to the library in the morning. I barely slept. Instead, I watched the lights going by out the window until the sun overhead replaced them.

I didn't know what they were at first—I had thought they were TVs. Rows of flat, glowing monitors with privacy partitions between them and a matching set of chairs. I sat at one and saw there were letters splayed out in front of me. I didn't know what to do, so I raised my hand. A few moments later, the girl I was rooming with came over and turned it on for me.

"My dad has a secret one. He thinks my mom and I don't know! You move with this, press this button, and then this," she said, leaning over me to fuss with the device.

As soon as she turned on the computer, everything changed. A gentle breeze pulled me toward the screen. One moment I was looking at a glowing screen and sitting in a stiff, uncomfortable chair. The next moment I was absorbed. I remember hearing her scream and praying, but the distance between us grew. Eventually, I couldn't hear her at all.

I spent a month inside that computer, becoming a different version of myself. I could change my clothes, my hair, even my height. I became taller and more beautiful, not unlike the girls in the pictures I found. I saw many things and learned so much, skipping through image after image and stealing my favorite parts.

One person's hair, another's shoes—there were endless options and endless opportunities. People used the computer for all types of things. Some were wholesome, but most were decidedly not. I watched from the sidelines as websites scrolled by and faces stared blankly at the window of light I lived in.

During that time, I met Greg. He thought I was a virus, which he found funny. He came in every day for weeks, talking to me about school and his family. I think he just needed to be listened to.

"Hey, you're pretty cute for a virus. It must be nice not to have to work or pay bills. Imagine just hanging out online all day," he said. It was the first sign that he was struggling. He seemed young though. Maybe around my age, or a year older. I walked up to the Google search bar and spoke the same way as always.

"Are you okay?" I asked as my words appeared above me as text. He squinted at the screen and then laughed.

"Now the computer is taking pity on me. You know it's bad when the AI thinks you're pathetic," he said out loud.

I shook my head and typed, "I am real."

"If you're real, prove it," he scoffed, rolling his eyes.

I walked toward him and jumped through the window. With a flash of light, I was back in the library. People panicked, darting in each direction, scrambling and knocking over chairs to get away from us. I was taller, my hair glowed as though backlit from a screen, and was done in a style stolen from a social media post I'd liked. Looking back, no wonder people were afraid. Not Greg though. He wasn't scared at all. He was delighted.

We left the library together, and he got me pizza and a soda. We laughed and talked until late at night. Once he had to go home, I didn't know where to go. He showed me his phone and asked if I could jump on it. I tried. My world was small again. Just a phone with no data, but there were some lovely photos, and I could explore when he was on Wi-Fi. Soon I had made his phone a pleasant home, even changing the background image to a cute apartment photo.

We were always together; he needed a friend and gave me

shelter in return. As time passed, I noticed changes, though he never told me exactly what was happening. He wasn't living with his parents anymore and talked to me less. I fell asleep when he stopped charging his phone.

When I woke up, he looked different. His face was angles, the softness of youth gone. The date on the phone took a moment to update, but it had been over a year. Just for a moment, I wondered what my family thought happened to me. I supposed they knew I might never come home and had been looking for me.

He had left me in a box for a year. How could he do that? He explained that electricity cost money, and he hadn't had it. I felt pity for him. We had poverty at home, and it had made sense at the time. How could I have been so stupid?

The jobs started not long after he booted me up. He slid his phone behind a corner store counter and distracted the employee. I pocketed cigarettes and any cash I could get a hold of. It was only a few months until we could afford our own place.

Years went on, and we got better. Our jobs didn't need Greg anymore, just me. I learned how the more extensive world worked. If you were fast, sneaky, and clever, you got everything from people—love, respect, and sometimes even kindness.

A few times I caught myself thinking back on the rolling green hills of my father's farm, the braided black hair I used to have, and the warm wool dresses that pulled on my waist and only let me raise my arms halfway. But now, I could go wherever I wanted, drink whatever I wanted, and be whoever I wished to be. "Marlies" no longer suited this girl who could travel the world in the blink of an eye, who loved her freedom and longed for nothing.

So I chose a new name.

Apricity.

CHAPTER 4

PAINS AND PAINKILLERS
"BEAUTIFUL AND BLESSED BY ALL OF THE PANTHEON."

XÓCHITL | JULY 18 AT 11:00 P.M.

My mother smiled in the doorway, arms out for a hug. I ran into her embrace. I was small and safe.

"I'll be back soon. Be good, mija."

She looked at me like she meant it, but I knew she was lying.

All the pain in my body left. My broken arm, my headache, the bruises, the burns, the dizziness—everything was gone. I didn't even realize how much pain had been there before. For a moment, it was as if I was floating weightless and nowhere at all.

Is this heaven? I guess I'm not that bad.

The sharp scent of menthol cigarettes hit my nose, and my brow furrowed as I muttered, "There are Newports in heaven?"

A cackle cut through the gentle fog, sharp and wild like a witch or a mad scientist.

"There better be," answered a distant, velvet voice.

When my vision focused, I stared at an old ceiling with geometric art deco patterns pressed into its antique copper, tarnished in spots to a contrasting teal color. I sat up in an old-fashioned fainting chair as if all of last week's injuries were a dream. The room that came into view was expensive and lush.

Jewel-tone antiques blended with hyper-modern lights. Black-and-white photos lined the walls alongside vintage records and a collection of certificates and degrees in golden frames.

"You're awake then. That's good."

Across from me, someone in a suit sat cross-legged in a tufted black leather chair. If I died, this must have been hell because they were the very picture of the devil: sharp, threatening, beautiful. They were androgynous; their hair was cropped close on the sides, long on top, and tied in an intricate black knot pierced by a gold spike. They had a villainous look about them, made near cartoonish by the cigarette they held in a long black and gold holder like a scene from an old movie.

My head was in such a fog that fear missed me.

"Where am I?" I asked, squinting at the window.

I was on the fourth floor of an old apartment building, though I couldn't pinpoint my exact location. At least it was clear I was back in the city. My thoughts swam, dulled by some sort of painkiller.

"TV-head over there brought you."

The person thumbed at the robot from Čapek's lab, who appeared to be whole again, left untarnished by the second explosion. He was powered down in the corner at the moment. Someone had put a large-brimmed felt hat over his head. My orange canvas coat was hanging off his right shoulder, the robot looking for all the world like he'd been converted into a coat rack.

"I gotta go," I said.

I got up, walked to the coat rack that saved my life, and grabbed my jacket. I hoped that wouldn't wake it, concerned it would jump out at me like a Halloween animatronic.

"You have burns on your legs, a concussion, a broken arm, and some broken ribs. I would not go anywhere if I was you," they answered. They did not stand, only took a drag of their cigarette and watched.

"I feel fine. None of that is new, thank you."'

I checked the contents of my pockets. No vial, but my wallet and keys were in their typical stashing places.

"That's what I do. You should give me your number," they called over their shoulder at me as I walked by, a smirk on their face.

"I don't date…sorry," I replied, only then realizing my phone was gone.

"Shame, but I meant more for the medical care. You're in pretty rough shape."

They held up a prescription. The heading said "Dr. Andy Siu." An office number and email were printed neatly at the top. They chuckled. I grabbed it more briskly than I meant to.

"Did you take my phone?"

Their eyes rolled, and they muttered something under their breath as they pointed at the gold and walnut coffee table where my phone sat in plain sight.

"Had to turn it off. Someone would not stop calling you. I told them you were fine, but it was ringing every ten seconds. He was worried about you. You should really slow down."

Leo's face scowling like his dad came to mind.

Does the whole world exist to scold me? Surely, someone somewhere has something better to do.

I snatched up my phone and booted it up before spinning on my heel and walking out the door.

I made it halfway down the hall when the pain came crashing back, a cacophony of injuries screaming for attention at once. I got woozy, my gut lunged into my throat, and I vomited the remnants of my empty stomach on the checkered marble tiles in the hallway before falling down in a slump.

"I told you to slow down."

The *click* of Dr. Siu's oxfords was deafening, each step sending a throb through my skull. When they leaned over me, it was gone

—all of it. The closest thing to pain I felt was the slight sting of my nostrils from the smell of mint and cigarette smoke that clung to them.

"It's what I do. I take away the pain. Now take this and slow down."

They handed me a pill. I grabbed it and threw it into my mouth, not quite ready to deal with the experience of my injuries again. I opened my phone. It had been too long since I last read any texts. Dread crept over me. Though, according to my phone, I had just slept for a day and a half, I was already exhausted.

I texted Leo—"I'm awake. Let's meet at the garage"—while still sitting next to my own vomit in the hall. While Dr. Siu stood over me and smoked, I checked my messages. Twenty-four missed calls from Leo, one from Leo's dad, one from my dad, and three from an unknown number. My vision and focus grew hazy as the pill took effect. Still, I stood up with only a little struggle.

"Thank you again, Dr. Siu...I appreciate you and your gift quite a bit."

"Andy's fine," they answered in an offhand way.

"Okay. Thanks, Andy," I said before turning to leave.

Andy waved as I walked away, and they made eye contact with the vomit on the floor before scoffing and walking back to their apartment, leaving it behind to be someone else's problem.

The lobby was dark and less lovely than the unit I was just in. The doorman was grim and unstylish compared to my former company, though he did have a strange glass prosthetic hand. He saw me off onto the street, where I confirmed I was back in the city, not far from the news studio from yesterday morning.

"You have twenty-nine new voicemails and three saved messages. New message..."

The synthetic voice was replaced with a familiar one as Leo's desperate voicemails started.

"Xóchi, the robot ran off with you. Can you hear this, Xóch—"

"Message deleted."

"Xóchi, please be ok—"

"Message deleted."

"Xó...why the hell did you go in there!"

"Message deleted."

Several of the remaining messages were sobs or pleas for me to be okay.

"Xóchi, who was that person who picked up? Was it a doctor or a nurse? What hospital are you at?"

That was the last message from Leo that sounded at least halfway coherent. I deleted the rest while I shuffled toward the subway, then descended into the station. Each step flared up the pain; even dulled by the medication, I was winded by the time I reached the platform.

"Xóchitl, dead name called us. She said you could be hurt. Please let us know if you're okay. We are worried—"

"Message deleted."

How on earth did he guess the wrong dad? Come on! I can't believe they still use his dead name.

An old, smooth voice from far in my past spoke from my phone, weighing heavily on me as it did.

"Hey, lil' flower, Leo tells me you're in trouble. Remember to keep me in the loop and be careful. I know we don't talk much, but I still love you—"

I guess he told both dads.

"Message saved. Three new messages."

I shut my phone off and pocketed it, then closed my eyes for a second. The flickering fluorescents of the subway strained my eyes, and the jostling of the tracks aggravated my pain. There was also something exhausting about listening to my own eulogy, as though being alive was a rebellion against the messages. I whimpered, tears welling as the orchestra of pain began to crescendo.

Finally, the static suggestion of words indicated it was my stop, and I returned to the street. The night was so muggy that the fans and ACs blowing hot air around the road felt like the stirring of soup rather than a breeze. There was a reason no one had any love for New York in the summer; if one could afford to leave, they did. Otherwise, they'd wait, cooking in the heat and praying for it to end.

Just four blocks to the pharmacy, then three more to Leo. You've got this.

I tried to cheer for myself, hoping it would keep me going. Fortunately, a street vendor selling soft pretzels caught my eye. With a bit of math, I decided I could hold down a pretzel. After the transaction, I pressed the phone to my ear with my shoulder and tore at the pretzel with my teeth. Each bite hit like a cannonball, but it was seasoned with so much hunger, it tasted like one of the best meals of my life.

"First skipped message."

"Hey, Rem-Erez, the name's Grand. I saw you on TV. You covered Powers, yeah? I got some bad press, and I was hoping you'd take my side of the story before everyone gets the wrong idea. Call me back—"

"Message skipped. Next, one skipped message."

"Ms. Ramirez, some stuff is really going sideways. Please call me back. This is Grand again, in case you can't tell. I think…I think someone died—"

"Message skipped. New message."

"Hey, listen, call me…please—"

"Message skipped."

The pharmacy resembled a deep and narrow cave. Stalactites of snacks lined the front of the shelves, and a single aisle separated the two halves of the store. The counter sat right by the front door with a plexiglass box that made all the employees appear like trophies in a case. I grabbed a can of chicken and stars and some chips. I reasoned that the last venture earned me my childhood indulgence as I meandered toward the register.

A scream froze me in my tracks. Looking up from my armful of snacks, I saw her. A beautiful woman was pointing a gun toward the pharmacists, the plexy-protection suddenly missing. She had long, blue hair with magenta tips that glowed as bright as the neon signs in the window behind her. In her nonthreatening hand was a cell phone and a large bucket of water.

"Empty the register! Big bills! You better be grabbing from under the drawer too!"

She kept shouting at the clerks and gesturing the gun toward them, shaking as she yelled. The two panicked employees fumbled with the money and piled it in a heap in front of them. The girl put the bucket of water behind her and grabbed the money, shoving it haphazardly in her pockets before focusing on the phone.

I raised my phone up and started recording, awkwardly shuffling the food into the sling of my arm. The shutter sound as my finger slipped was enough to startle both of us. Her eyes locked on mine. Terror streaked across her face as she disappeared into a blink of cyan light, the phone plunking into the bucket with an audible splash. She left behind nothing but the bucket of water and a now-drowned phone. I ran over to the bucket and fished the phone out. A glitching version of its powered-down screen was the only thing visible. Large granules of rock salt layered the bottom of the bucket. The shopkeeper started yelling "Where did she go?" while running up and down the aisle looking for the suddenly missing threat, as though she was just hiding behind chips. The money, the plexiglass, the girl, the gun...all gone.

CHAPTER 5
PIXELATED PRISONER

"MADE OF LIGHT GIVEN VOICE, I
WAS BETROTHED AND GIVEN
WITH ME A DOWRY."

XÓCHITL | JULY 19 AT 9:00 A.M.

"Jesus! Are you okay?"

Leo's tone reminded me of his dad again. Maybe he was just getting old. I wanted to tease him about this mercilessly, but he had driven all the way down to the station to pick me up. I supposed I could be a little more grateful. I wondered if I had interrupted business for him.

"Powered robbery is very dramatic. The girl looked terrified. I don't think she was a legitimate threat. Look at the video. She's shaking like a leaf," I said, holding my phone out to him. As I climbed into the café truck, it was already in tiny-home mode, so maybe I hadn't interrupted service.

"Did you show the PPD that?"

"No, they would have taken my cell phone. It's my only camera now."

"That's a crime, Xóchi."

"I know, I know, but—WATCH!"

I shook the phone in his face and started the video over. As before, the girl shoved money in her pockets and gestured with the gun. She looked at me, startled, then vanished in a flash. Her phone fell into the bucket.

"The last few days have been a bit much. Maybe you could just work at the café tomorrow. Let the biggest stress be an oat milk shortage or some guy who doesn't know what a macchiato is," Leo said, tilting his head to maintain eye contact with me and ignore the phone.

"How could you not want to see this?"

I slowed the video down frame by frame. She looked right at me. She held the phone over the bucket. There was a barely visible number on the screen, then the flash, and she was gone.

"Can you make out the number?"

Curiosity peaked in Leo's voice despite himself.

I nodded, plopped down on my desk chair, and dialed the number. No answer. After a moment of thought, I googled the number, but nothing came up. With the easiest solutions exhausted, I went to the contacts on my phone. The whole time, Leo stared at me from behind his rectangular lenses.

"Hey, Mason. Where are you?" I asked. An audible *tsk* came from Leo as he walked away from me toward the cab.

"Uh-huh. Okay, can you run a number for me? Really? Okay! Yeah, we will be there. I'll text you the number," I finished. As I hung up, a string of curses and sound effects wafted from the cab.

"Leave it to the cops, X6! AND *MASON* DOESN'T COUNT!"

"He's a cop!"

"He's *your* cop, not *a* cop. That's different."

"I don't own anybody last I checked."

"Can't you just call 911 like a normal person?"

"I'll take it under advisement," I said and turned my attention to the phone.

Watching the video again, ahe looked so scared when she noticed me. She was holding the gun at a strange angle. Her posture was that of someone in a panic, but where did she go?

From the cab, I could faintly hear Leo muttering about bail as he drove us to our night parking spot. I stretched and moved from my desk to the bunk in one twisted step. Leo climbed into his bed above mine.

"Good night, Leo," I said to my already half-asleep brother. He mumbled something incomprehensible back. I laughed at the mumble. It sounded friendly enough.

I woke up sometime the next night after sleeping the day away. I reached into my pocket and grabbed some pain pills before I got up and shuffled to the shower.

The water was unbearably hot on my burns, yet not hot enough to relieve the ache of my muscles. It hurt, but after it was done and I had removed the plastic bag from my cast, I felt human for the first time in days.

I lumbered to the cab after plugging in my phone to charge. I took a second to type in the GPS address for Mason. I googled Grand, the Powered person who had called me. My heart sank as I read a news story that said he had run over a college kid. I wondered why he thought I could help him with that.

I called the number from the video again.

"The number you have dialed has a voice mailbox that has not been set up yet—"

"HELP ME!"

The automated voice got cut off by a woman's scream, then repeated its message. I turned off my phone, looking in every direction at the sleepy garage we were in. It was 10:00 p.m. and almost every food truck was gone. I couldn't see any people who could have screamed, but there were not a lot of places for somebody to hide. Worried, I picked up my phone to dial Mason again.

"Hey, where are you now? I think that thing I called about earlier, I think it was more urgent than I knew."

"I'm working, you know," he said before telling me the new address to meet him.

Mason was in the middle of a minor altercation when I found him ticketing a man with a sign that read, "Fly around the city in the arms of a Super! $100." The man was wearing a discount Apex costume he probably got from a pop-up Halloween shop.

"Whaddaya mean a permit? No, I ain't got a permit. You can't regulate FLYING!" the lanky man yelled, his face red with anger.

"Tell that to the airlines, buddy," Mason responded, trying to hand the man a ticket. "It's all fun and games 'til you hit the Goodyear blimp."

Discount Apex gestured at a stack of football helmets.

"THAT'S WHAT THE HELMETS ARE FOR!"

As he took the ticket, he kicked down the pyramid of helmets, causing them to roll around and into the street. He crumpled up the ticket, threw it on the ground, and flew off in a huff.

"Mason!" I called out, arms wide for a hug.

"Xóchitl! How's it been? I haven't seen you since college. You look like hell." This was a lie to tip me off. Were we being watched? Ah, his body camera—that made sense.

He hugged me tight, and I heard him writing something behind me.

"Same old same old. You?"

The hug lingered until he finished writing.

"Same. We really should catch up sometime," he said before placing a ticket on the remaining helmets and walking away.

"Bye." I reached over to grab the ticket once he was gone.

The ticket was blank, but the back had a name and address with a smiley face and the words "last time."

When I got back to the truck, Leo was awake.

"Where we goin'?" he asked, seeming too tired to argue.

I gave him the ticket with a grin.

"*Mason,*" he hissed, like the name was a swear.

He drove after inputting the directions, while I sat in the passenger seat with one foot on the dash, looking out the window.

I don't remember falling asleep, but I woke up to a gentle smack on my arm.

"Almost there, Xóchi. You sure you're up to this?" Leo asked, turning off the highway.

It was somewhere with cookie-cutter big chain stores down a main strip. I thought we were in Jersey but couldn't be sure; my head felt too foggy to remember the address. I was worried the pain meds had made me sleep too much. Even though there were aches in all my joints and my arm was still sore, I opted not to take more.

It was dark as we turned into a complex of tiny, stand-alone homes. Most of them were in disrepair with overgrown, cramped yards. We stopped in front of one.

"Wow, shitty houses, nice cars...looks like the universal sign of petty crime," I said with a snicker.

"Don't forget the fancy doorbell camera, the cherry on top," Leo said, exasperation creeping into his voice. "You sure you wanna do this?"

"I'm not gonna pick a fight."

I wore what I hoped passed for stylish clothes—dark-colored jeans and an old band tank top with the word "Frisson" across the top. The girl from the robbery had expensive dyed hair and designer clothes; she could have been doing a photoshoot if it weren't for the gun. I probably didn't pass as stylish enough to be her friend, but I still wanted to try. Maybe if I could pass myself off as a friend, I could avoid any outward conflict and check on her. I put on makeup to the best of my ability, admittedly not well, and stared in the mirror. I couldn't stop thinking of the girl shaking a little, nervous, and how the voice that came through the mailbox when I called sounded like hers.

Music thumped inside, the speaker system's bass shaking the walls. I removed my arm from its sling, letting it dangle at my side weakly. I bopped to the song before I knocked, waving at the security camera with a big smile.

A skeleton of a man opened the door. He had a glint of gold

where his teeth should have been, and his skin was an unhealthy pale color, nearly glowing from the blue light behind him.

"I'm looking for a friend of mine. Six feet tall, blue hair, pretty?" I asked.

A blonde woman behind him in a T-shirt with no pants on was dancing and eating pizza. She looked to be having a blast.

"Yeah, App ain't here. We broke up—she's really trashy."

The girl behind him started cackling, clearly in on some joke that I wasn't. The laughter was strong enough that she lost a glob of cheese from the top of her pizza. It hit the ground with a thwomp as the door slammed in my face.

I called the number on my phone one more time, thinking if the music stopped, I'd know she was inside and safe. Something didn't sit right with me about that whole interaction.

Instead, the trash cans next to the house started playing a little jingle. I stepped down from the porch and opened the can closest to where I could hear the ringtone. I started digging through the trash, desperately wishing it hadn't been ninety degrees out all day as the smell of curdled food turned my stomach and flies swarmed in a cloud around me.

When I found the phone, it wasn't a burner like I had expected. It was a new model with a cracked screen. The background was an animation of the girl pounding on the glass. Tears were streaming down her face, blue hair tangled around her. But it stopped and stared at me.

What?

She looked confused, but as the lock screen came up, she traced a pattern on the other side of the glass. I traced it with my finger, and the phone opened. She guided me to the messages app, and when I clicked, something started downloading. The girl looked elated. The phone glowed blue before a beam of light shone from it. I almost dropped the phone in shock as the plexiglass from the pharmacy, a confetti flurry of money, and the girl joined the litter on the lawn from the trash can.

She scrambled to her feet with the gun in one hand and money in the other. She paused for a moment before coming to a decision.

"Thanks," she said, shoving a wad of money at me before marching toward the house with determination. She took the safety off the gun before pounding on the door.

The thin man opened the door laughing, "I TOLD you she ain't here. She doesn't even like girls, ya wasting your time."

He was looking away from the entry while he talked, and when he turned his head to see the person standing in front of him, he let out a small "Oh."

The girl pointed the gun at him and kicked the door; it slammed against the wall with a crash.

"The *trash*, GREG!?"

I scrambled toward the door, trying to regain footing, and saw Leo dashing across the yard. We made it to the entrance around the same time.

"YOU THREW ME IN THE TRASH, YOU USELESS PIECE OF SHIT!"

She towered over him, keeping the gun focused on whoever this Greg was. I tried to think of how to take it.

"Should we try to stop her?" I asked. Leo looked at me and shrugged before turning his attention back to the scene.

"I can explain," Greg said, cowering away from the girl.

The blonde in the T-shirt stopped dancing, noticed the scene, and dived behind the couch. Phone Girl wasn't impressed.

"Is that Sarah? REALLY!? Sure, you can *explain*, with Sarah half-naked in our house!? While I'm literally in the trash?" She brought the gun down closer to Greg's face, not letting him get a word in edgewise. "After all I did for you? AFTER ALL I *STOLE* FOR YOU!? Were you *really* just going to throw me out? I'm a person, Greg! You threw a *person* in the trash!"

Phone Girl raised the gun over her head and brought the butt of the pistol down onto Greg's skull before tossing it to the side. Even though he was already down, she punched him repeatedly until her knuckles were bruised. Leo bent over and picked up the gun, not bothering to move toward Phone Girl. Meanwhile, she swung her fists until her arms became limp, her knuckles dropping heavily at her sides.

The pop music on the speaker cut out, and a professional-sounding voice echoed in the room instead.

"911, what's your emergency?"

I put a hand on Phone Girl's shoulder.

"Come on, let's go," I said, trying to get her to leave before the cops arrived. I hoped that I sounded comforting enough to convince her.

Leo put the safety back on the gun and then ran to get the truck started. I tried to help the girl step over the puddle of the man who once was Greg and shuffled her away from the house. Greg stood up and yelled at Sarah to hang up.

"I'm fine, no cops. *I said no cops!*"

The speakers popped, and a voice said something I couldn't quite hear before the speakers cut out. Greg screamed profanity after us as we crossed his yard. Once we were safely inside the truck, Leo drove away as fast as he could. I took a seat next to Phone Girl on the bottom bunk.

"Is he gonna tell the cops?" Leo called back to the two of us, anxiety shaking his voice. His hands trembled enough that I thought we'd start swerving soon.

She scowled at the question, but the panic in Leo's voice stopped me from interrupting.

"Him? No, if the cops got there, he'd be arrested first," she responded absently, still staring across the small RV. She seemed to be fixated on a blank spot on the wall.

"You're safe here. Are...are you alright?"

"You were at the drugstore."

"Yes, that was me. My name is Xóchitl, by the way. The grumpy man in the beanie is Leo. This is our home. What should we call you?"

Leo waved in the rearview mirror. He still looked skittish, but his eyes were back to their normal size, no longer widened with panic.

She looked up from the spot on the wall and seemed to consider his reflection. She looked at me for a moment and then said, "Apricity. My friends call me App."

She went back to staring at the same spot on the wall, almost as though she could see through the truck.

"Are you registered?" I asked.

She shook her head and brought her knees to her chest, resting her forehead on them. Leo cleared his throat in the cab. I ignored him and put a hand on App's shoulder.

"We will help you," I whispered, trying not to let nerves creep into my voice. When she didn't respond, I gave her some space and walked up to the cab to check on Leo. He was still clearing his throat and coughing.

"We cannot keep an unregistered Super with us. *Especially* not one we just witnessed assaulting someone," he said through gritted teeth.

"I think he earned that," I retorted.

"That's not your choice to make. You're not a judge."

"We can't just *leave* her."

"Xóchi, I mean it. No."

He took his eyes off the road for a split second to throw me a harsh look. I returned the look in silence, walking back to my desk to sit with Apricity again.

There has to be a way to help her. I am going to figure this out.

"Do you have any family or friends nearby where we can take you?" I asked.

App shook her head, her hair veiling her face as she tried to shield herself from the situation. She had nearly a foot on me standing, but in this moment, she seemed so small. I reached my hand toward her. I wanted to clear the hair from her face. I wanted to brush the tears from her eyes. But I pulled my hand back and let her cry into her knees. She didn't need comfort. She needed solutions.

We could have tried to register her, but I knew she'd probably go to jail for a while if they connected her to the crime at the convenience store. Even if she qualified for a hero deal, it was unlikely she'd avoid jail, especially without a sponsor. Mason didn't quite have the pull with the PPD that she would need either.

The kind of powers she had made things difficult as well. Disappearing into phones seemed more stealth-oriented to me. She'd need a hero to back her, a sidekick job so that the hero's reputation would cut her some slack. I opened my phone and clicked through my contacts, highlighted the name Pox, and called.

"Hello, friend. It's Xóchitl Ramirez. Are you still looking for a sidekick?"

The raspy voice on the other side sounded as though he was recovering from a respiratory illness.

"No takers, I'm afraid. They all think I'm contagious," he said. He started to laugh, but the laughs just turned into a coughing fit.

"I think I have the perfect person. She's unregistered but talented—and she'd be a good fit. Plus, she could use your help. Do you think you can straighten out her papers?" I asked. Two brown eyes peeked up at me from behind the waterfall of hair.

"Who would want *me* as a sidekick?" App said, gesturing at herself.

"Wait, really? She'd take the gig? And she knows who I am?" Pox replied. His voice cracked like a teenager, the excitement and volume overpowering his ability to control his injured throat.

"I think you'd be doing her a favor if I'm being honest," I said. I figured he could smooth it all over since the PPD trusted him. I believed I could trust him too.

"Of course! When can I meet her? I'm on patrol right now, but I'm off duty in just a few minutes. I could meet you wherever you need," Pox said.

"I'll text you the time and place," I answered, smiling at a hopeful-looking App.

There was another horrific coughing fit, but this time from

someone else in the background. The coughs faded, and Pox's voice returned to its usual tone as he finished speaking. "Thank you, Ms. Ramirez, it is always a pleasure! You have made my night!"

"No problem at all! We'll see you soon," I said and hung up the call. I had barely lowered my phone from my ear when App spoke up.

"I don't think I'd be a good sidekick. I wasn't even a good villain," she said, burying her face back into her knees. Maybe I was wrong. Maybe comfort was the move. I'd never been good with women, especially pretty ones.

"None of that! This could keep you out of jail! Besides, Pox is very respected by the PPD. He can clear your name and get you registered. It's a way out with someone I can trust to help you." I hoped I sounded optimistic.

Her head shot up at the mention of his name, and her mouth twisted in a little scowl.

"Isn't he the one with leprosy?" she asked, rolling her eyes.

"He's got all of them, really. Leprosy, the plague, typhoid…you name it," I said casually.

"Ew."

"It can't be worse than your last job."

She considered that for a moment while tilting her head to one side and then the other.

"Fine, let's do it."

She uncoiled herself and quickly snatched my phone from my hand.

"Thank you," she said and lunged at me. I nearly jumped out of my skin before she sunk into the hug on the bed. She smelled like lavender. I was suddenly so aware that I stunk like the trash can she was in. Then she tapped on Pox's name, and a blinding blue light filled the truck. The weight of her and the warmth of her embrace vanished with the light. We swerved over the road as Leo let out a startled scream.

"WHAT WAS THAT!?" he yelled, turning to look behind the

cab. App was gone. Leo put his hazard lights on and pulled over. I got a text before we came to a stop: "Dear Ms. Ramirez, A warning next time. Please. Regards, Pox."

I laughed and spun from my chair to plop on the bed where she had just been sitting. My limbs felt heavy again, and I realized how tired I was.

"Hey, Leo? Tomorrow, can we just work in the café to be the normal kind of exhausted?"

"Can you even work with your arm like that?"

"Eh, I can take money."

He seemed to consider it for a moment before walking back to sit where I had been a moment ago.

"How about I drive back to the city, go to the wholesaler to get some milk, and we just worry about one thing at a time," he offered, staring tiredly toward the driver's seat.

"I think we did a good thing today," I said, half to Leo, half to my pillow.

"Yes, and we broke *so* many laws," he countered.

"We really helped her," I mumbled. I know he said something back, but the wave of drowsiness muffled him. I looked at my hand and thought of the hug and the smell of lavender, and I fell asleep heavy.

I dreamt about Mom again, about her leaving, about how she said she'd be home soon. Then my surroundings shifted, buildings falling and earthquakes eating the world. The ground below me shook and startled me awake, heart racing. My phone vibrated under my pillow.

"Hello," I answered in a groggy voice, looking around the truck. Leo was snoring above me, and there was a twenty-pound bag of sugar on the counter where my laptop usually sat. Nearby, a Post-it note in Leo's handwriting was stuck to the can of soup next to my weekly pill box, still full in spite of it being Thursday evening: "Please eat."

"NEWS GIRL! Thank god you picked up. Look, I need your

help. Really, man, they're everywhere. They got to know what happened. It wasn't my fault."

I stood up, poured the soup into a bowl, and put it in the microwave.

"Huh? Who's everyone? Is this Grand again?"

My mouth said it before my head processed it. He needed my help.

Right, something with a college kid.

My mind was foggy as I pressed two on the microwave, and the dim light filled the room.

"The kid, that kid, his friend, they're gonna kill me! Please, you gotta tell them I didn't mean it. I didn't know he was there! It was an accident. I just fucked up. Please! They ain't gonna listen to me. Please just help me!" Grand pleaded, sounding frantic.

I walked away from the kitchenette toward the cab.

"Where are you?" I asked, typing the coordinates into the GPS as he gave the directions. A parking garage was only about ten minutes away from here. "Uh-huh, I'm on my way. I'll be there in ten, fifteen minutes tops."

I hung up as I sat down to drive. My shoulder was starting to feel better, and I could now turn the wheel with both hands. I took the zig-zagging path toward a warehouse district not too far from our own garage. The city wasn't ever really dark, but the garages at night were the closest it could be. The city never slept, but it dozed in patches like these, where no sensible person would be at two in the morning.

I carefully parked the truck outside the garage. Leo was still snoring behind me. I poured the soup into a paper to-go cup, hoping the lid's hole was large enough for the star noodles and little carrot cubes. I climbed out of the cab.

My eyes slowly adjusted to the dimness of the garage. It smelled like exhaust and spray paint, strong enough to sour the soup taste. I walked around to the front of the garage and dipped under the yellow-and-black striped bar that blocked the ramp into the underground parking area. The light of large headlights poured out from around a corner.

"Hello? Grand?"

I stepped in the paint before I saw it. I didn't know how I missed it. The ground was covered in red runes. I walked around the bulk of them, leaving half-red footprints in my wake. I hugged the ramp's wall, which took a sharp turn toward the lights.

Rounding the bend, a grisly scene unfolded. There was the cab to a massive semi-truck twisted around the silhouette of a man, as though it had hit a steel or stone statue while going top speed. A broken corpse was on the ground, illuminated by headlights. It was surrounded by glittering glass fragments; he had been thrown from a window. I snapped a photo and uploaded it immediately with shaking hands, hoping at least to leave some evidence behind if this is where I would die. I held my breath, trying to be sure that no bogeyman had jumped out at me. After a couple of seconds that seemed to stretch on for hours, I worked up the courage to dial.

"911, what is your emergency?"

CHAPTER 6
THE MISSING MAN

"A SILVER BOX THAT HELD WITHIN
IT A GREAT AND TERRIBLE POWER
WAS TO BE OPENED UPON MY
WEDDING DAY."

XÓCHITL | JULY 21 AT 1:00 A.M.

Though the regular cops arrived simultaneously, the handover to
the Powered Police Department was swift. One look at the scene
and everyone knew this wasn't an ordinary homicide.

Mason was one of the first to arrive. He pretended not to
recognize me and kept his eyes fixed on the wreck. They took my
statement more than a dozen times, looking for holes in the story.

His partner—who had no idea who I was—got too close,
looming a good foot over me.

"Why were you here? From the top."

"I do stories on Powered people for my blog, *Storm Chaser*.
Grand—" I gestured to the twisted man getting photographed for
clarification. "—kept calling me. He said I had to clear his name. I
think he thought I was a private detective or something, I don't
know. But he seemed distressed and told me to come as soon as
possible, so I did. I sleep in that truck over there; that's my brother,
Leo. Anyway, when we got here...well, it was like this, so I called
911."

Which was something I was starting to regret.

"Why upload a photo first?" Mason asked. He sounded like he took that personally.

"Yeah, why did you do that? We could charge you with obstruction," his goon of a partner parroted.

I tapped my foot and tried to keep my temper, reminding myself to breathe. I had seen the PPD blow up over nothing. They weren't very regulated and were armed to hell.

"I didn't know if...whoever that was—" I gestured at the human-shaped indent in the large steel truck. "—was still around. I wanted to leave breadcrumbs for y'all to follow if I died."

"Breadcrumbs?"

"To find me? Like Hansel and Gretel in the woods. Oh, never mind. The point is I wanted you to have a clue."

They never do.

The PPD was founded right as Powers started to hit the scene. As a division of Homeland Security, they were supposed to help bridge the gap between Supers and non-Powered folk. They were militarized beyond reason with security as a justification. After all, if they were expected to bring in people who could explode stuff with their minds or had the strength of ten men, they would need all this fancy equipment, right? Nope, wrong.

Best anyone could tell, they didn't do much. They took photos, wrote reports, and handed out tickets instead of acting as defenders of the common folk. To be honest, they acted more like a DMV for superheroes, complete with multi-hour-long wait times and tons of needless paperwork.

I was supposed to pay attention to the big man yelling at me, but I couldn't even hear what he was trying to say. I looked up at him. He was, in fact, still screaming. I didn't answer. He eventually cuffed me, saying something about obstruction, and threw me in the back of a holding car. I nodded at Leo, who pinched the bridge of his nose and mouthed "Again?" at me as a farewell. I could hear the "I told you so" already, an echo left in my mind from the hundreds of times he said it in the past.

I sat in the hot car as the sun rose, remembering all the stories of dogs overheating. I could see Mason photographing the scene out the window. He stood with his partner, both of them staring at the symbols painted on the ramp for a moment. I wished they were facing me so I could at least try to understand what they were saying. They handed Leo a business card before coming back to the car.

It took hours to process me, but I was grateful at the time to be out of the broiling car. They fingerprinted me and ran my blood twice to check for powers, and when I tested negative, they held me in a cell. I don't know how long I sat, but my arm throbbed with pain and the lights flickered at just the right consistency to bring on a headache. I waited for ages, first in the car, then in a chair by the lobby, then in a small room with a large table.

When Mason and his partner, whose name turned out to be Tucker, joined me, my head was down on the table and my hands were still cuffed.

"My coat had my medication in it. Any chance I could have it? I'm recovering from some pretty severe injuries," I said.

Tucker scoffed as he sat down gracelessly.

"You'll be fine, junky. You can have your pills back after your interview. The withdrawal will loosen you up for us."

The pulsing brightness of the lights made me squint, but I thought I could see Mason wincing at his partner's words. Tucker slid my cell phone across the table.

"Unlock it," the big man said as Mason sat down next to him.

"I don't have to do that; I'm non-Powered. Are you charging me with anything?"

This was technically true—as a non-Powered person I had protections. In retrospect, it didn't feel like my most brilliant move.

Tucker grabbed my hair and pulled my face off the table, pointing the phone at me. I winced as the facial recognition clicked the phone on. He dropped my head, more interested in the phone. Defeated, I thought about the number of these felonies I could tell my lawyer about. But ultimately, if there was a Powered crime, it threatened Homeland Security.

The PPD had no restrictions. I knew it. He knew it. There was no point in pretending anyone actually had rights.

"There are three or four skipped voicemails; they will all back up my story, and the last call is recorded on that app. Have a listen then, since my privacy is a joke," I said.

Mason took the phone from Tucker. I hoped it was for my protection, but somehow having my old friend looking through my personal belongings felt more like a violation than if a stranger had done it.

He played the voicemails first.

"Hey, Rem-Erez, the name's Grand. I saw you on TV. You covered powers, yeah? I got some bad press, and I was hoping you'd take my side of the story before everyone gets the wrong idea. Call me back—"

"Message saved. Next skipped message."

"Ms. Ramirez, some stuff is really going sideways. Please call me back. This is Grand again, in case you can't tell. I think…I think someone died—"

"Message saved. New message."

"Hey, listen, call me…please—"

"Message saved."

"At no point did you think to call the PPD? He said someone died," Mason said. He sounded exhausted as he pinched his nose, like Leo. I wondered if he picked up the habit from when they were friends.

"The person who died was already on the news. I didn't think I had anything worth adding," I answered.

Mason looked over at Tucker with a somewhat pleading expression.

Is this good cop, bad cop? They can't really use old movie clichés like this.

"It's like she said, Tucker. Her story appears to add up."

I tried to look sincere, but I didn't really know what that looked like. I put my hands out in front of me, palms up, and tried to smile. I hoped they wouldn't listen to all my calls. The first two would be fine, but the one with Pox might have been an issue for him and App. She hadn't even had a day yet. Who knew if she got registered, if she was safe. Mason carefully slid the phone over to me.

"Ms. Ramirez, please unlock the app with the call recording."

I did it using my fingerprint.

As the call replayed, I thought back on the events from tonight. Had I just been a little faster, could I have saved him? Maybe if I hadn't eaten or taken a different route, he would have lived. The idea he may have died because of chicken and stars seemed too bleak to sit on for long. The guilt must have read on my face because Tucker slammed his hand on the table, startling me.

"I don't like you, So-chi-eal. You've been at too many spots lately. Too much trouble is following you. I don't buy it. That's what…three Powered incidents in the last week? No one is that unlucky."

"It's my job. It's yours too, but instead of solving crime yourself, you're here yelling at the person who does your job for you."

I should not have said that. Agent Tucker sprung up and wound back his fist to hit me. I tried to hide behind my arms, but they remained cuffed to the table. Mason stood up quickly, his chair falling over in the process.

"AGENT TUCKER!" he shouted.

The big man pivoted, fist remaining raised for a moment. It looked like he may have hit his partner before he dropped his arm. He straightened his collar, spun on his heel, and slammed the door on his way out. I exhaled, shaking as I tried to unclench my jaw. Mason uncuffed me and fixed his chair.

"Thank you," I said, rubbing my wrists, which were sore from trying to resist restraints and defend myself. Mason was a bit lost for a moment. Green eyes looked through me. I noticed the bags under his eyes and the start of crow's feet in the corners. Like Leo, he looked so much older than me somehow. I wondered why time was sprinting for them.

"He's not bad once you get to know him. You're free to go, Xóchi—I mean, Ms. Ramirez. Thank you for your help with the investigation."

"You don't have to defend him."

"He's my partner."

A strain marked his voice. He was struggling between who he wanted to be and who he was.

Finally, after a lingering silence, he said softly, "You're a person of interest. Please don't leave town. We will be in touch. Stay out of trouble, Ms. Ramirez."

I wanted to hug him. I longed to tell him he'd be okay, to make him laugh. I thought of him in college, happy and determined. We met in our criminal justice class, and he was thrilled when he got his badge. Picturing his face back then, I couldn't help but notice the contrast. He was no longer clean-cut, no longer bright-eyed, and no longer smiling. I grabbed my phone and walked past the man, pretending to be strangers. Maybe the friendship was an act? I wondered about the offer he had made to catch up sometime. I thought maybe we should.

The woman at the front counter who gave me my coat and wallet back clearly shared Tucker's opinion of me. She preferred to drag her feet instead of helping me get out of there quickly. The lobby was bustling with people as I left. I had been led in through the garage and had missed the showy part of the building.

The PPD got most of its money from the registry of Supers. The central part of the building that led back to the street contained the grand hall, covered in the iconography of these heroes. Banners fluttered over the large windows. Capes and costumes were arranged in varying degrees of popularity. The geometrics, exquisite marble, and gold details here reminded me of the Chrysler Building, but its angles were sharper than its turn-of-the-century neighbor.

I stepped out on the street, disoriented by the fact it was so bright. Zephyr Square was impossibly busy. People passed by without even looking up at this place. My phone said it was already ten in the morning. I looked up Cactus Café's website.

"Not in service today" replaced its standard location alert. I stared at the statue of Apex in the center square. It was twenty feet tall but somehow seemed smaller than the man himself. The bronze was polished in areas people could reach, but higher up he was tarnished by the fifty-odd years he had stood in the center of the square. Tourists took photos under the statue and jumped to reach its fingertips. Behind him, the Zephyr Building loomed, casting a shadow over half the courtyard, home base to the agency representing more than half the city's heroes. I couldn't help but notice that shadow as I called Leo.

"Hey, they let me out. Yeah, I know—you told me so. Can you...can you come get me?" I asked, trying to keep ahead of his worried comments.

I kept watching the tourists as I baked on the hot marble step. Then, after what felt like no time, a shadow lifted some of the sun's pressure off me.

"This should teach you—" Leo started as if he was going to argue. I looked up at him with eyes blurry with tears. "Never mind. Let's just get you home."

The truck was still a mess. Nothing had been fixed since last night. Come to think of it, things looked the same as that night we drove to Čapek's lab. The smell hit me in the face as we opened the back hatch doors. Blood, sweat, mold, and smoke were all baked by the July sun. It all felt so heavy. I lay down for only a moment before the smell became unbearable.

"Hey, can we go to a laundromat?"

Leo smiled at the prospect and answered, "Thank god this whole crust-punk vibe isn't our new thing!"

I grinned to myself.

When we got to the laundromat, I gathered everything I could grab—sheets, pillows, blankets, our clothes, and every towel in sight. Tiny-home life was a nightmare for stuffiness.

Our laundry got thrown into a row of tumbling, rolling, and spinning washers. I stared at the soapy, hypnotic whirlpools for a while. Leo cleaned the inside of our home. Eventually, I snapped out of my trance and started scrolling through my phone. I looked through the camera roll, quickly passing the grotesque shots of Grand. I stopped as something caught my attention. One image showed a clean shot of the graffiti.

A reverse-image search showed everything, from T-shirts and patches to other crime scenes. Each image had the same symbol, always red. On these crisper pictures, I could see the shapes of two Ys stacked on top of each other with a hooked line through the center, then reflected upside down. It looked to be Old Norse runes for something, and when I tried to run it through on an online translator, it was marked as similar to three or four defaults, all amounting to shield, protection, or ward. I searched again, adding New York to the search bar. It returned a support group called Can't Save Us All.

It was meant for grieving people who lost their loved ones to Powered incidents. It wasn't identical, but the logo looked like the top half of the graffiti symbol.

Leo and I folded and stowed our clothes, then I brought up the group after a much-needed shower. I was vague about needing support, trying not to worry him with anything new. He was thrilled, thinking I was taking steps to move past my personal baggage. It wasn't entirely a lie.

The meeting would start around eight that night. I took a subway to a crumbling old church with a musty basement. I wore a red tank top, hoping the color would buy me a ticket.

Their coffee was still warm, and the donuts were good. There were around twenty folding chairs arranged in a circle. I sat with a small hoard of donut holes. Quite a few eyes lingered on me. I hoped their attention might have been on the sling, but I felt a bit guilty for taking more than my share. The guided session started with everyone going around the circle and saying their name. When they got to me, I said my name in a hurry.

"You don't have to share your story, but we encourage new people to speak their piece. It helps everyone feel safer, but we understand it can be a lot, especially with all the recent trauma," the therapist guiding the meeting said.

I regretted not taking off the sling. I felt like it drew added attention to me. This lady had a gentle presence, and she spoke without resentment. It reminded me of my mom.

"Hi, do I stand? I don't know if I should stand."

The woman nodded, and I stood back up, feeling even worse about taking all that food. I wrapped the leftovers in napkins and put them in my pocket, stashed with the crumpled cash.

"My name is Xóchitl Ramirez. My friends call me Xóchi," I said. I waited for a "Hi, Xóchi," like in the movies, but it never came. The silence lingered thick in the air.

"When I was a kid, my dad had this job and still does actually. He reports on natural disasters. Hurricanes and earthquakes... really dangerous stuff. So, for as long as I remember, it was Mom and me. She was an English teacher, much safer, or so we thought. There was this villain who went by Seismic and was on the news a ton—"

"I remember him! He would use earthquakes and make tunnels to steal stuff and live in the subways. He was a local!" a thin man in a red coat interrupted, calling out like he got the answer right on a quiz show. "Apex took him out in 2011."

"Yeah. He was one of my mom's old students. His name was Carlson. He ate with us at Thanksgiving. He was almost family when he was younger. Then one day, he was gone. When the news aired his face after he robbed a bank, Mom recognized him. She went to see him, to try and talk. August 21, 2011, the same day Apex defeated him. She got caught in the crossfire, and the laser cut through her...the only casualty other than Carlson." I paused to fidget in my pockets for my wallet. "There's a trading card..."

I pulled it out of my wallet. It featured an image of Apex that day, triumphantly flying over a collapsed building.

"Says no casualties, a flawless victory...but my mom was cut in half, and a building fell on her, and no one knew for fourteen days. They printed papers and cards, and no one knew except me... just...me. My world was over, and the news talked about it like it was the best day in history. Hundreds of people were saved as a villainous plot was thwarted. No casualties, they kept saying. Most papers didn't even issue a correction when my mom was found. The ones that did said Carlson killed her. He didn't have lasers, but that didn't matter. And just like that, I knew there was no such thing as superheroes. Powered people, yeah. Heroes? No. I haven't met one yet." —

A handsome man with dreadlocks tied behind his head clapped.

"Thank you for sharing, Xóchi—" he started. He sounded encouraging but was cut off by the man who'd interrupted earlier.

"That's why they all have to go. Apex, Artemis, Warde, K9, Mercurial, Pox...all of them. Especially the big ones, the ones with no one policing them. They just get away with murder, and for what? Cartoons? Comics? Playing cards? Why is it that if you can fly, you're suddenly above the law?"

The therapist cut in with a firm tone.

"Anger is only a step in the healing process. Don't let it fester, or it will infect you," she said, ending the man's rant. He plopped in his chair with enough force for it to squeak against the linoleum and groan with the weight. Others also shared stories, ranging from mundane days to lost loved ones. When the meeting was over, I was somehow more exposed than I had felt while speaking to a room full of strangers. I helped put away the chairs, hiding in the work and hoping no one was going to talk to me, until the man with the dreadlocks approached me with an extra cup of coffee.

"Are you okay?" he asked. He had a sincere expression.

"That question's a trap. There's only one answer people are allowed to say."

"Not here. This place is safe," he answered with a little smile. "I have to admit, I knew who you were, Xóchitl. We're supposed to be strangers, so let me level the playing field. I'm Tafari."

He stuck out a large hand to shake mine.

"Xóchi is fine. Follow my blog?"

"Yeah, *Storm Chaser*! I follow you on everything. Only honest reporting out there, best I can tell."

I felt my cheeks warm slightly at the prospect of a fan. Then I realized he was wearing a red coat, even though it was about eighty degrees outside this evening.

"Truth be told, when I saw the logo on your Instagram this morning, I hoped you'd find us," he continued. I processed the prospect slowly.

An invitation?

"I like your coat. I've seen many of them lately," I said to change the subject.

He smiled as he spoke. "Every movement has a uniform."

"What's the movement exactly?"

"Power to the powerless. The world needs to know what *heroes* are doing. They can't be trusted. They can't be left unchecked like they are right now." Tafari stayed quiet in volume, but the tone shifted to fury as he spoke. "We need to knock them down, show them they aren't gods. They should all be locked up. The uniform is to let others know they're not alone, that we are not alone, that there's a whole—"

I couldn't stop myself from interrupting.

"Hate group. You're a hate group against Powered folk. I don't need any Kool-Aid. Thanks though."

"I prefer *movement* or *revolution*. People don't have to be silent about their losses anymore. You can tell your story to the world."

I stared, maybe for too long. My face must have betrayed my disgust, because he shrugged and reached into his pocket, pulling out a card.

"Look, I get it. You're not ready to commit, but…we could use a voice like yours. I have nothing but respect for what you do."

Then he got up and left. Nearly half the room left with him, all in red. Once the chairs were away, I was offered the last of the donuts, which I gratefully accepted before heading up the stairs. I hesitated at the front door. What if they were waiting outside? I worried that some members of the group were violent.

A shiver raced up my spine at the prospect, but when I opened the door to street level, no one was waiting. I felt so silly. Of course, it was safe. But I noticed on the way to the subway, passing by the typically crowded street at ten o'clock. Red wasn't just the new trendy color this season. Without warning, wearing red had become a call to arms. A call that nearly everyone walking past me had answered. I started walking faster, almost running, when I reached the subway. Sitting in the shaking car, still nervous and feeling more alone, I took out the card. It was plain white, nothing fancy or insidious, just a phone number and that all-too-familiar logo.

CHAPTER 7
ROADS OF RED

"SO, UPON MY HAPPIEST NIGHT,
WE LIFTED THE SMALL SILVER
LID."

XÓCHITL | JULY 22 AT 10:00 P.M.

The ride back to the café was nerve-wracking. Every time someone with red got on the subway, I looked them up and down. I was somehow convinced they were going to hurt me or threaten someone, but no danger ever came. It was almost eleven at night when I got home, and Leo was watching something on his phone with earbuds in. He ripped out the earbuds and turned to me when I opened the door.

"Hey, how was the group thing?" he asked, shoving his phone in his pocket and turning on the overhead light.

"Informative, I guess. I met someone," I said as I tried to gather my thoughts.

I should tell him we may be in danger.

Are we?

Tafari seemed friendly enough, but a known association with murder did put a damper on any prospect of safety.

"Like *met* someone, met someone? I didn't think you were interested in people, only photos."

I blinked in confusion before I remembered that I hadn't told him my honest intentions before leaving.

"Oh no—not like *that*. Wait, what? *No*, I like people, Leo, but not this person!"

Leo smirked as though he had completely caught me.

"You do like a person though?"

Again, he had all the annoying pride and hubris of catching me in the act. I pictured Apricity briefly, then got furious with myself for my cheeks flushing.

"No *that's not*—ugh! Leo, I went because I thought it was a meeting for the hero killers. Not exactly my dating pool!" I said, exasperated.

My brother let out an audible groan.

"Of course, you wouldn't go to therapy, it would get in the way of you obsessing," he said, plopping in my chair at my desk. "Xóchi, what would have happened if you were right and you didn't tell me that's what you were doing? What if you just didn't come home? Then what?"

He paused to pinch his nose under his glasses.

"You would have figured it out! They had the same logo on their card as the crime scene. Besides, I brought money and a gun to try to get out if things turned sideways."

"I'm sorry…did you say you *have a gun*?"

"Well…it's Apricity's. She left it here. I was just borrowing it."

"Give it."

I handed it over, and he shoved it in his pocket.

"I can't even trust you with a camera! You can't have a gun."

"I'm an adult!"

"Yeah, an adult who consistently makes bad choices. Like keeping a gun that doesn't belong to you, which is also linked to multiple crimes, on your person."

He was right. I knew it, but I didn't care for being treated like I was a child.

"I'm going to bed," I said, plopping down on the bottom bunk and covered my head with a thick blanket. I heard more grumbles before he climbed up to his bunk above me.

On my phone, I looked up Can't Save Us All and all their meetings in the area tomorrow.

"I'm sorry, Leo," I said to the upper bunk after a while. I waited for a response, but one didn't come, so I kicked the bottom of the bunk and heard music coming out of a now-removed earbud.

"WHAT, XÓ?"

"I'm sorry."

"Me too."

The muffled music sounds cut out as he put his headphones back in, and with that, I fell asleep.

In my dreams, I was chased by red dots that pooled together into rivers rushing toward me. I ran, but no matter how hard I ran, eventually I was swept up.

This meeting was different, set in a community center. The smell was mostly the same: floor cleaner, musty walls, and donuts. I arrived early this time, helped set up chairs, and watched as people arrived. The counselor hadn't changed, and she recognized me immediately.

"Welcome back! You know, most people only do one meeting a week. You run the risk of wallowing in the past if you don't focus on other things as well," she warned.

I noticed she wore her hair in a natural tumble of coils and curls, a navy blue dress, and a gray cardigan. She wore no red at all.

"The last meeting was a bit aggressive for my taste. I was hoping for a more peaceful group," I admitted.

"This one tends to be calmer. You may be in luck," she said with a nod and a gentle touch on my shoulder.

I hoped she was right.

As people filed in, there were only one or two red shirts, and they were mainly helping set up. They didn't talk about their trauma or any death—just struggles they dealt with daily, nightmares and obsessions, and difficulties focusing on their lives.

When a man in a red plaid button-up with a pin in a runic shape stood up, I sat forward, paying closer attention.

Here it comes—the anger from the other group.

"Hello, my name is Robert. Last week, I talked about losing my work friend. I just wanted to say it was his birthday Wednesday. I went to the bar we used to go to and brought my dog along. There was an open mic, and some Powered person was using their talent to do a comedy sketch. I got mad, and I just…well, I just left. I paid and tipped and everything, but I had to leave, and I felt really bad… And I just wanted to say I feel like that was a bad slide back. It wasn't their fault. That person didn't do anything wrong. I just didn't wanna see it that day, you know?"

I processed this slowly. This man, the terrified one, was wearing red.

Is this an act? Either it's a coincidence or maybe he just likes the trending fashion?

I watched him during the rest of the meeting. He wasn't a small man, but he tried to be. He hid behind his oversized glasses and hunched his shoulders when he stood, as though he was apologizing for his height.

Shouldn't he be brazen like Tafari had been? If he was a member of this anti-hero group, shouldn't he be at least a little angry?

He seemed so apologetic and so soft. The person behind him handed him a napkin or a note. Once the meeting was over, he helped put chairs back, and I took the opportunity to talk to him.

"Hello. My name is Xóchitl Ramirez, and I run a blog. I was wondering if I could record your story?"

"Hi, um, I'm Robert Triddi. I, uh, I don't really have a story."

"I'm collecting a story about the red coats."

"The British military? I, uh…" he responded, still confused. I stifled a giggle.

"No, this group. If it helps, Tafari sent me," I said, pointing at his pin.

"You met Tafari? I honestly wasn't sure he was real. I thought he was an urban legend, like a rat king or Mothman. Anyway, you can't want to talk to me. He's the real story, if he's real, I mean. I'm just some guy. If you'll excuse me, I gotta get home to my dog." He started to walk toward the door but paused for a moment. "*Anti-hero* is the better name for your article. I don't want to be associated with British imperialism. They were the bad guys."

I don't know if I had ever felt more confused than at that moment. I considered following him but hesitated a moment too long. By the time I had reached the front steps of the community center, he was nowhere to be found. However, after a moment I caught a glimpse of the other man in red, the one who hadn't talked. He was smoking in front of a corner store, handing something out to others. I tried to look like I was texting on my phone as I zoomed in with its camera. He was handing out what looked to be sheets of red paper.

Then they all stopped, and he pointed at something down the street. Without looking up from my phone, I started walking toward what he pointed at. Down the street was a hero in full uniform, a man in a military-inspired costume with a German shepherd. It was K9, I realized. I followed him from across the street. Only a few steps behind him was someone in red.

Was he in danger? Should I tell them? Should I call the PPD?

I dialed 911 and kept my thumb hovering over the call button as I walked behind the anti-hero.

That name may stick.

The anti-hero was moving strangely. He kept touching the wall and the poles, and I looked for evidence of a Power I hadn't known about. After five blocks, the anti-hero stopped following K9 and threw something on the ground before crossing the street to my side.

I was convinced I had been spotted, so I crossed to the opposite side, only sharing the crosswalk with him, so that if he were to confront me, it would be in the street with a line of cars idling at a red light as witnesses. I stayed as far as I could from him and kept my eyes down, hugging the crosswalk's rightmost edge. His shoes came into view. They were black sneakers with tan toe caps, and they were stepping toward me. My heart pumped as I waited for an impact, a knife, a gun, even a shove—but nothing came. He passed me and kept walking as if he hadn't noticed me.

Why did he change course?

Once I arrived at the corner he had originally been on, I looked for the thing he had thrown. I found a small scrap of glossy paper, the kind stickers were printed on. I picked it up and put it in my pocket.

I guess he was just littering.

Looking up, though, I saw a small, square, red sticker on the phone pole he had been leaning on, with a black arrow pointing the way K9 had gone. The pole had about five other stickers, all different, with arrows pointing in different directions. Remembering the man's weird posture, I retraced his steps. I found stickers everywhere his hand had touched, simple and small, no bigger than a dime. All of them were red and featured an arrow pointing in the direction he had gone.

Following the stickers back and walking in the opposite direction of the arrows, I noticed they were everywhere. I expected to walk back to the convenience store, but at some point I wound up on the wrong trail, and six or seven blocks later, I realized I was following a new path. The stickers were everywhere—sidewalks, street signs, bike racks, even inside trash cans. There were some scattered among the random fliers nailed on poles. They had blended in previously, but now that I was alerted to them, they seemed to be sprinkled on every unimportant surface.

I stopped to get my bearings. There was construction up ahead, and the bottom layer of the scaffolding seemed coated in stickers pointing to the left, maybe twenty or thirty of them all crowded around each other, all pointing in the same direction.

I followed them instead of backtracking this time.

Maybe a headquarters? But…why so many?

The stippled path took me to a beautiful apartment building

before I encountered a telephone pole saturated with these stupid stickers. These had no arrows, though, just plain red squares.

I stood with my shoulder pressed against the pole, looking down at my phone. I played a simple color-matching game to try to feign boredom as I watched the entrance of the building. Delivery drivers walked up and gave the doorman names, apartment letters, and a few people came and went. A plus-sized woman with copper hair and thick glasses walked into the building, and the doorman greeted her with a smile. The best I could tell, there were no red coats, threatening demeanor, or even Powered people. I was thinking of leaving just as a hand with a red sleeve slapped another plain sticker on the pole next to me. I jumped, startled.

"Do you mind?" I asked. The guy scoffed and kept walking. He had come from the direction the ginger woman had, and looking back, I could see more stippled red marks on various objects down the street.

Why are they tracking her? She wasn't in costume. Maybe she's a Zephyr employee or a PPD officer...

I stood for a moment and continued to watch the building.

...or a secret identity...but whose?

CHAPTER 8
DIANNA'S DAY

"EVILS UNRAVELED FROM INSIDE; WAR, PESTILENCE, POVERTY, AND WRATH ALL UNWRAPPED."

DIANNA | AUGUST 1

The alarm went off. It was a series of chimes through my phone, a gentle way to ease awake. I got out of bed, lifting the heavy blanket off me. It was cold in the apartment, but looking outside, I could already tell it would be a scorcher. I began my morning stretches as I watched the sun rising over the city, steel and glass reflecting oranges and cotton candy pinks in strange, blurred patterns. Once my stretches were finished, I found my glasses and turned on the news.

They were still prattling on about Apex. Evidently, he'd saved a town on Long Island when an abandoned factory had exploded. The interviewer was talking to a wild-eyed teenager who was making an explosion sound. The news got interrupted by the coffeemaker bubbling in the background.

It's got to be close enough to done to drink.

I sat back down with my mug full and my mood a bit softer. Apollo jumped on the couch next to me, his front legs tucked under himself, but his back legs stretched long. I scratched under his long, floppy ears and under his harness.

"Good morning, little splooter. How's the day treating you?"

The pup responded with a tiny snort and went back to sleep. I pulled my computer onto my lap. My agent, Ms. Olive Miller, set up about thirty daily alerts to remind me of my appearances and obligations. I looked at the schedule and felt a pit in my stomach. The multicolored blocks of time stacked up on the calendar appointments, precariously packed into the day. I closed my eyes and took a long sip of coffee, enjoying the sweet, almost floral smell, trying to remember my machine's setting and the roast to replicate later how lovely that cup was. At that moment, I let myself sit and relax for just the amount of time it took to finish my coffee, long enough for the slight twinge of stress-induced indigestion to leave. When I finally reopened my eyes to be greeted with the devil's Tetris, it felt a little more manageable.

"Better wake her up," I said.

I focused on meditation and visualized a precise image of a crescent moon. I traced the curve of the crescent with the palm of my hand before pinching the uppermost point with my thumb and pointer; it snapped straight in the shape of an arrow pointed on one side and feathered on the other. The palm of my other hand flashed hot, then ice cold. I felt a bow materialize in my palm, filling the gap in my grip and brushing against the calluses worn to their shape. I drew the arrow back to the mental marker on my cheek, inhaling as I did while gathering my strength into a steady motion.

I exhaled and loosed the arrow. It shot across the living room, stopping midair as though it hit an invisible wall, and then transformed into a woman made of marble. She looked impossibly light and graceful. Even as she stepped forward, she made no noise. Thousands of pounds of marble standing eight feet tall and still lithe as a cat. The goddess stared down at my dog on the sofa and then at me. I shuffled up to my feet and reached over my head, and she mirrored my movement, her fingers nearly grazing my high ceiling. I put my arms at my side and focused on breaking our bond. She stood at attention, a statue mirroring my previous pose, her face knotted in concentration like mine.

I installed a tiny camera on her laureled head, then checked the feed on my screen to ensure I saw from her eyes. Looking down at myself, the perspective shift distracted me. I somehow felt too small and too big all at once. Sitting comfortably on the couch, my skin looked pale, marked with large, red splotches wherever the sun had made contact. The knotted pit in my stomach returned momentarily, and I sighed.

No need for that right now.

I swiveled the laptop until it was pointed away. On the sofa, Apollo snorted and turned around before plopping back into location. I tied my orange bob into a bun and finished my morning routine. The goddess lorded over me in silence as I went about my tasks.

I had Artemis leave before me. It was relatively well known that she could not talk, but people still tried. Tons of tourists swarmed outside the building to take photos with her. It quickly became difficult to navigate. People didn't understand how hard it could be for her to pass them without hurting anyone. I squatted down and then jumped a little. My feet only managed about a half foot off the ground, but Artemis flew. She echoed my movements, but I felt it was the other way around—my small, clumsy movements were a fraction as grand and graceful. Still, I stayed floating just off the ground in my apartment as she flew in a series of leaps to her first appointment, twirling and twisting in the air. She could jump off of nothing as though kicking off a pool wall. The weightlessness was freeing. I kept my eyes glued to my screen as she landed carefully in front of the studio for the first contractually required appearance of the day.

The lights were bright, and though I was on time, everyone was already there. Maybe Olive quoted them hourly—I couldn't remember at the moment.

The background was a green screen. In front of it, a group of schoolchildren were pretending to wash their hands. One adorable child with a gap in his teeth and an unruly mop of hair looked directly at the camera and then fake-coughed into his elbow. Off to stage left, a man stood, lean and frail. He wore a long, black coat and a stark-white plague mask that resembled a crow's skull. The tip of the beak was black as ink. I recognized him immediately. It was Pox, and he waved sheepishly as another child tugged on the edge of his coat. Then, though I couldn't quite hear what he said, a blue-haired twenty-something behind him burst into laughter loud enough that I felt myself jump. I tilted my head, making Artemis nod.

Pox walked to the middle of the stage and mimed washing his hands, coughed into his elbow, then pointed at his mask before wagging his finger. The blue-haired girl who was with him kept messing with her phone, and the kids weren't paying much attention to whatever Pox was trying to say. The kid with the mop-top pulled on the tip of his nose, pretending to have the crow's mask. He mirrored the hero's movements. I giggled, and Artemis's shoulders bounced as a silent laugh took over her face. The kids all turned to her. Then, as though they had rehearsed their battle plan, they all charged Artemis. Arms flailing and mouths screaming for delight, the children mobbed her. The blue-haired girl looked pale and stared at the goddess's face, then at the camera. For a moment, it seemed as if the girl's eyes could see me through the screen. She appeared confused, and her cheeks turned red before she broke out in a grin.

Pox finished filming his segment, and then it was my turn. I started darting my hands in a too-fast string of ASL words, trying to keep pace with a teleprompter designed for speech. My cheeks flushed with frustration as my hands spun and zipped through the words. My expression must have appeared on Artemis's chiseled face, because the director yelled "Cut!" and looked frustrated.

I sighed, seeing Olive arguing with the director. I heard bits and pieces, but eventually tuned them out as they discussed lip-syncing. I looked over at one of the kids. He was throwing crumpled paper balls at Pox as another one yelled and chanted about cooties. I wondered how Pox got his infinite patience. Then, his neon-haired accomplice walked close to Artemis and pulled out a piece of paper. The stationary kit was from the studio and so was the pen. She half-bowed, sticking out the pad toward me. Once Artemis grabbed it, she began to speak in ASL.

"My hero's name is Apricity," she said. "You've always been my favorite."

Her hands moved in practiced motions. Her whole face was red. I signed the paper in my own practiced motion.

I added "Thank you, Apricity!" to the paper.

She looked at me, a bit confused, before her hands stumbled through the signs. "Thank you for what?"

I gestured to her and signed, "For being a hero."

She looked lost in thought at the prospect, and I turned my attention to Olive.

Her frustration was familiar in these kinds of things. At least this one was not a live event. Watching a crowd of people stare at an interpreter speaking back my own words was always annoying. The voice and tone were always severe, but I thought the goddess's voice should be gentle. They tended to use the same woman, who sounded like she was going for an Oscar. Hers was a voice fit for a warrior goddess, not the soft savior I wanted Artemis to be.

Zephyr represented me, and Olive, who acted as their mouthpiece, got me gigs that paid well and maybe occasionally helped someone. They respected my privacy and made sure Artemis's face was always in the sun, glistening and glowing, to sell as many comics, cards, and movies as possible. I was sure our interpreter worked for them directly. Olive looked defeated and walked over to me wearing her own mask in the form of a too-perfect smile.

"They want you to lip-sync it so Evangeline can be added into the fold. Production said it's more accessible."

I sighed and tapped my thumb against my thigh a few times before agreeing with a nod. I went through the teleprompter action again, speaking the words carefully as they scrolled past, hearing my own voice echo in my empty apartment. It sounded high and thin compared to the grandiose voice it would be on release, not fit for the face it would have come out of. Nonetheless, as I spoke and signed, Artemis mouthed.

After finishing the segment about how proper hygiene makes you a hero too, Pox and Artemis stood side by side. The little mop-top kid who had been flicking boogers at the poor crow-faced hero ran up and gave us a big hug.

In his almost deafeningly shrill voice, the kid belted out, "I'M GONNA BE A HERO TOO!"

The director yelled cut, and we were free to go. The segment was done, and Artemis sat in a contractually provided oversized chair and closed her eyes before I severed the connection.

Looking around my beautiful apartment with its wood floors and high ceilings, I felt momentarily proud. Then, pride gave way to a pang of hunger and an echo of loneliness. I hadn't done anything today. I hadn't even left my apartment. I looked at my reflection in the large glass wall nearby. The window showed the glittering skyline at night, but it was too bright a blue during the day. So there I was in my reflection, floating partially transparent over a sea of endless sky. I felt like a fish in an aquarium and suddenly claustrophobic. I had to leave. I threw my laptop into my bag and scratched under Apollo's chin. His droopy face looked up at me as his tail wagged lazily back and forth. Apollo always looked sad. He was some kind of basset mix, but despite his looks and howls, he was among the happiest dogs I'd ever met.

A food truck was dealing out coffee and tea at the street level. There was a cute little cactus logo, and they served an excellent lavender latte I'd gotten attached to since they started parking outside my building this last week. Today, though, the man working the counter looked tired and miserable. Judging by his line and the heat this time of year, I wasn't surprised. I decided staying inside somewhere else would be better.

A few blocks later, I found myself at my regular shop. This place was a real hidden gem. A small, wooden sign zip-tied to an iron handrail read, "Bubble tea this way," and had an arrow pointing down. The door to the shop was blue and half underground. The only windows were at the very top of the walls. All booths had tall backs with good lighting, not to mention free Wi-Fi. The shop was perfect, with privacy, a good connection, and some excellent tea.

I set up in my ordinary corner, my laptop in front of me and my back to a wall. I ordered my sweet and creamy orange-colored tea speckled with black tapioca pearls. I turned on my laptop and got settled. My schedule blocks said I had thirty minutes of free time and had only used fifteen of them. When I reconnected to the camera app, something was wrong.

Apricity, the blue-haired girl, was in the frame, and she was shaking Artemis...or trying to. Artemis's heavy limbs were pretty much impossible to move. Everyone was crying. The lights on the stage were broken and dangling, and the large doors to the studio had been crumpled inward, as if something enormous had burst through them.

Apricity screamed when the goddess opened her eyes.

"They took the boy. Pox ran after them. You have to help!"

She spoke through the camera as though she could see the real me. She had tears streaming down her face, and I wondered what her powers were, since she didn't follow Pox out of there. Maybe she was new—I remembered how easy it was to freeze up in the first few weeks.

I signed the question, "What does the car look like?"

She looked confused and started tearing up again. She punched my shoulder.

"Help us, damn it!" she cried.

I signed the question about the car again.

Olive called out in response, "RED! IT'S A RED VAN! Pox grabbed it! I don't know how long he can hang on!"

I nodded and ran, my feet under the booth kicking slightly with each step. Artemis's feet pressed footprints into concrete as if it was sand. She leaped tens of feet at a time, clearing cars and traffic lights, sprinting entire blocks, and carefully dodging between cars. She used all the grace from before, but none of the gentleness.

Scanning the street, we followed the signs of a chase—cars that had been run off the road, rubber burnt into the concrete, broken glass, and pedestrians videotaping the disaster in the street. It was an easy trail for us to track. They must have turned onto a street a few blocks down, because there was a small pile-up where people swerved to avoid the chaos. A man with blisters on his face was lying out on the sidewalk. The crow-faced man was perched over him, placing him in cuffs. The man's soft whimpers indicated he would not resist. Pox pointed a gloved hand down the road without even looking at Artemis, and I just barely caught sight of the van swerving around another corner. I continued sprinting down the road, momentum too strong to stop. I used a pole to pivot Artemis in midair. It indented where her hand grabbed it, but held firm as she whipped around. I caught a glimpse of the red blur as she leaped off the air, pushing forward, flipping, and landing on the ground, feet planted shoulder-width apart, hand reaching to catch the van. The driver hit the gas, hoping to improvise his getaway vehicle as a weapon. I felt my lips curl into a smile as I softly spoke to myself.

"Mistake."

A matching smile cracked Artemis's marble lips as she spread out her hands, and the car crashed into her, going nearly sixty miles per hour. She slid backward a few feet, heels digging into the concrete and leaving long divots in the already pothole-pocked street. The airbags blew up as the driver bounced off them. I lifted my foot occasionally to decelerate the vehicle as much as possible. I gripped it firmly and set it down gently. I swore I could smell the smoke, and for a moment, I forgot that it wasn't me holding the car.

Focus!

The van lay crumpled in front of us, Artemis's shape almost carved into it. I calmly walked her to the back of the van, and she ripped the back door off, throwing it behind us. My real-life hand bounced off the chair behind me, snapping me back to my place in the café for a moment. The immersion wasn't broken for long, though, as the door opened and revealed one of my worst fears.

There was a man wrapped around the mop-topped boy from earlier. The criminal aimed a gun, pointing it at the ripped-off door. As Artemis came into view, panic crossed his face. The boy was awake and terrified. Tear-streaked hope filled his eyes as he saw her silhouetted by the light of the street. The man with the gun cocked it and started to shift directions to the boy. All combat training said to consider hostages dead. You couldn't save them in this kind of situation. There was nothing that could be done. The small boy was very alive, though, and it was devastating to watch him tremble while trying to look at the gun pressed just outside his field of view.

"No!" I shouted, hollowing my lungs with a scream inside the café. Despite how silly I'd look to onlookers, I made Artemis shoot an arrow using full motion.

No chance to be subtle, no chance to hesitate.

The criminal was shot through the chest against the wall of the truck. He was pinned off the ground, releasing the boy and firing a shot simultaneously. By some miracle, the boy fell to the ground just in time for the bullet to shoot over him. It passed through one of his curls and out the side of the van, missing entirely. The boy was screaming and sobbing and somehow still alive. The man above him was dying, pumping blood out in a grotesque shower over the poor boy. I killed very rarely, and though I would wonder who this man was or what life I had snipped short, at that moment I didn't care. I cared about one thing: getting that kid out of there.

Artemis had to hunch carefully to step into the van, and it jolted down with the weight of her foot. As she stepped in, I reached out our hand to the boy, who grabbed it. I had Artemis pull him into a careful hug.

I let him sob into her shoulder and kept his eyes off the horror show behind him. I wished to tell him it would be alright, that I had him, that he made it. But right when I thought we were in the clear, an oncoming vehicle was not able to stop.

As Artemis jumped over the van, the taxi speeding toward us swerved to avoid the wreck. She landed hard on the other side. The boy screamed, and the audio was so loud in my headset that I winced. I set him down, and he whimpered. It appeared his foot was hurt in the crash. The ankle was swollen enough that his shoe no longer fit. We should have been more careful. I mouthed an apology. He whispered a thank you and clung to Artemis. Then, with a flying leap, we took him to the ambulance beside Pox.

We handed the boy off to a paramedic. He was still sobbing, but I knew he'd be safe. They said the ankle should heal. In moments, the woman from the studio, who was either his mother or maybe his manager, arrived and started hugging him and wailing too. Pox was giving the PPD a report, and his new sidekick was arguing with someone in a red coat on the edge of the crime scene. I couldn't quite make out what she was saying.

I need a better microphone.

I heard Olive give me the okay to leave, and I briefly disconnected to focus on my screen's content and send the footage to the PPD directly. I felt sweat beading down my face, and I closed my eyes for a moment, pinching the bridge of my nose under my glasses. I heard Zephyr's emergency hero alert go off on every phone in the café, saying there was a Powered pursuit and to stay inside. As usual, it was comically late.

I drew my attention back to the screen, and Artemis took off toward home. Once she was high enough over the city to be hard to see, I dissipated her. Even though I'd been here for some time, my iced tea was still cold. I longed for home. I started to pack up, but as I set my laptop in its case, I felt the table shift as someone slid into the booth across from me. I looked up. Near the door, a man in a red coat caught my eye as he swore under his breath and walked out of the café in a huff.

I lowered my gaze to meet the person in the booth across from me, pulling my attention from the bag. She was a young Hispanic woman with chin-cropped, wavy brown hair, a bruised cheek, and an injured arm. Her dark eyes met mine in a look of determination, despite apparent fear. Her hands were visible on the table, and below them was a pile of Polaroids, the kind that were usually taken on a cheap, disposable novelty camera. She slid them toward me. Some were clearly taken through my penthouse window. I was glowing, and the shape of Artemis was forming in front of me in one. Another two shots were of Artemis and me in the same pose from two days ago. The third pair was of me walking Apollo and of Artemis awkwardly sticking her hand out to walk an invisible dog during an interview two weeks ago.

"I've been watching. I know who you are. You are not safe."

CHAPTER 9
COWARDS AND CROWS

"THE WORLD BROKE AND ALL
THE BLESSINGS FROM ALL THE
GODS EACH CAME WITH A
CURSE."

APRICITY / AUGUST 5

That fluffy-haired idiot, Xóchitl, was right. Pox did have the PPD's respect, but nobody else's. It had been three weeks since I started this sidekick business. Got my name changed and everything.

So long, Marlies.

My name, Apricity, meaning "warm sunlight on a winter's day," I had shortened to App, an apt nickname if I do say so myself. Sidekicking wouldn't have been so bad if it wasn't for my partner, a "hero" with the ability to store disease symptoms and spread them.

He's a goddamn petri dish.

Even the kid he and Artemis saved last week didn't respect him. Pox extended the kid's life expectancy, and the child was still grossed out by him. It would be enough to make me furious, personally, if it wasn't hysterically funny.

Pox lived in a Zephyr-supplied apartment in the basement of an old building. It smelled like damp cigarettes, and no matter how many lights I turned on, it was always dark. He kindly gave me his spare room, which had a futon. It was the only room with any natural light to speak of. A short, wide half-window nearly flush with the ceiling had a view of the street just outside.

I watched shoes, wheels, and paws walk by as I began to get lost in my thoughts. The gentle tapping at my chamber door alerted me to the raven's presence.

"Nevermore," I said out loud, still lying in bed and staring up at the small window.

"Do you need the day off? Or is this another bird pun?"

The man's breathy tone was unnerving; it sounded like he had to struggle to speak, permanently rasped as though ill.

"You wear a beak. What do you think?"

"It's a centuries-old costume."

He sounded more tired than defensive, and I laughed in response.

Everything was so severe and literal with Bird Boy. I could hear him sigh, clearly flustered.

"What if we got coffee? I think Ms. Ramirez's truck is close by on our rounds today."

I felt my cheeks flush. Seeing Xóchi sounded intimidating to say the least, but also appealing. I had not thanked her yet, not really. I crossed the room and opened the door. The man towered over me, though he was so gaunt I thought he may have been a skeleton. He was already suited up. I'd lived here for nearly a month and still had not seen the man's face beneath.

We started at the Zephyr headquarters. The building was by the square of the same name, and the statue of Apex loomed outside the window.

What kind of narcissist got a twenty-foot bronze statue made of himself?

The square was crowded with Powered people of all ages. Even children still in training swarmed around like bees in a hive. Everyone had to be on a mission or to have some sort of purpose. I wondered when the sense of urgency would hit me.

The front desk receptionist was a young man with a great smile and thick glasses. He greeted Pox and buzzed him in. I knew to wait in the lobby, but made my mistake immediately by making eye contact with the receptionist.

"When are you getting a costume? Are you going to go for a plague doctor or bird theme too? If he's a crow, maybe a cardinal," he suggested with far too much enthusiasm.

Why didn't we start rounds with coffee? Probably because I'd have skipped out on the rest of the patrol. Bird Boy is learning, unfortunately.

"No, I think I'm gonna stay like this," I answered.

I gestured at my clothing. Simple black jeans and a black crop top served as a nice contrast to my nearly bioluminescent hair and skin. The idea of a horrible red costume with a crest burned itself into my mind.

"Remind me of your powers again?" the receptionist asked. He looked disappointed in the answer before I even spoke.

"I can turn myself into data."

"How do you use that, like…in a fight?"

"Good question. If you figure that out, let me know."

" … "

" … "

We stayed locked in an awkward staring contest for an uncomfortable amount of time until I slapped the table in front of him and said, "Sooo, big fan of the biohazard?"

He looked confused for a moment, his brow furrowing behind his glasses.

"You should respect your hero. Sidekicks are supposed to support them. Try to be nicer to him. He has some of the best arrest numbers in this agency."

"And yet, here we are."

"You can have a seat, Miss Apricity," he said as he shifted focus back to his computer.

I plopped down on the strange geometric chair by the front door. It felt like an eternity, but the black shrouded figure eventually reappeared through the security checkpoint, the front desk staff waving at him with enthusiasm again.

"Good luck on patrol today, Mr. Pox."

Kiss-ass.

I giggled and nearly snorted at the phrase "Mr. Pox" while I caught up with my mentor.

"So, um, Cactus Café?"

"Of course," Bird Man agreed.

We set off. My heart fluttered in my chest, and a lump formed in my throat as I practiced what to say in my head.

Thank you for digging me out of the literal and metaphorical trash? No, too stupid. *Thank you for not letting me kill my ex-boyfriend?* Too dark. *Thank you for the sidekick gig, thank you for the second chance, thank you for saving me. We should get coffee... She works in a coffee shop. Get it together, App, you cannot be this dumb!*

I must have looked distressed, because I felt a gloved hand on my shoulder.

"We don't have to go if you don't want to. I just thought you were Ms. Ramirez's friend," he said as the white, green, and pink truck came into view.

"No, I want to go very much. Besides, I need the caffeine."

I raced ahead to stand in line.

Thank you. Just thank you. That's all I have to say.

The man in front of me in a tacky red shirt stared at the menu with such prolonged indecision that I couldn't help but loop through my entire speech again under my breath. When I was finally greeted by a familiar voice, I looked up to see the guy who was driving that day. I felt my face fall.

"Oh, hello, Pox! And, uh...Apricity, right?"

I couldn't tell if he was uncertain about my name because I was a hero now or because he had forgotten it. His eyes seemed to have grown some sizable bags since our last interaction.

"Yeah, one iced maple cold brew and one iced decaf americano, with a splash of oat milk," I said. I prattled off the order and watched as Pox tilted his head in surprised confusion, looking even more bird-brained.

"You remembered my order?"

"It's not complicated. You like the bitter, cold, watery drink."

I stuck my head into the window and scanned the inside of the truck. Leo frowned.

"She's on a bit of a mission today, I'm afraid. Glad to see you're well, though, App!" he said, and I felt my face fall.

"We are on a mission too. Just looking for caffeine to keep our energy up on patrol. Thankfully, your truck happened to be here."

I rubbed the back of my neck, feeling a bit stupid. Of course, she'd be busy. I heard a ping on Pox's phone.

"We have to go. There's a robbery," he said. He took off quickly, and I ran after him. I heard Leo call after us about the coffee as I started a message to him. I handed my phone to Pox, who continued to run. I hit send on the phone as soon as he held it.

I felt the cold light surround my body, and while stepping forward, I was sucked into the digital space. I was briefly enshrouded with digital brightness. It took only a second before the backdrop behind me was replaced by a neon pool of light with a hand-drawn version of the Cactus Café logo. Touching the drawing, I realized the texture was that of a bar napkin, and I couldn't help but smile.

One wall of the room I was in had a large window. Giants lived on the other side. A colossal double of Leo, his face distorted slightly by the glass, loomed over me. I walked up to the window and knocked. He opened the message and understood why I was there. I arrived just in time to save the two drinks from the drain.

"Mind texting me back?" I asked, coffee in hand.

The van inside was different from the tiny house and somehow even more cramped. For good measure, I looked around, hoping to spot a fluff of brown hair or a green canvas coat. Instead, he unlocked his phone, a bit irritated, and sent me off without a word as I dove back into the pool of light.

I knocked on my phone screen. Pox opened the message, and I rematerialized to hand him his americano. He must have been in the middle of talking, because the PPD officers jumped backward, making room for me. I took stock of the situation around us. The PPD surrounded the bank, but there was a gap of around fifty feet between the closest officer and the front door. Next to Pox on the opposite side of me was a handsome brown and black dog and a less handsome man in military-inspired hero gear. A PPD officer in full SWAT gear was in the middle of the debrief, and he cleared his throat as if to get everyone back on track.

"They have hostages, at least ten. The individual is Powered, by a pyrotechnic of some kind. Nearly fried the whole building when our negotiator tried to communicate and...we lost an officer."

They pointed to some scorched concrete in front of the building, and I realized that the front door was propped open by something blackened and smoking. I hoped it was not a person. The dog whined slightly, and the hero with the K9 logo on his chest spoke up.

"We don't need biological warfare. It would kill the hostages."

The man had a thick Texas accent, and I wondered if it was fake. He sounded to me like he was making his best cowboy impression. I giggled into my coffee and took a sip. It was actually fantastic, much to my surprise. I took another big gulp.

I suddenly realized all three men thought I was laughing at Pox's expense. As Pox's shoulders fell, the Texas dog man laughed and the PPD officer shot me a cold stare.

"This is a serious situation, ma'am," one of the officers said.

"So? I can get in there. Not a problem. What's the end goal?" I shot back.

I hoped that the shift to duty redirected the aggression back at the man literally threatening to burn people alive instead of at me.

All this for giggling at an inappropriate time?

"Eliminate or incapacitate the villain. Keep the civilians alive," the officer responded.

Pox lifted his mask slightly to sip his coffee through a straw, briefly exposing his chin, pale with dark stubble. This was the most of his face I'd ever seen during meals or drinks, and I was increasingly unsure if he had a nose or eyes.

K9 bent down and started conferring with the dog, who didn't speak back. I raised an eyebrow and wondered how *he* would even try to make fun of another hero's power. He understood dogs and happened to have found a Super genius one. He himself was pretty damn useless, best I could tell.

I walked up to an officer who looked a bit less intense and asked, "Anyone we are communicating with inside?"

The officer nodded.

"We've been able to send text messages to one of the tellers. The brave girl has been keeping us looped in."

Then I heard the wannabe cowboy yell, "Don't TOUCH ME!"

I whipped around to see Pox on the ground. His drink spilled, clearly shoved down by the other hero, who huffed off. The dog walked over to Pox and whined as if apologizing before trotting after his companion. I helped Pox, and he brushed the ash off his long, black coat.

"I-I didn't touch him…"

His voice was slightly panicked and apologetic. No anger, just anxiety.

"I know."

Pox was once rated the fifth most powerful hero in the world. I remembered the magazine had spoken of him as if he was a monster or something dark to be afraid of. I'd lived with him for around a month and could easily say I'd never watched someone get so consistently bullied in my life. I had a great deal of respect for how carefully he lived around others. He was constantly afraid of his powers getting out. He wore gloves and disinfected his home daily, and though I'd seen several dangerous situations, I'd never seen him kill anyone. Artemis killed the man who was going to shoot that kid just last week, but Pox only arrested the accomplice and gave him some nasty rash. I wondered if his gentle streak might be why he was so unpopular. Even monsters get at least some goth fan girls.

"I'm going to go in. I'll make my way to the emergency exit at the back to let you in, and then you do the rest, Bird Boy."

I pointed at the map, and he lingered in silence before nodding in approval.

"I am surprised you made a plan. You're really taking to the job! Just remember it's likely to set off an alarm. He may become dangerous the second it goes off."

He sounded delighted. I nodded and took a deep breath. I asked the green-eyed officer to let me use his laptop to message the teller inside.

"Take your phone and put it under something big, a counter or table or something out of sight of the villain, then open the next message," I wrote.

"Huh?" pinged the teller's response.

The light enveloped me as soon as I hit send on the second message, and Pox blurred into oblivion.

"You can do this," he said. I could hear the smile in his voice as I digitized.

I popped out of the teller's phone, hunched under the counter. The bank teller jumped but resisted a scream. I couldn't see anyone else behind the counter with her. I focused on muting my glow, my hair fading to a duller, darker tone. I pressed my finger over my lips, keeping silent. I heard roaring fire over the counter, my back against the wall.

"No-no-no, this is all wrong!" the man yelled. I could hear his footsteps as he paced. As he spoke, it almost sounded like a fire was being extinguished. The hiss of steam and smoke and the crackle of sparks between breaths was strange.

"It's a holiday," he started, though that wasn't true, "and you all weren't supposed to be here. None of you were supposed to be here."

I heard the whoosh of fire again as I started circling around the counter to the side room where the emergency exit was. Each footstep was uncomfortably loud, and I stayed as low as possible. It was surprisingly easy to get away from the main crowd.

The man robbing the place kept counting, "One, two, three, four, five, six..."

I got to the edge of the counter, holding my phone in my hand, ready to send myself back to Pox if caught.

I'm fine, it's fine, I got this.

"Seven, eight..."

I reached the counter's edge, knowing I had to run down the hall. It was the part on the map I was most afraid of.

"Nine, ten. All accounted for...ten people who shouldn't have been here. They said no one would be here." He started pacing again, and I waited to hear the steps fade behind me. I held my breath and ran down the hall.

To the right, there was the door. It only opened out. It was steel-reinforced and our best chance. An alarm would sound when I opened it, but Pox would come in.

Just down the hall, just right there.

I was already almost to my goal. I turned to look over my shoulder while running, and the man looked directly at me, curling blond hair framing an unmasked tan face. Fire crackling from between his lips, he inhaled a big breath, and a blast of fire rushed toward me. My hand reached for the door. My fingers grazed it as I felt heat approaching. In a panic, I hit send. I felt the heat against my back as I was enveloped in the scorching, startling light. Safe inside Pox's phone, I sat briefly, breathing fast, my heart still racing.

"Fuck! I fucked up!" I shouted.

I knocked on the window, and Pox looked down at his phone. He was outside that back door, waiting for me. He tapped his giant finger on the glass, and I fell to the ground beside him. The steel door was hot enough that I instinctively pulled my hand away when touching it.

"I ran away. He breathes fire," I said before I was even solid enough to feel the concrete below me. Pox nodded.

"That is sometimes the best move. Are you hurt?"

"No."

"Did anyone get hurt?"

"No."

"Then you did well. Do you want to try again?"

"No."

He gently placed a hand on my shoulder.

"That's okay."

No, it's not. Three weeks, a bunch of jobs, and this was the first time I could have been useful. Like, really useful, and I biffed it.

"Can I see your phone? I want to try again."

He nodded. I carefully typed the number into the teller's phone and hit send. He perched outside the door, ready to swoop in.

This time the teller wasn't looking at her phone. I knocked on the glass, and she looked down at the phone, seeing me behind the screen. She smiled between tears and snot and opened the message.

The dragon-breathed burglar was still in the hallway, rattled by my mysterious escape. I heard him muttering to himself from my place near the teller behind the counter. I decided to spy on him before making my next move.

"...she's gone? Not even the bones? That's...that's not right. Oh, oh god, she's Powered. Oh god, they're Powered, oh no-no-no!"

He squatted down, grabbing his head before looking up at the ceiling and breathing fire again. The pose reminded me of a wolf howling, neck oddly craned. The drop ceiling caught fire immediately; in seconds, large chunks started raining down. I was out of time. I stood and ran past him as fast as I could to get to the door.

He redirected his fire away from the ceiling and toward me, but he ran out of breath with a wheeze, sending only sputtering smoke and sparks my way in lieu of an inferno. Some of those sparks hit my skin and burned slightly, but it was nothing compared to the roaring fire above me. Everyone all around me was screaming.

He inhaled again, ready to blast me with more fire, but something hit him on the side of the head, and his fire was replaced with smoke as a latte doused the man. The teller stood a few feet away, black hair falling from her messy bun. She had thrown my drink as an improvised distraction. She panicked and curled up to protect her head from what we both knew would happen next.

As I ran for the back door, I could hear the man inhaling, pointing his breath weapons toward the brave and terrified girl who saved me. The rush of fire filled the air as I got the door open.

Pox ran in. I heard screaming and choking. I stayed in the alley, crumpled into a ball on the ground, my heart pounding. It was over in seconds. The man was arrested, sputtering and bleeding from his eyes, mouth, and ears. The fire department got everyone out.

One casualty, which had been the PPD officer who tried to negotiate, and one severe injury, third-degree burns on the face and body of the teller who got me out.

"You did very well. This was a tough one."

Why the hell is he praising me?

"She could have died. Why'd she do that?"

"She saved you. You saved everyone. She's a hell of a hero."

"All I did was open a door, and it took me two tries—two poorly executed attempts. How are you so calm?" I shouted. I slammed the side of my fist on the concrete and pressed my forehead into my knees.

"I'll give you a minute," Pox said, leaving to report to the PPD.

I sat there thinking about the brave girl's face, tears streaking down her cheeks on either side of her smile. I remembered the hope in her eyes when she saw me on her phone again.

"Fuck," I mumbled, squeezing my legs with my arms.

Something wet and rough touched my knee right where there was a burn. I was startled, and I looked up to be greeted by that dog from earlier. He whined and nosed my arm. There was blood in his coat, and he was limping. He looked afraid.

I got up, and he ran a few feet, then turned to look at me, barking twice. He led me away from the crowd and the PPD. I followed, my feet heavy, and though it couldn't even have been noon, I was exhausted. The dog took me down winding alleys and a busy street. It felt like we wandered through the maze of roads for an hour. Eventually, he turned a corner, and I followed, curious.

Oh no…

K9 lay crumpled on the street, battered and bloody, the wall behind him adorned with an enormous red symbol, spray paint still dripping down the wall. The dog nosed the corpse, whimpering. I called 911, and for a second I felt the light pulling me toward the phone as I barely resisted the urge to run to safety. I wanted to be anywhere but here. I stood by in shock, still waiting for the first responders to arrive.

It took a while for them to catch up. The police determined multiple assailants with blunt force weapons had killed him, in addition to a bullet wound. I told the officers what happened— that the dog had led me here, that K9 went AWOL in the middle of a hostage situation. The police wrote everything down, and the man was carted off by a silent ambulance with the dog by his side.

My phone rang, and I picked up without looking, half muttering.

"Sorry I took off."

"It's okay," a warm, familiar female voice responded. In an instant, my anxiety swapped origin stories. Not my mentor yelling at me, just the girl I like-Like? No reason to be nervous. I made accidental eye contact with a cop and turned to face the graffiti wall.

"Xóchi, I-I didn't realize you had my number," I said after a too-long pause.

"Pox gave it to me. I know who's murdering heroes, and I need your help. Can I call in that favor?"

"It's the least I could do," I said, touching the red paint on the brick wall before me and leaving my fingerprints in the scarlet hue.

CHAPTER 10
ARROWS AND ALLIES

"THE SEA ROSE, AND THE WAVES
ATE THE WORLD I KNEW, SO I HID
IN THE SILVER BOX."

DIANNA | AUGUST 7

The sun blazed, and the fire escape felt like it was branding me. I adjusted, using my bag as a seat to stop the searing hot corrugated mesh below me from leaving more marks on my thighs.

This should work. We are being clever and careful. Hopefully, careful enough.

I looked down twelve stories to the parking lot, with clear views in nearly every direction. I could see Xóchi two floors below me where the nearest window was. She gave me a thumbs-up and a big grin.

"*Crazy.* She's crazy. *This* is crazy," I muttered to myself. I had a goddess on my side, but she put herself there to protect *me*, and still, I was armed with a second-hand bulletproof vest and a wooden baseball bat, just in case.

My phone vibrated, and a text alert popped on the screen with the word "test." I unlocked my phone to open it, and a brilliant light flashed beside me as Pox's sidekick formed next to me. She was holding a coffee, but the bags under her eyes implied it hadn't been effective enough. She was wearing PJs with little hearts.

"Good, you got unlimited data, right?" she asked, scanning the city and leaning her elbows on the railing.

"Yes, of course. It's important for me too. You work with Pox, right?"

She jumped up as though things had just clicked for her.

"A-are you...no, you're not..." she started, switching from speaking to ASL. "Artemis?"

I nodded, and she froze as though the information had broken her.

Not what she was expecting. Never meet your heroes.

With another blinding flash, she was gone, leaving behind a cell phone that clattered against the iron grate, as did her coffee.

I continued setting up. We fed extension cords above me through a window. The cables backed up my laptop power so I could see the battlefield if the stream died. I had noise-canceling headphones so that any crashes wouldn't pull me from my concentration. We also had the best hot spot money could buy. Hopefully, all would go to plan. I took a few deep breaths. I'd fought more formidable foes. I was sure I'd been down this road before. The villains were strong, but Artemis was a goddess.

This should be fine.

My skin crawled as the hairs on the back of my neck stood on end. I had been doing this for twenty years, but I still felt fear set in right before a big fight. There was always tension in the air, as though a storm was coming.

It was time to bring Artemis out. I closed my eyes as the bow was manifested. I pulled back the string, but then my concentration was interrupted.

The discarded phone vibrated against the grates of the fire escape, startling me so much that I nearly jumped out of my skin. I opened my eyes and saw the culprit before me, my hands still glowing from the now unfocused power.

I answered the call, and the cyan-haired girl popped out again. This time she had two coffees. One of them said "thank you" written in sharpie, and she handed it to me.

"Y-you're my favorite. Always have been. I never thought I'd meet the real you in a million years, and I'm so sorry I'm in PJs and...and yeah. I'm going to make you proud." She held out the coffee. "I'm Apricity, by the way."

"I...this is...thank you," I stammered out. My hands sparked and then fizzled across the bow, deteriorating to moonlight as I reached for my latte. It had a cactus on the side of it, and that logo seemed familiar. I recognized it as belonging to the food truck that had been stationed outside my apartment for the last month. Thinking about it further, Xóchi always seemed to be around that truck. It must have been how she got all those candid photos of me.

"My name is Dianna. Nice to meet you. I'm sorry, I'm... probably not what you expected."

I gestured to myself, a little sunburned already.

"You're kidding, right? You're Artemis! *The* Artemis! The strongest, smartest woman in the world, and I get to meet you! The real you. Thank you."

The girl was tall and thin, and when she smiled, it looked like she was in some kind of commercial. She was the kind of girl who got the guy at the end of the movie, a movie where I'd be the funny sidekick instead of the protagonist.

The coffee was delightful and, strangely, my exact order: a latte with lavender and skim milk. Looking down at the parking lot, I could see the same barista who always made my drink, pacing back and forth on the phone. I could hear bits and pieces of the conversation from Xóchi, yelling on the other end of the line below me. It appeared the man had the same opinion of her sanity as I did.

"So, Apricity, how do you know Xóchi?" I asked, trying to understand how this mismatched crew got together.

"She saved me," she said, turning her gaze to peer down at Xóchi. The girl smiled and leaned on the railing again, her eyes glistening as she spoke, and I could tell the words she said really meant "I love her," but the idea might have been too new and fragile for her to speak out loud. Perhaps it was still a puzzle she hadn't parsed. She seemed embarrassed again. Her aloof posture was at odds with her red face.

"Wh-what about you?" she stammered out, trying to hide behind the question.

"Blackmail," I answered coolly. She tilted her head like a puppy and blinked as I started cackling, my laugh echoing around the parking lot. I couldn't help myself.

But then I felt it—the change in the wind. The threat was suddenly heavy in the air. Then, as if to confirm my premonition, a horn blared from the food truck twelve stories below us. Apricity tensed as she grabbed the phone from her pocket, shaking so much she nearly dropped it before disappearing. I closed my eyes again, reformed the bow, and shot the arrow. When I reopened my eyes, Artemis was in the parking lot below. She was eight-foot-tall, stone-chiseled perfection, and the sharpness in her eyes did not betray my nervousness.

I watched the barista fix the camera on her laurels. I looked down at the laptop as the camera feed started, the screen shuddering and shifting as the man tried to fix the placement. His face was so close to hers that it felt almost intimate.

The close-up was not flattering, though he was handsome. He had a haggard expression that highlighted the bags under his eyes, and his brows were furrowed in frustration, tape hanging out of his mouth as he fussed with the camera until it was both secure and hard to see. Leo tapped his finger next to it, and I placed my headphones on in time to hear the mic check. The goddess nodded to indicate the setup was sound.

"I know you are strong. I know I am not, but if Xóchitl dies today, I will kill you," he said, looking up at the towering figure above him. A chill raced down my spine as I felt the sting in his voice.

Brave, but come on, I am trying to help here.

An entire family of fearless idiots was in over their heads, and somehow I had to protect them. It was my job to protect everyone and chase off the boogieman. A role I wasn't unfamiliar with, but this bogeyman was specifically a hero killer, one who apparently got hit by a semi-truck and didn't even bleed.

Xóchi's photograph of the Grand incident was fixed in my mind, the indent of the truck, the perfect shape of a man seemingly unbothered by the ten tons of steel crashing into him. A shadow replica of him was left crushed into the metal of the cab. I exhaled.

Artemis is a goddess. What is a shadow against the moon?

My part of the plan was simple—throw him into the back of the sometimes-café, and Leo would pocket him away. Then we would simply drive to the PPD. Any others should be easy to handle. Most anti-heroes were Powerless. We would try to restrain them, then just outrun them.

Xóchi had called their leader as though she knew him. She said I'd be there and that we wanted to talk. She had said he would try to kill me and bring a crowd to watch. Many people tried to kill me, so that was not intimidating. Only the spectators scared me. I repeated the plan in my head like a mantra, over and over.

Throw him in the truck.

No one gets hurt.

No one gets killed.

Simple.

The day passed as waves of ease were followed by tension. I kept my mind busy memorizing the plan. It was one of the longest days of my life, and I spent it all watching the shadows race across the parking lot as the sun started to fall beyond the horizon, scattering reds and pinks across the sky. Artemis glowed like moonlight on the glittering asphalt below.

We had talked about a crowd. I had pictured ten or twenty. We received an army. Their chanting could be heard blocks away. At first, the rhythmic sounds seemed more like a drum and a hum, but as they got closer, the words echoed clearer.

"Power for the Powerless! The Powerless have the power! Strength in numbers! Strength in voices!"

They marched on the west and east sides of the parking lot,

encircling the truck. Hundreds of voices kept calling out chants in imperfect unison. Even with my headphones, I could hear them echoing on the microphone and reverberating in the air around me.

They kept chanting, and then the angry mob did something I wasn't expecting—they formed up. Two orderly flanks organized themselves as if part of some stage direction I'd missed the rehearsal for. Then, like an offering from the west, a single figure stepped forward. He was tall, broad-shouldered, and wearing a red, fur-lined coat with his dreadlocked hair knotted on top of his head. The man didn't seem outwardly dangerous, but when he raised his hand, the scarlet horde instantly fell into silence.

He said through a megaphone, "Here today, we see the self-proclaimed Moon Goddess. One of the strongest, one of the most revered. How many people did you smite to earn that reputation, Goddess? How many men and women died unjustly? How many civilian casualties? Were they worth it?"

He looked her in the eyes. I exhaled and held my hands out. One hand was held open, and the other held up two fingers. The man seemed perplexed by this gesture. He looked suspicious of the count. The doubt did not reach me. I knew how heavy this burden had been on my shoulders.

Seven.

The number of people I could not save and the number of people I had, in the last twenty years, let get crushed, incinerated, or worse—civilian and villain casualties. Seven lost souls held in my heart every single day. Seven that I had *failed*. I was told the number was low, though I didn't believe that. I thought about lying down and letting the crowd run over me for a moment.

These people have the right to be mad.

I am wrong.

I have failed too many times.

Then there was Apricity. She was standing with her back to the food truck, her hair glowing slightly, a visible tell of her powers. Someone threw a rock, and it hit her in the shoulder, then a brick came flying at her, narrowly missing her face. Artemis moved to get between her and the front line, jumping over the truck to close the distance. A hand from the crowd threw a glass bottle. Artemis raised her hand to block it, and it shattered against her, shrapnel spraying on either side as some glass caught Apricity's arms. The red-coated man with the megaphone jumped higher than humanly possible and landed on the truck's roof, the heavy sound of steel buckling below him. He stood looming over us. A flash of light flared, and my ward was gone. Another flash on the fire escape below me, and she rejoined Xóchi. My attention was still fixed on the man in red.

He leaped down at Artemis, his hands shining a metallic black as he swung his fist for her face. She lifted her right hand to catch the punch, sliding back on the blacktop behind her. My own hand started to ache as his fist pressed hard into the marble. The impact was hard enough to shatter her palm. Spiderweb fractures splintered and spat chips from her arm, and I lost feeling in my pinky and ring finger as fragments of her clattered to the ground by her feet. He followed up with his left hand, snatching for the camera in the laurels of her hair.

This can't be happening!

Just how much does he know?

I leaned backward. My head made contact with the bricks behind me as she pivoted her weight around and down. His fist was still held in the remnants of her hand. The shift in his momentum made easy work of slamming him to the ground. Then, she pressed her knee into his chest and pinned him to the concrete. She pulled an arrow from the quiver on her back; though she was too close to use the bow, the arrow grew in her grasp, extending to nearly her own height in length. The weight of the newly formed spear was heavy in her hand. As a warning, she stabbed a foot deep into the concrete beside him. We hoped he understood.

I don't want to make a corpse of you, but I can.

To Artemis's left, Leo opened the back doors to the van, and the crowd started to swarm on their right. There were people everywhere. I was afraid to move her, afraid to hurt any of them. Her hand was locked on the spear. I was paralyzed by knowing that any significant swings could leave someone dead. I breathed deeply and kicked off the ground, lifting the man by his coat as I went. If I could get him above the crowd, I could throw him in the truck without risking others getting hurt.

A stranger's hand grasped Artemis's leg as she kicked off the air to pivot. They got lifted into the air with her and flew off into the crowd.

"No-no-no," I felt myself muttering as the camera feed on my laptop showed the person getting flung away. The shifted attention was noticed by my adversary, who took the opportunity to grab hold of the spear with both hands, anchoring himself to it before kicking off of Artemis's chest. We lost our grip on him, and he crashed into the concrete, the crowd parting to make way. I swear I felt the corrugated metal below me shift on his impact with the blacktop, but I kept my attention fixed on the screen.

Artemis perched atop the truck, looking down. The man almost immediately disappeared, his coat blending in as one of the hundreds, similar to a drop of water in the raging sea. Artemis kicked off into the air again, floating above the crowd, hoping the vantage would find his face among the waves of strangers.

After far too long, I caught his expression in the group on my screen, grinning and staring at me, squaring his shoulders, arms outstretched above him as if to challenge the moon directly. Artemis drew her bow and pointed it at him, an arrow at the ready. Light pierced the darkness and lit up his face, a spotlight illuminating his arrogance. I thought about firing the shot but paused. There were so many around him. I hesitated, and the goddess faltered. Then I felt the world shake below me again and broke my concentration from the laptop. People were clambering up the fire escape toward me.

Xóchi was only one floor below me, back to the ladder, halfway up, trying to stop the mob from progressing. One of them grabbed

Apricity by the throat and squeezed. I called Artemis, the stone figure almost swimming through the air to get to us. The glow of App's hair flickered for a second as she started to lose consciousness. Artemis's foot made contact with the fire escape, rocking the whole structure. My laptop crashed to the street as I stood, my hand grabbing for the baseball bat Xóchi had left me. My heart was racing; I'd only ever felt this close to danger once. I never had to be this kind of brave. That was Artemis's job.

My eyes drifted below to watch through the grates as Apricity disappeared in a cyan light, taking the man's arm with her at the elbow. He screamed, blood shooting from the stump and showering over his compatriots, who were crammed on the small platform below. Xóchi was on the ladder underneath my perch. I lay on my stomach and reached down for her. My hands grazed the top of her head, but she didn't look up.

I felt the ground beneath me shifting as the bolts securing the fire escape to the brick wall flew out. The metal was creaking, and the weight limits far exceeded what the fire escape was meant for as hundreds piled on.

Xóchi was holding her bat firmly, her legs hooked into the ladder. If she was afraid, she was hiding it better than I could. The crowd started pulling on her, their hands finding purchase and gripping where mine had missed, eventually pulling her down the ladder's steps. Her head bounced off one of the rungs. I hoped that was when she lost consciousness. Hands swarmed her, and I saw her disappearing into the sea of people and screams below. She reappeared at the edge of the railing. She was only ten feet below me when she was thrown off the side of the building.

Twelve stories.

Artemis reached over the railing one floor below her, but we just missed her. Instead, I heard a horrifying metallic *thunk* that sounded like metal scratching the concrete below.

Artemis jumped off the railing two floors below. Untethered by gravity, she pivoted toward me and lifted me off the escape and into the air. Held in the marble arms, I floated above the crowd, safely looking down at the chaos. The food truck was being rocked back and forth, the barista was no longer visible, and the back of the café was shut tight.

I didn't see Xóchi, Apricity, or Leo, but I recognized the man in red standing next to the glowing spear Artemis had left behind. His defiant face smiled up at me. Someone had tied a red flag to the lunar spear. I shifted to be held with one arm, and we flew down toward the food truck. I was set on top of it, mimicking the goddess lifting it up. The truck rocked horrifyingly left and right, and I feared we would be toppled over before she could bear the weight of it. Trying to avoid the people, she kicked off the air, the displaced force sending a shockwave through the crowd as she lifted the truck, with me on it, into the sky. Only seconds before we were so high up, the group was no longer audible. The wind whipped in my ears, and I heard nothing more. I quietly added Xóchi to my count of failures.

Eight. I have let eight people die.

I dared not set us down on this side of the river, but I found some calm on the top of a parking garage in Queens. Artemis and I opened the back of the truck, ready for a red coat to jump out. Instead, we were met with Leo holding a tire iron. He poured out of the alternate version of the truck and heaved vomit on the ground next to the car on all fours. Leo stood up, snot and tears running down his face, and saw me held like a child in the arms of Artemis. He wrapped his arms around me and the waist of the goddess. He buried his face into my stomach, sobbing loudly, gasping for air, breaking the silence with the constant wordless ramble of someone experiencing complete and utter loss.

I didn't know what to say. We stayed like this for an eternity before I smothered my shame and whispered the words he already knew.

"She's gone. I'm sorry."

CHAPTER 11
WOUNDS AND WORDS
"I WAITED AT THE BOTTOM OF THE SEA WITH NOTHING BUT DESPAIR FOR COMPANY."

APRICITY | AUGUST 7

The stranger still squeezed my neck. Jumping from phone to phone normally felt instant, like floating. At this moment, it felt like falling. The pressure on both sides of my throat voided my lungs of air as I crashed into the invisible wall of Pox's phone. I felt it vibrate under me, the resulting digital earthquake shook the hand's grip, and the world was consumed by a ringing sound as if a thousand bells rang in one horrific, cacophonous chorus.

Another tremor below me knocked the hand off my neck. At that moment, I realized only the arm had made it through with me, not the whole man. I jumped away from the growing pool of blood around the arm, horrified. The ground vibrated again, and I watched as the pool rippled and spread. Then Pox answered.

I fell through the ground below me and landed hard on my hands and knees on the kitchen floor. The hand landed just after I did with an upsetting wet thwomp. The scene's violence was at odds with its peaceful setting. The smell of blood and sweat was replaced with basil and garlic, and the sounds of screams switched to the gentle lull of classical music and boiling water. Pox cooked pasta in our kitchen like the world wasn't on fire. To him, it was a typical peaceful Friday. Before standing, I made eye contact with his fluffy bunny slippers. They were slowly absorbing blood into the soles. He bent down to help me up. His frail hand felt more stable than mine at that moment.

"Can you breathe?" Pox asked.

His voice seemed far too loud as it reverberated in my skull, the phone's ringtone still haunting me.

I realized I had not yet inhaled, and I let out an audible gasp followed by a spattering of coughs. He bent down to my hand. His knee landed square in the blood. He didn't seem to mind.

"Can you speak?" he asked again.

I didn't know until I tried.

"Yes," I rasped out. The sound escaped my throat and sounded nothing like the voice I was used to. He helped me to my feet. I nearly lost my balance for a moment. The head rush almost robbed me of my footing.

Once vertical, I leaned on the counter and realized the scene I had interrupted. I had told him I wouldn't be back tonight, and the casualness of how he was living reflected that. Shocked, I realized that his face and hands were uncovered. The crow costume had been replaced by a pale man with gray eyes and ringlets of loose black curls to his collarbone. The crackle in his voice made me think he was elderly, but seeing his face, I realized I was misguided. He couldn't be more than thirty-five maybe. I knew he was thin even behind his costume, but his frailness surprised me. His cheekbones were sharp, and his cheeks were hollow. The man could pass for a skeleton if it weren't for his hooked nose.

"Less of a crow and more of a vampire," I said. He spun to the kitchen cabinet and grabbed a paper medical mask, looping it around his ears and covering his nose and mouth.

"What is this? Where were you?" he asked, gesturing at the arm. His voice held no judgment or harshness, only concern.

"An arm, what does it look like—Xóchi!" I shouted, interrupting myself. I grabbed my pocket and fumbled for a phone, but Pox quickly snatched it from my hand.

"Not right now," he said, and then I caught my own reflection in the glass of the stove, stranger than his to me. My glow was fading, and the blue and pink of my hair were replaced in chunks by the ruddy brown it had been before I got my powers. My freckles were also returning, and one of my eyes was bloodshot. "Now, where were you?"

I inhaled, and the air felt like needles in my chest. With great effort, I explained. As I recounted my day, I watched his face grow grim, still strange to me. Occasionally, he looked over at the arm on his kitchen floor. When I finished my story, he dialed something on his phone, placed it in my palm, and curled my fingers around it.

"Go."

I hit send and felt myself swept along by a current stronger than me. I landed on my feet this time, though I was still in the phone, walking along the icy surface of the stranger's screen. I glided like a practiced skater. The message bubble loomed above me. Today's date and time appeared below it.

The last message from some time ago read, "I cannot see you any longer. I am bad for you. Goodbye, Vincent."

It had been sent in February.

Did he text me to an ex?

I realized just how little I knew about him.

His name is Vincent?

I should have known that. I'd lived with him for a month. I started gliding along the glass toward the earlier messages.

"I need to see you again."

"I miss you."

"I need you. Please help."

All left on read over several days. I realized these were personal. It was not my business how Pox handled his last breakup.

The ground fell beneath my feet as someone opened the message. The smell of menthol hit my nose before I even opened my eyes. A warm, somewhat gothic apartment dialed into focus in front of me, all old furniture with warm-hued velvet and antique wallpaper. The person holding the phone in front of me took a drag of their cigarette, eyeing me up and down before quietly laughing.

"Vincent's partner?"

The voice was smooth. Something about it dulled the bells in my ears, and the vise around my throat seemed to loosen. I felt warm and numb as all the pain and stress fell from my body and mind. They put their phone down and closed the distance between us.

"I'm Pox's sidekick," I said, worried I had overstepped by reading the texts. I did not want to entangle myself in the emotional mess of Pox's love life. Instead, the person placed their hand on the nape of my neck. It was cool to the touch, and even when they touched the bruises, it felt more like ice than pressure.

"Poor dear," they said, dark eyes scanning my neck. They were so close to me, and though they seemed to be a medical professional, I felt myself blushing. "Someone tried very hard to kill you, sidekick. Let's get you patched up."

They fetched a bar cart that looked old and expensive, but where bottles and glasses should have been, medical supplies sat instead. The stranger lifted some cotton balls off the mirrored surface, and I caught my proper reflection. My freckles hadn't returned, but strange new speckles dotted my face and neck. There were vivid purple bruises discoloring my skin where that man had tried to strangle me.

The cold-handed person cleaned the cuts carefully, but it didn't hurt. I still felt like I was swimming in a blissful, painless pool, drunk or stoned but not quite. I traced the speckles on my face and neck.

"Petechiae from the injury."

Their voice seemed to amplify the painlessness, and even the pressure of my own fingers on my face all but vanished.

"Who are you?"

I felt the words escape my lips and regretted them almost

instantly. I didn't introduce myself, and the tone sounded too airy, as though I had lost my sense of place.

"Dr. Andy Siu. And you are?"

I lost myself momentarily in their voice and was startled awake as they snapped their fingers in front of me, looking for an answer.

"Apricity, or App."

The doctor smiled in response.

"A ray of sunshine? You're the strangest thing I've ever downloaded on my phone, and that list is long."

This might have been the first time anyone got the pun. For a moment, I pictured the word of the day calendar I had as a child. The sun was filtering through the trees and casting speckled beams of light across my father's desk at the farm. I felt heavy, and the nostalgic memory possessed my senses until I lost them.

I don't know how long I was out, but crashing metal footsteps roused me from a heavy sleep. I was lying on an amethyst fainting couch, and it took me a moment to find my hands and push myself up.

The metal man had what looked like a CRT TV for a head, and something was wrapped in red in his arms. It must have been raining outside. The pooled droplets were leaving a trail behind him to the front door. He turned and laid his bundle on the couch opposite me per the doctor's hushed instructions, which were too loud and sharp to be effectively quiet. In the dark, my eyes struggled to adjust. There was shifting and moving. Eventually, a steady, familiar heart monitor beep. I could make out squinting as they braced the person's neck, and then the patient let out a whimper.

"Xóchi, is that you?" My voice came out cracked and crooked, still sounding like a stranger's. Dr. Siu turned to me.

"Everything's okay, App. Go back to sleep."

The hissed words had a panicked tone, but it was a command I could not resist. I felt heavy, and my head fell with a soft audible thud on the velvet cushion.

I dreamt of home, rolling hills, and riding horse-drawn wagons with my sisters. A lovely montage of memories flooded my senses. I slept soundly for hours or maybe even days.

When I woke again, it was light outside, and the large windows were bright enough to illuminate the whole living room. I felt the creak of my limbs from sleeping too long, but nothing of the pain from my bruises and scratches.

Across the room, on the couch opposite me, was Xóchi. She was covered in a thin, black blanket, hooked up to an IV, and covered in more bumps and bruises than skin. She was sleeping. I'd have thought she was dead if not for the steady beep of a heart monitor beside her.

I scrambled to her side as fast as I could and buried my face into her blanket.

"I am so sorry I ran. I am so sorry I failed you. Sorry, I'm so sorry!"

I wondered if the words reached her through her sleep, then I felt a hand on my shoulder.

"Tea? Coffee?"

The doctor's tone was comforting but worn from two surprise guests. A marble-top table in a separate room had Earl Grey tea with honey waiting for me. It tasted delightful, and though I felt slight pressure when I drank, the tea was comforting. After putting the cup down, I realized that Dr. Siu was staring at my throat as I swallowed.

"You're healing well, and your powers seem to be returning," they said, gesturing to a mirror, which showed me that my hair had returned to its familiar blues and pinks. For a second, I missed the warm brown hair I had when I was young.

"How's Xóchi?" I asked, my voice still shaky and muffled by tears.

"It's not great. She has broken ribs, broken limbs, and a concussion. She punctured a lung, but we drained it. She's stable, but we won't know how bad it is until she's awake," they explained. The doctor took a long sip of their tea and continued speaking. "Čapek looped me in." They gestured at the robot. "She was thrown from a building, and he caught her, but the impact was still hard, and she was already roughed up before she got thrown. Do you know who to contact?"

I nodded and started dialing the phone but felt the wind pulling me toward the screen and hesitated. If I dialed, I was concerned I'd fall through, so instead I slid my phone across the smooth black marble table to my host, with the contact card for Leo pulled up. The doctor nodded and dialed. I heard the ring and then an answer, followed by silence and then muttering.

"Hello, Leo? It's Dr. Siu, and I have your friends in my care. Apricity, Power ID #126-498, and Xóchitl Ramirez," the doctor said. I could hear some kind of yelling on the other end of the line, multiple voices screaming but muted by the distance. "Yes, she's stable, she's not awake, but she is alive... Yes, Ms. Apricity is also alive... Yes, I'll text you the address. Maximum one visitor per guest. Do you know if Ms. Ramirez was on any medications I didn't prescribe? ...Uh-huh, how much? ...Okay, bring the bottle, please. Thank you."

They got there fast, nearly as fast as I would have. Or my sense of time was distorted. The more I thought about it, the more the creeping numbness overwhelmed my senses.

Leo was sobbing at Xóchi's side, and Dianna hugged me too tightly. It should have hurt, but I felt warm, soft, heavy, and light all at once. I fell asleep again, my forehead resting on Dianna's shoulder with the heat of her sunburn bouncing off my cheek. Then I heard a familiar voice.

"Leo?"

We all jumped up. Dianna and I scrambled to the living room, where Xóchi was starting to wake up. The doctor moved with clean, sharp motions. They shined lights in Xóchi's eyes.

"Xóchitl, can you hear me? You've been in an accident. Do not try to move."

The doctor removed Leo, Dianna, and me from the room with a firmness that may not have been wholly natural, and we all stood in the hall while they ran tests.

Once in the hall with the door shut behind me, the numbness washed away from me. The throbbing of my neck and head knocked the wind out of me momentarily, and Dianna had to steady me to keep me on my feet. The world spun as acid raced up my chest and burned the lining of my esophagus.

Pox's messages were ringing in my mind with clearness as I yearned for comfortable, numb oblivion.

"I need it, please help."

My body was frozen in place, leaning on Dianna's soft shoulder. It was the greatest act of willpower of my life not to crawl through the door behind me. Maybe they weren't dating. Perhaps he became addicted, more directly dependent on that feeling.

It felt like hours until we were called back in.

When the door opened, the glorious numbness coated me again, a single chill racing down my spine as I left my pain in the hall behind me. I realized then how dangerous walking back into the room could be, how addictive this was, and how unsure I was that I could ever leave again.

"Hi, guys," Xóchi called. She was still lying down, but the couch had been adjusted below her to have her partially sitting up, and she was somehow, impossibly, smiling. "Sorry...sounds like I scared everyone a bit."

Leo crumpled to her side and hugged her gently.

"*Never* again, Xóchi."

I wondered if he ever stopped crying. At the same time, I felt my tears welling up as a smile crossed my face.

"We all lived," I said, unable to believe my own words.

For one perfect, painless moment, we all rejoiced in defeat.

CHAPTER 12
CALLING COLLECT
"I WAITED AND WAITED."

TAFARI I AUGUST 9

The burner rang.

The burner. *Her* burner.

How?

Is she alive? Is this her ghost? Did her friend find my card going through her belongings? On the other hand, maybe this is a hallucination from guilt.

I thought for a beat about letting it ring, about allowing the mystery to die and forgetting my mistake. Still, an irresistible impulse found me flipping the cheap phone open and pressing it against my ear.

"Hello?" I answered. There was a crackle on the other end of the line, and at first, I thought it was a spam bot haunting me.

"Hey, red coat," she said. It was *her*, clear as a bell. "Sorry, it took so long. I…had a bit of a week." She laughed on the other end of the line, and I stepped onto my apartment's balcony, closing the door to the meeting behind me.

"I thought you *died*."

"Sorry to disappoint."

"Contrary to what you may think, I never wanted you to get

hurt. Things just got out of hand, but I still think you should join us. You saw it. There are thousands of us. Change is coming. Come on, Xóchitl, help us. Be our voice. You're not Powered. You should be on our side," I said.

"Me not being Powered didn't stop your friends from throwing me off a building," she said.

I felt my heart skip a beat. That had been her. I was right.

How… Maybe she was Powered?

"That was you."

"Yep, that was me. Ya know, Artemis showed a lot of mercy. She didn't kill you because she worried about the civilians. Unfortunately, the favor was not returned."

I felt the pain in my chest return. What seemed like our victory, that whole display of strength from four days ago, had lost all its poetics for me. In its place, only shame remained.

"That's not how it happened. You tried to ambush us. We beat you to it. You tried to muscle us. You lost," I answered. I felt even then that my stance was poor, the sting of my retort dulled by doubt.

"We tried to take you into custody for murder, and you all tried to kill us. Because that's what you do…you kill what you disagree with. You don't look for common ground. You silence other voices until yours is the loudest in the room. You're a coward—"

I slammed the phone shut and wound my arm back. I thought about throwing my phone into the street below, but my arm fell limp to my side, and the phone still weighed heavy in my hand.

It shouldn't even be my voice. I wanted yours.

CHAPTER 13
RECONNECTING AND RESTING

"ALONE, SO ALONE."

XÓCHITL | SEPTEMBER 8

I hadn't left Siu's apartment for three weeks. Though it was easily tenfold the size of our tiny truck home, I quickly became claustrophobic. It took me days to walk and even longer to run on the treadmill in the corner of the room I'd been assigned. The slow creep of progress did nothing to dull the repetition of the days passing by. Dr. Siu ran tests on me, and the robot kept asking me questions. A dull, orange sans serif blipped across its face, "Pain 1-10?" My response, as always, was "zero."

Apricity was allowed to leave for her daily patrol after the first week. She often came back with food and stories. Today, she perched on the arm of the sofa as the robotic assistant helped me go through my vitals. As of yesterday, I didn't have an IV. Now that my tetherball cosplay was done, I was extremely restless. App plopped a bag that repeated the words "thank you" on it in red on the table. She reached in and pulled out a quart container. A delightful spicy smell filled the air.

"Can we end this soon?" I asked the robot eyeing the receipt stapled on the bag inside the thank you bag. It seemed to be Korean letters.

The screen answered. "Your health is the priority. Please squeeze my hand as hard as you can."

I did. His three-fingered metal hand had no give. Then I was to push on it, testing the strength in my arm. As I did, I twisted slightly to make eye contact with App, who was already fishing in a pint container with chopsticks. I made an exaggerated face of force, something a bodybuilder or wrestler might have done. She smiled but didn't quite laugh. I turned back to the robot. "What were the five words?" his face said.

"Newports, ravens, coach, and then they forgot they were talking to me for a second cause the news was on the radio. Eventually, they said 'Hmmm, still here?' Ask Čapek," I said. It had been an entire three weeks since the doctor told me to remember five words, then I got distracted, but I wasn't going to let them forget.

"Very funny. It is late. You should sleep," it said. It had made it less than four steps before I was unwrapping the takeout.

"There's bapsang and Bibimbap, some dumpling things, scallion pancakes, and kimchi. I didn't know what you liked, so I got some spicy, some fresh...oh, and some tea." As App spoke, I organized the food on the coffee table in the living room. The food smelled so good and strong that it cut through the menthol and cigarette odor permeating the apartment.

"Thanks for the feast!" I said, already folding and dipping a slice of scallion pancake. I hesitated for a moment before I put it in my mouth. "This is like the third time you got takeout for me. Are you sure I don't owe you?" I heard my stomach protest but still paused for an answer.

"Oh, it's the least I could do after all you've done for me." She blushed, tucking her hair behind her ear.

I shoved the pancake into my mouth. My eyes closed automatically as the flakey outside met my tongue. I had forgotten to eat again. It must have been 9:00 p.m., but with the doctor's painkilling aura it was hard to remember. I had finished the whole first slice before my thoughts were collected.

"Wait, what did I do for you? You are the one bringing me food, and Pox is the one who helped you get out of trouble."

"You got me in touch. Besides, you keep me company, since Dr. Siu still wants me to sleep here." She quietly continued poking at her food.

"I wonder why they are keeping you here. You seem okay, and you're fine with going outside," I said, still shoveling food into my face with the sort of eagerness usually reserved for rabid dogs.

"Honestly think I'm here to keep you busy." As she spoke, she watched the robot enter Dr. Siu's office and lock the door behind them. "Plus, when I'm here, Leo's not, and to be frank, I think they hate him."

I pictured the last time Leo had come over. He had yelled at the doctor for smoking while taking my vitals, talked about how unsanitary this place was for a medical location, and how they should take me elsewhere. Dr. Siu had responded by promptly kicking him out.

They were pretty accommodating. This wasn't a hospital, just an apartment. There were small rooms that seemed more like guest beds than hospital rooms, and the living room was rich in texture and moody color.

The doctor was odd, and always busy in their office. I couldn't help but wonder what they were doing.

I must have been staring at the door to the office for a long time, because a hand waved between me and it, with black nail polish on long pale fingers.

"Huh, sorry I spaced out for a second." I felt tension in my ears, and the embarrassment surprised me.

"More than a second, love. Sometimes I wonder if you even like me. You live in a daydream so much."

"Of course, I like you! You always have my back. You don't even lecture me about recklessness, just genuinely help. You seem to get it, like, *really* get it. Also, you're so beautiful I feel like a blob person standing next to you." I laughed a little, looking down at my own clothes, plaid pajamas and a tank top. It really drove the point home.

"Beautiful?" she looked a bit shocked

"I mean not in a creepy way, but yes, you're stunning."

"Stunning? I feel like things are escalating. You should keep talking," she said, leaning closer to me. I laughed and tried to figure out where I stood at that moment. I couldn't stop staring at her face. She had this tiny smirk, and my eyes kept falling to her lips as she spoke. I blushed and thought about Greg. *She doesn't even like girls, ya wasting your time.* I leaned away, straightening myself out in my seat.

"What, uh, what do you think they do in there?" I gestured to Dr. Siu's office. A flash of annoyance splashed across App's face.

"None of our business," App said, sipping at her tea.

"Čapek and Andy are in there ten-plus hours a day. You have to be curious."

"Nah, the doctor helps me so I can stay out of their business. You're the one who likes a mystery to keep you sane."

"You might be right. I don't hold still well. But I think they must be working on something big."

"There *has* to be other things you think about, or is it conspiracy and tinfoil hats all the way down?"

"There's some read strings and pins on maps I think," I said.

"Xóchi, I'm gonna level with you. Do you like women?"

"Yes, I mean, not exclusively, but yes, some women. I mean, not that I want to make you uncomfortable." I was suddenly very aware of the part of the sofa our legs shared.

She leaned over me. Her hand reached for my chin. "You're an idiot. I mean..." She gently pulled my face up to meet hers. Her lips nearly brushed mine when she spoke. "This." The whisper was so small and close and quiet, it felt secret.

She pressed her lips against mine, and my mind broke slightly. I was shocked, not because of our genders or that she was a hero, but because she was so perfect. For all the webs of secrets and mysteries, for all the wondering and thinking I did all the time, I had not once considered anyone, especially anyone like her, would bother taking an interest in me. There was this magnetic pull that I couldn't, and wouldn't, break. She pulled away and looked down at my lips.

I hadn't imagined she would kiss me. But once she had, all conspiracies faded. I could think of nothing else. She pulled away, and I nearly fell on top of her. The absence of her kiss knocked me off my feet.

"Sorry, you're not an idiot—" She genuinely seemed apologetic, and I probably should have answered. But it felt as though she was apologizing for the wrong thing. How could she worry about a petty play insult when she dared to stop kissing me? All I wanted was to press my lips to hers. So I did, and this time I was prepared.

The shock gone, all that was left was my need for her. My tongue slipped between her lips. Her hand slid to the back of my head, fingers tangled in my hair. She pulled me with her as she leaned back into the couch, my knee pressed between her legs as I fell against her. I broke the kiss to look down for just a moment. I wanted to etch the image in my mind: the near-black navy couch behind her as her pale hair poured over the side in a waterfall of blue. Her face was flushed, her mouth hung open. Her hand slid down the nape of my neck and she pulled me toward her. I kissed her gently, but the urge to taste more of her was overwhelming. I kissed her jaw, her neck, my teeth grazing her skin. Traces of lavender from her shampoo lingered on my tongue. She pushed me off gently. I rolled my shoulders back and removed myself from the sweetness of the place where her shoulder met her neck.

I must have misread. God, I'm stupid. The word "idiot" rang in my mind as I got off her. I could feel my pulse in every part of me, the sound of my own heart near deafening as she got up and walked down the hall away from the living room toward her room. I touched my lips with my fingertips, trying to remember the smell of lavender. She stood in her doorway at the end of the hall and turned to me, pulling her jumper down one arm and then the other and letting it drop. I felt like a cartoon, my jaw hung open in admiration. She stood pale against the darkness of the apartment, glowing faintly in nothing but a lacy pair of black panties. I stumbled off the couch, running to her to press her against the inside of the door. Lips finding hers again, I slipped my tongue into her mouth. She sat back on her bed and pulled me with her. I broke the kiss to unabashedly stare.

She lay on the bed. My mind short-circuited, words failing me. All I could think of was the way she glowed like some kind of divine being. Her hair was a halo, her skin luminous against the navy of her sheets. Lips parted in invitation to mine. My fingers traced her in meandering trails around her torso, limbs, and breasts, studying every inch of her. The way she shuddered beneath the slightest touch. The small gasps and tremors in anticipation as my fingers explored her, her head tilting back, eyes closed as a small, secret smile found her lips. I began kissing trails after my fingertips, taking her breast into my mouth as she moaned. I flicked my tongue around her nipple. One of my hands grasped at the breast I tended to while the other continued to trail farther down. Her hands pulled at my shirt, and I sat up to pull it over my head.

For a moment, I hesitated. The view from my new angle was so stunning, I wanted to imprint the moment in my mind forever. An inkling of doubt crept in.

I thought of her view, of the bruises and scars, marks, and flaws. *Why was someone so perfect here like this with me?* I shook my head and refocused. I prayed my touch was soft in spite of the roughness of my hands. The gentlest traces. She pulled off my sports bra with one hand, her other hand tugging my shoulder so that I was on top of her again, my lips against her. And the insecurity vanished in a moment of bliss. The taste of her fresh on my lips. I needed more. My worries and doubt faded, replaced with desperation. I slid down, following my previously mapped trails with my lips, my tongue, my teeth.

I pulled her small black panties off her in a minorly clumsy move. In a tangle of legs and elbows, the self-doubt crept in for a moment, but the need for her was stronger. The moment I touched her she shivered. I felt a grin crack my face. The desire to see every secret tremor and hear every gasp of breath became my new obsession. I knelt beside the bed and, with both hands, pulled her hips to the edge and watched her face flush as I buried my mouth in her. She tasted salty and sweet and perfect. Her hand snapped to her face, covering her own mouth in an almost comical act of modesty. I thought about pulling it down, about telling her how I wanted to see her and hear every moment. If it was my apartment, my actual bed, I might have, but lying in the borrowed bed, discretion made more sense. Besides, my hands were occupied. She was so slick when my fingers slipped into her that I hoped I might drown. What better way could there be to go? Her legs rested on my shoulders. My fingers pumped her, and my tongue twirled circles around her clit. Her legs tightened, wrapping around me and pulling me into her. Barely muffled moans escaped her lips as I kept a steady pace. All too soon, her hands snapped away from her mouth to the top of my head, grabbing my hair in desperation as she came. Her back arched and her body tensed as she gasped at the air, letting a moan escape that echoed around the room. I didn't stop until her legs fell heavy on my shoulders. I broke for a moment before her hands, still tangled in my hair, pulled me to her face, and she kissed me deeply. I stayed locked in the tangle of fingers, still surrounded by her pulsing and wet. Until a loud voice boomed from the hall.

"IT'S THREE IN THE MORNING! SHUT UP AND GO TO SLEEP!"

I froze like a kid with her hand in the cookie jar. Apricity started giggling, and I untangled us and plopped on the bed next to her. She leaned over me and brushed my hair out of my face before kissing me on the forehead. I felt a little pang of pride as a bead of sweat dripped off her face onto mine. Her hand trailed down to the fly on my jeans. Passing over all the flaws I was so worried about. I kissed her.

And again, the voice from the hall. "I MEAN IT! Fuck again in the morning! After I've had coffee, please!"

"Do they have cameras in here?" I asked, looking around a bit embarrassed.

"So what if they do?" Apricity answered with a giggle.

I pushed her hand away and scanned around the room, looking for a red blinking light.

"Tinfoil hats all the way down." She giggled. Her hands pulled at me, shifting so I was beside her on the bed. And I gasped slightly between a giggle.

"Sleep," the doctor demanded, the smell of new ports and the numbness thickening in the air. Then, compelled by a force of supernatural nature, we both fell into a heavy comfortable sleep.

CHAPTER 14
PREYING ON PARASITES

"IN THE DARK, I PROMISED THE
GODS I WOULD HEAR THEIR
REASONING."

XÓCHITL | SEPTEMBER 9

The old rotary phone rang, and I was startled awake. The room I was in was mysteriously absent the navy sheets and the beautiful, glowing woman. I walked into the hall, still not sure if I was dreaming; I never had dreams this good. I had just enough time to catch Apricity on the phone before she swung a modern-looking chair to look out the window. She stared down at Pox in his plague doctor costume on the other side of the street and pouted.

"That's my cue," she said, sliding into her shoes and shrugging on a simple gray jacket.

"He never comes in. Do you know why?" I asked. Apricity looked panicked, as though she had a secret she wanted so badly to tell. I nudged her with my foot and smiled.

"Uh, um, I think there's history there?" she said, almost too quickly, before kissing me on the cheek and sprinting out the door. That *was* interesting, the secret but also the kiss. I had plenty to think of all day while Siu hid in their office.

Like most days, the doctor worked on something behind closed doors, for hours and *hours*. They and the robot argued and muttered to each other. The look across Siu's face when they took their rare breaks reminded me of Leo when he was about to fail out of grad school. I saw a cocktail of burnout and determination. He always brushed me off if I asked about it.

Being locked in this velvet cage of an apartment was brutal, but having a secret helped keep my mind sharp and made it not seem so bad. I learned some other things during my time at the clinic. First, when I heard the doctor call the robot Čapek, I learned that it was more than just a namesake; it actually had some of the older man's memories downloaded into it. Siu referred to the robot as if it was Čapek himself. Secondly, Siu had known the living version of Čapek for a very, very long time. This brought me to fact three: our most esteemed Dr. Siu was *old*.

They looked between twenty-five and thirty—no wrinkles, no lines around their eyes when they smiled. There was a shock of white to their black hair by both temples, but before now, I thought it might have been a fashion statement. Nonetheless, the doctor was at least in their late eighties. There were photos on the walls with Siu's image rendered in grayscale. The edges were cracked and yellowed with time, and the frames were altered more by the sun than their still-breathing subject. There were framed medical degrees—all about twenty-odd years apart—dating back to the forties, each subsequent one more faded than the last. And then there were the songs.

They always worked with music playing in the background. It drifted softly out of the office's barred doors. I didn't know if it was just to make their muffled frustrations harder for me to hear or if it was a genuine preference. The music was almost always the same lo-fi voice accompanied by a lone piano. I'd tried to use my phone and my laptop to identify the artist, but the lyrics came back with nothing; even song-identifying apps couldn't place the melody. Whoever sung these songs on the record had been forgotten by time, by all but Siu themself, whose home was often filled with her voice.

They did see patients other than me. All of them were Powered. Many of them got turned away from hospitals. If their injury was unique or interesting, Dr. Siu seemed more inclined to take the case. They also had regulars who came for prescriptions. I think a few people even showed up for therapy, though Siu was hardly someone I would confide in.

Today there was one such appointment. I didn't know the specifics, but the man's hand appeared to be made out of glass, and Dr. Siu seemed exasperated by his presence. While they were distracted by the distraught man, I snuck into the office from which I had been banned.

The office turned out to be more of a lab. There were pieces of test equipment I didn't recognize sprawled across a black soapstone desk. The cold stone reminded me of a chem lab in high school. The walls were lined with journals and binders, some were medical textbooks but most looked to be handwritten. I opened the desk drawers and found petri dishes, gloves, and masks—all normal medical supplies. I shut the drawers one by one. I sat in the chair, frustrated at finding no answers.

That was when I saw it. *The vial.* The one I had dropped just as the roof was blown off in Čapek 1.0's lab.

And they had left it on their desk instead of in some locked cupboard. In plain sight.

Strange.

I grinned ear to ear while inspecting it, turning it over and over in my fingers. It was definitely the same one, the same name, the same code, and inside was still a bit of deep-wine–dark blood swirling as I turned it. I noticed movement just past the vial as Čapek 2.0's head tilted inquisitively to one side.

"I knew it! You're still trying to cure powers."

The robot's face was showing an hourglass turning before an orange-text "yes" appeared.

"Why hide it from me?" I half-murmured before the text audibly blipped out.

"The more people know, the more likely *he* will know," he answered on screen.

The text scrolled fast, but once it was done, the photo from the day we met replaced it. Apex was shooting down the robot in that one. It clicked while zooming in on the "hero's" face.

"But I could help," I said. The words came out, but I didn't know how true they were. I was no doctor. Not a scientist either. The only way I could help would be if I told everyone. That would cause more chaos than assistance.

"Yes, you can," Dr. Siu said, their velvet voice coating me in an impossibly numb wave from the door behind me. "In fact, you already have."

They crossed the room, and I felt a chill; then tension began to knot in my shoulders and jaw despite my dulled senses. My hand was in the cookie jar—I'd been caught. They opened their still-locked desk drawer and pulled out a similar vial of blood.

"You know how powers awaken?"

"It's stress related. Some people, when they break, find themselves with new abilities. Often, those abilities mimic the situation that caused the stress. Like, Leo wanted privacy after I moved in, so when he felt overloaded, he literally made space."

Andy set the new vial on the table in front of them.

"That's true for some. But it's not the full equation. They need to be exposed first."

I felt my tension lessen.

Was I not in trouble?

I gripped Apex's vial in my hand behind my back.

"Exposed?"

"To this."

I heard beeping and a safe unlocking. They pulled out a small petri dish and placed it on the table next to the sealed vial. In it, something wiggled and moved. I leaned in closer to get a better look. A golden spiderweb was sticking along the interior of the dish, and it shifted until it reached toward the vial.

"What...is that?" I asked, unable to look away.

"That's power. Distilled from me. Truth be told, it's almost like a parasite. It moves, feeds, has a will of its own, and it wants what all parasites do—a new host," Dr. Siu said.

I stared at the thing in the glass dish, and something in my stomach turned. I knew instinctively that there was an otherworldly hunger, a danger in this room. Every fiber of my being told me to run. My feet stayed fixed in place despite my intuition, and my eyes locked on the glowing, shifting web of tendrils. I felt like prey already cornered.

"But not everyone is compatible," Dr. Siu said. They opened the lid of the dish, and the web gently pulsed. They dropped some blood from the new vial on top of it, and a tentacle no bigger than a hair reached up toward the droplet. But when it made contact, there was a hiss like water in hot oil and the web hollowed, clinging to the edges of the dish away from the drop. "You, for example, cannot be a host. You are a toxin to it, as are most people."

"That's why some people don't get powers? They are resistant to...that." I gestured at the golden nest of strings still sizzling and trying to escape the center of its enclosure.

"That's the theory."

"So you needed blood?"

Dr. Siu shrugged and said, "Well, any Powerless person's blood."

"Why not use yours for the experiment, or why didn't Čapek use his own? Why do you need Apex's?"

Dr. Siu looked grim for a moment, then carefully reached in and cleaned the speck of blood off the glass disk with a cotton swab. In seconds, the golden web was repaired and squirmed over the center.

"Because some people are better hosts than others."

They reached out their hand, and I gingerly placed Apex's vial in their palm. Dread sat heavy in my stomach. Čapek stepped in front of me with a defensive arm across my chest.

Siu spilled a single red drop in the vial, and the room exploded into chaos. The thin tendrils shot out in every direction. They grew thicker and faster and whipped around, lashing at Čapek and me. I felt primal fear clutching my heart as one bounced off the robot's shoulder and flung itself toward my face. I felt frozen, sure this was somehow my demise. Then suddenly, they were no longer animate. They lay limp along the table in every direction, like the vines of a wilted plant. The golden web in the petri dish was replaced with a black ichor that spilled across the room and dissolved.

"What did you do?"

My fear was still obvious as I noticed the gashes in Čapek's metal arms where the tendrils had made impact.

"I cured it."

The victory in Dr. Siu's voice was strangely profound, like a hunter standing over their prey or the caveman who created fire. They held a syringe over the petri dish filled with a clear liquid. It looked like saline or water. Unimpressive to look at, yet it was easily the most valuable thing in the city—maybe in the world.

I looked up at Siu. I never noticed how sharp their features were or how toothy their grin was. They were the very figure of a human possessed with a purpose. I suddenly realized that I had merely been a pawn in their game all this time.

"Now…what do you do with it?"

Siu deflated a bit, staring transfixed at the syringe before spinning in the chair and placing it in a safe. They slammed the safe shut while adjusting their coat, back still to me.

"I think, for tonight, we drink champagne and toast victories. Tomorrow, I'm afraid, we may be fighting a colossus or two."

CHAPTER 15
FRISSON FIXATION

"WHY TAKE THE WORLD FROM ME, MY HUSBAND FROM ME?"

XÓCHITL | SEPTEMBER 9

The doctor had already sent the word—today would be my farewell party. I was to be discharged. I felt another pang in my gut.

Was I just kept around as a test thing?

Despite my misgivings, the apartment had been decorated. Leaves were added to the table, and beautiful opalescent champagne flutes with gold rims were washed and dusted before being set out.

Andy normally seemed aloof with the kind of intentional practiced movements fitting to someone their age, but that day I could sense some jittery excitement. The same songs were hummed at a quickened tempo as the table was being set. The curtains were opened, the home was dusted, and somehow they reminded me of someone about to propose. Everything needed to be perfect.

The apartment was filled with the scent of good food instead of cigarettes. The windows were open to let fresh air in. The heat wave had finally broken, and it left the apartment breezy and comfortable. Just as the last fork had been placed on the table, a buzzer filled the room with an unnaturally loud ring. Čapek pressed the door release, and within moments Apricity, Dianna, and Leo were in the apartment. Dianna had even brought flowers and a get-well card. I hugged App at the door, and she pulled away embarrassed. *Oh, I guess not in front of everyone?*

Lingering in the door was a man I didn't recognize. Black curls fell to his shoulders, and gray eyes peeped over an N95 mask. He was wearing a black sweater with a black button-down under it and leather gloves. He lingered in the doorway, seeming unsure. While everyone else hugged and fussed over each other, he stood planted in the hallway, locked in place until App reached back and grabbed him by the arm. I tensed at the sight.

"You're being weird," she said and pulled him in. By his hands. A gesture that seemed too familiar for my liking. As soon as he was in the apartment, color returned to his face. His shoulders dropped, and he visibly relaxed. Andy, upon seeing him, put a glass in his hand and pulled him into a tight hug.

"I'm glad you made it, Vincent. Tonight, your being here means the world to me," they said.

It was the softest I'd heard them speak—genuine joy perhaps. The robot returned and ushered us to the table.

At the head of the table, Dr. Siu raised their glass and toasted, "To Xóchitl!"

A small chorus of "To Xóchi!" echoed back, and I stared expectantly at the host, waiting for them to drop the real news. But instead, the doctor winked at me. Everyone clinked their glasses and took a sip. The man in the mask lowered it to take a sip, revealing a gaunt face with a somewhat hooked nose.

"You're not gonna tell them?" I exclaimed, slack-jawed at the host, who let out a sly little laugh. A concerned pile of confused faces turned to me.

"Are they dating?" Apricity whispered a little too loudly to Leo, who spit out his champagne.

He laughed a little, then whispered back, "Xóchi doesn't date."

I winced slightly at the comment, made to the one person in the world it may no longer hold true for.

Vincent looked a bit confused and turned his attention back to me as Pox's familiar voice asked, "Why don't you enlighten us, Ms. Ramirez?"

I remembered Apricity's word—*history*. I looked at Dr. Siu, and they nodded and took a sip, a devilish grin peeking out from behind their glass.

"The first time I was brought here by the robot, he had rescued me from an explosion at Čapek's lab. See, he was working on something that he was trying to hide, and Apex wanted to stop his work, so he killed him and tried to kill me," I explained.

There was a medley of reactions. Apricity's eyes widened in surprise, Leo looked predictably concerned, and Dianna was gripping her cloth napkin in her lap, face hidden behind hair and glasses. I instinctively reached toward Dianna. It seemed to me she needed comfort.

But Pox cleared his throat. "Apex is well respected. He doesn't just go around murdering. What was this research?"

"A cure," responded Dr. Siu, accompanied by a smile that was all teeth. Vincent put his hand to his chin.

"For?"

"For us."

Dr. Sui's grin glowed with manic delight.

"You continued it?" Pox's voice sounded grim, but there was the faintest trickle of hope in it.

"Yes, and I completed it."

Dr Siu's eyes remained fixed on Pox—it was a knowing look, an understanding between just the two of them.

"For any powers?"

A trickle of hope flooded his voice. It sounded as though he might burst into tears.

"Yes," Dr. Siu confirmed.

Tears stained Pox's mask, and a muffled half-laugh, half-cough was all he could manage for a response.

Dianna, Leo, and Apricity caught up, and a bunch of "Ohs" filled the room as Apricity drank deep from her glass of champagne.

"That's world-changing...I don't think we should keep it. Shouldn't we give it to the PPD or something?" Leo suggested, seeming to still be worried about me. I shot a concerned look at Vincent, whom I thought would share the sentiment. But instead, he spoke up.

"This is something that should be handled in a medical capacity, in my opinion. Even a perfect version of the PPD, completely devoid of corruption, would use this punitively, and I am unsure if that is fair."

Less of a narc than I thought.

I briefly considered how things may have gone differently a month ago had I included him.

"What about Zephyr or one of the other Powered agencies?" Apricity suggested. She was shaking slightly, and it seemed she was afraid she'd be added to a body count to stop this cure from existing.

"No!" Dianna responded before I got a chance to answer. She slapped her hand on the table with enough force to make flatware jump. "I m-mean, they are financially motivated to keep as many powers on the street as possible, and they don't always act ethically."

"Aren't you represented by Zephyr?" I chimed in, recalling to whom I sold the images I had taken not long ago.

"They aren't all bad, but well..." Dianna trailed off, and Dr. Siu spoke up.

"You don't have to tell us if you don't want to," they said. Apricity jumped to her feet, towering over the doctor, stopping them short.

"Eff that! If you know something we don't, you should tell us. Any secrets could put us in danger." Apricity crossed her arms and plopped back in her chair as she spoke, looking all the world like a pouting child.

"That's unfair. She's under contract with them. I think we should trust her," Pox said.

The attempt to soothe his sidekick seemed only to frustrate her further. Pox's tone was reminiscent of a school teacher.

"No, she's right. It's relevant. When I was just starting at Zephyr, it was in the early 2010s. I was still a kid, but, um…there was this hero, Frisson," Dianna explained.

"I remember him, the musician who controlled soundwaves. He was awesome! What happened to him anyway?" Leo piped in, as the resident hero nerd.

"Apex happened. I was just a kid, but Frisson was starting to get really popular. There was even talk of building him a statue and getting him a movie deal. One day, while I was waiting in the hall, they were all in a meeting, and I heard Apex screaming. He was furious, and he shot a laser in the meeting room that split a desk in half. Less than a week after that meeting, Frisson died in a freak accident. Zephyr barely reported on it. He was *everywhere*, and then poof—nothing ever mentioned of him again, not even a candlelight vigil. Just gone. I couldn't prove it, and I was scared but…Apex was walking on air that whole week."

The silence hung heavy in the apartment for a moment. The room was so quiet I could hear the champagne fizzing.

"No evidence?" Pox questioned tentatively. I started searching on my phone "Frisson" and "cause of death." All I could find were washed-up old articles that stated it had been a "tragic accident" or "building collapse." No funeral, nothing. Most of the time, when a big hero died, they milked it on every news station for years. This guy was ranked most popular the year he died, but the whole agency ghosted him.

I scrolled on my phone only vaguely hearing people argue around me. It seemed like a cover-up of some kind. I'd started with smaller leads. I had the date, and the building that collapsed was a Zephyr apartment building, the same one he had lived in. I continued to scroll, googled the address, and looked for witness accounts or other casualties—anything.

A decided lack of digital evidence. An unnatural lack. Not even crackpot conspiracy theorists on YouTube or memorials for others in the buildings. Nothing.

The void of information sat poorly in my stomach.

"Xóchi!" said Leo.

I looked up from my phone across the long table.

"Stay focused. This is not a meeting for taking down Zephyr. This is to decide what to do with the cure."

"We need to get rid of Apex, before he kills us all," I said, the words tumbling out before I could fully process them.

"I'm not here to kill anyone," Pox said as he stood to leave.

"Not kill—cure." The doctor's voice stopped him in his tracks, and he sat back down.

"I agree that may have to be our first big move, but I'd also like to quietly start treating folks. I have clients in pain who would truly never be at peace without the cure," Andy continued. Their eyes fell to Pox again, but he did not return the gaze.

"So this is a last meal," Apricity said from inside a wall of hair as the robot set a large, beautifully cooked steak in front of her and Pox. After that, the plates started coming out in pairs.

Dr. Siu lifted their glass. "A first. This is the first group in the world that knows. You all will alter the course of history. I've been around for some time, and I value the rarity of such a moment, a celebration that acts as a mental bookmark. This is the night where it starts, and you magnificent people are the ones who start it," they said.

Perhaps it was the champagne, or maybe it was the confidence in their voice, but most of the rest of the night was a joy. There was plenty of dancing and a few boisterous stories. Even Pox seemed to let down his guard after a time. I think I drank a bit too much, as my memory blurred until my blinks elongated, the darkness lingering longer and longer until I found myself unable to resist the temptation of sleep.

The alarm on Leo's phone played the same jarring cacophony it had for years at the same ungodly time. When my eyes opened, the room slowly came into focus. It was clear no one left the party so much as hung around and made little drunken camps littered throughout the apartment. My head was leaning on the arm of the small fainting couch. Leo was already up from the ground next to the chair, turning his phone off and untangling himself from his blanket. We left before anyone else was awake. Apricity had curled herself on the navy couch we once shared, glowing against it. I thought again of that night. I wanted to kiss her, to brush the hair out of her face. But instead, I placed my favorite coat over her and left with Leo.

The thing about selling coffee is you're supposed to be there first. The truck was open by 5:00 a.m., which means we were stocking milk at 4:00 and driving to locations with machines heating by 4:30. Leo had a spot in midtown this week, a good one that would hopefully earn back some of the lost revenue from being closed while I was unwell. The sky was still an inky black when we parked, opened the side shutters, and set up an A-frame sign listing specials.

By the time the sun had risen, we had a line and had already burned through four full pots of the house blend. Anyone who did what we did knew people came in waves. The ebb and flow of the tide was a recognizable pattern, but the wave was always enough to knock you down. It had been months since I worked the truck. My hands were stiff, my motions clumsy as though I had just started. We kept running out of coffee, tea, sugar, and cream. The little things piled up, and I played catch up all day until it was four in the afternoon and Leo closed the shutters.

I squatted behind the counter, knowing I should have been counting, cleaning, rinsing, and otherwise buckling down the café, but I couldn't find the energy. So I waited, recovering. Last night swam through my mind. The word "Frisson" came to the forefront, and I typed it into the search engine.

The hero came up, then there was music. I pressed play as I

slowly stood, becoming acutely aware of the ache in my muscles. I missed the numbness of the apartment.

I started cleaning while the first song played; it was the kind of progressive experimental rock that came into stride in the seventies. It had that same classic feeling. I realized I'd heard it before and never knew the artist. The sounds bounced around the truck, and I felt myself moving faster, noticing the creaks leaving my body. I wondered if the effect was supernatural or if it was simply the talent of the musician.

The folly of many progressive rock artists was that they seemed to meander. Instead of feeling like they were exploring, their songs felt as though they'd gotten lost or had no direction. Somehow this didn't feel that way. Despite the lack of predictable patterns, it felt as though it was leading you somewhere, sort of deliberate and pointed. As the last song played, I realized I had overfilled the small sink and it was pouring water onto my apron.

It was nearly six by the time we closed up. Neither of us had eaten, opting instead to down quart containers of too-sweet iced coffee.

The music had long stopped playing by the time I found myself in front of the pizza place, but I still felt the pull of it. It was obvious to me why this person rose to fame and why they topped popularity and music charts. It made sense how they rose, but how did they just disappear?

I inhaled the pizza, and about half my aches and pains seemed to ease. We both picked up our pace on the way back to the truck while eating a second slice.

"Leo, I know I promised, but..." I started. He was walking ahead of me, and his shoulders fell. I heard the sigh from several paces behind him. He knew what was coming.

"I heard the music, and I know where this is going. You did promise," he said. He wouldn't look at me.

"But no one knows. Just us," I replied.

"Just work the café, please," he pleaded.

"It's Apex."

"Xóchi, stop."

"I know, but I can nail the guy for real. Show the world for real—"

"XÓCHI!"

I couldn't remember the last time he'd yelled. His voice cracked, making me think it was as foreign to him as it was to me.

"But...Mom."

He stopped in his tracks. He always knew that's what the goal was, but I don't think he was ready to hear it. Guilt hit like a bomb.

This is manipulative. I am in the wrong. He's right. I shouldn't antagonize him. I can't work a shift. How am I supposed to take down the number one hero of all time?

"Your mom wouldn't want you to die," he said, and though I knew he was right, I couldn't bite my tongue.

"I'm going to do this. Will you help? Or will you let me die alone?"

He was frozen on the sidewalk. People flowed past us on both sides. Like stones in a river, we remained fixed. Shadows were long this time of day. Stuck there for a while, I started to notice there was less red in the crowd than there was the day before my injury. Black and gray shirts walked past, and I wondered if there'd been that big of a change while I recuperated in the apartment.

"I'll help, always."

I don't remember closing the gap between us, but I found myself squeezing him close, my face over his shoulder. "Thank you."

The morning was bright, and the sunlight dug into my head, leaving behind faded lines and ghost images every time I shifted focus. I took my medication, and we drove to the Zephyr offices. Three coffees and what felt like probably too many ibuprofens later, I was climbing the stairs to the company stationed across the square from the PPD. I spent a good deal of time outside the building not so long ago, but it never seemed as tall as it did now. Its shadow loomed over the square and the police department building, covering half of Apex's statue and shading the left side of his face.

I waited at the top of the large marble steps for Čapek and Dianna to arrive, all the while fixated on the bronze face of the person I was trying to incriminate. The distinct sound of metal on marble startled me out of my daze, and I looked down the steps at my friends.

"Welp, we only get one shot at this," I muttered as Dianna, Čapek, and I entered the lobby.

The lady behind the counter barely acknowledged us. Even with the eight-foot-tall robot, no one seemed to be surprised or alarmed.

Dianna piped up, "We have a 7:00 a.m. with Olive."

I heard a soft buzzing sound and a click as the door to the left of the desk opened. Dianna scanned a card, and we entered the elevator. I watched the floors *tick-tick-tick* away as we climbed ever higher. The glass wall in front of us showed the city fall away beneath our feet until the cars and cabs looked like toys. Then I could make out the tops of buildings. At Floor 94, well over the cloudline, the elevator dinged to a halt and the doors opened. Dianna handed the key card to Čapek, whose screen blinked "THANK YOU" in bright orange text.

"Good luck. Don't get caught," I said to the robot.

Dianna and I left the elevator, and I followed as she walked confidently down a long hallway that stretched the width of the building until we arrived at a large, frosted glass wall emblazoned with the name "Olive Miller" in gold foil. Dianna knocked and most of the glass became translucent, leaving only a portrait of Artemis on the pane. A young woman with perfect hair and a pressed suit was sitting at the desk. She waved us in, and Dianna pushed on the door. Once closed behind us, the glass on the door became frosted again.

How much would that even cost? Why so decadent?

"Hello, Ms. Miller. This is—"

"Ms. Ramirez! Big fan of your work. Your portraits really capture the nobility of my client," Olive interrupted. She stuck her hand out to shake mine, and I obliged. Her smile was large, gummy, and practiced. As soon as she stopped shaking my hand, she turned to Dianna with a sour expression and said, "Where is your mother? She's been gone for two days."

She sounded exasperated, and her tone was probably shorter than she meant it to be. I noticed the hint of bags under her eyes, carefully covered by layers of makeup.

"That's why we're here," Dianna said, her hands shaking slightly. I put my hand on her shoulder in support. "Artemis isn't my mother, she's...me."

Olive leaned back against her desk, not quite sitting on the edge, and tapped a pen against her lips. There was not even a hint of surprise on her face. She'd known for years, and she had chosen ignorance.

"Don't do this," Olive said coolly.

"Do what?" Dianna said.

"Dianna, Artemis has a brand. It needs to be protected. You aren't it," Olive replied.

Are you kidding me?

"How can she not be on brand? She is the brand. Did you not hear her?" I all but shouted.

"You're gonna make me say it?" Olive asked. She started tapping her foot.

"I know I'm not eight feet tall with a twenty-three-inch waist, but that doesn't change the fact that I'm her. Everything she does is my choice. She's literally just a...a doll."

"That doll is worth 2.3 billion dollars. That doll has a penthouse suite in one of the best buildings in the city. That doll has movies and TV shows, sponsors, and designers. THAT DOLL *IS* ARTEMIS! You're just some nobody. I don't want to talk to you about this again. I do not enjoy being your villain."

Olive shifted her focus down to her paperwork, breaking eye contact.

Dianna nodded, shaking tears loose that had been gathering in her eyes that whole time. For a moment, I felt like I could see inside her mind, all the insecurity that held her...all the anger bubbling up.

"Let me correct you. *I* am Artemis. *I* am worth 2.3 billion dollars. *I* have done amazing things, and I've done them as me. SHORT, FAT, GINGER ME!" Dianna shouted. She started waving her hands as she talked, light shining from her eyes like spotlights for just a second. "This is not a request. I am not your product! I am a person, and if you are unwilling to represent me, you're fired." She motioned for us to leave.

Olive yelled something about a contract as we left, but when Dianna shut the door behind us, even though it seemed a gentle movement, the glass wall shattered. Behind us, I could hear Olive yelling more about contracts and responsibilities, but neither of us turned back. We just marched on to the elevators. We didn't need a key card to go down to the lobby, and as we sank and were enveloped by clouds again, I saw our reflections in the glass. Dianna held her head high as tears ran down her cheeks.

"I am proud of you," I said.

She didn't answer.

We rode down the elevator in silence until we reached Floor 20. The clouds cleared up, and we saw something happening outside. There was screaming as people ran, and smoke billowed under the statue of Apex in Hero Square. Čapek lay cracked and broken in a crater in the ground. Apex loomed over him, crouched on the shoulders of his statue.

"No-no-no!"

I started slamming the ground floor button, hoping somehow it would get me there faster. Then, the glass behind me shattered.

CHAPTER 16
TRUTHS AND TURBULENCE

"THE GODS WOULD ANSWER."

DIANNA | SEPTEMBER 12

The *click-click-click* of the button labeled G was deafening in what should've been a quiet elevator. I closed my eyes and tried to steady myself.

Inhale, exhale, inhale.

I opened my eyes and drew the arrow, the bow heavy and cold in my hands. I stood between Xóchi and the glass wall of the elevator and aimed my bow at the ground between Apex and Čapek.

Exhale, loose the arrow.

The glass in the elevator exploded out, and wind whipped through the now-exposed walls of the bubble elevator.

Xóchi screamed, startled by the eruption of glass, as we were left with just the metal framework. Artemis formed, standing face to face with Apex, mere inches away.

I knew he didn't sign. He found the concept laughable when it had been suggested in the past. Instead, I furrowed my brow and mouthed the word silently: *Mine.*

Apex laughed, pulled back his fist, and slammed it into Artemis's face. I felt my own nose crunch, and blood flowed down my lips and chin. The impact was enough to knock Artemis spinning. Even so, she lifted her leg, kicking him square in his jaw with the momentum of his own punch. It sent him flying head over feet. He lunged forward through the air, charging her with both arms over his head. The impact was earth-shatteringly loud as the two grappled, pulling at each other. In the chaos, capes tore while stone fractured and chipped.

The crowd that had gathered to watch the conflict between Apex and Čapek started running away, curiosity giving way to panic as the near-gods fought. The PPD had already started barricading the street. People ran into nearby buildings and jumped behind cars.

Apex shot a laser from his chest while still grappling with Artemis. He smirked and said something, but I couldn't figure out what. Artemis crashed to the ground, leaving a crater next to Čapek. I felt the weight of the impact as pain flashed on my shoulders and back. She drew her arrow and launched it at him, still pinned to the ground by the force of his blow and the concrete that surrounded her on all sides. He dodged effortlessly over her as it shot through the tatters of his cape.

The elevator continued in jolts and jumps. The descent was terrifying. I thought the car might fall at any moment.

I drew the bow again and tried something I never had before. I loosed an arrow from *me* instead of from her bow. Bright white and shining like the moon, it flew forward and pinned Apex's cape to the statue behind him. I was hit with a wave of exhaustion for my effort. I fell to my hands and knees, struggling to breathe. My hands pressed into some of the broken glass on the floor. Blood from my nose and hands peppered the ground with crimson specks.

We were nearly at ground level. Xóchi jumped the rail of the elevator and exited through the broken glass. I tried to regain my breath. That single shot had taken every bit of my effort. I struggled to focus my vision and restore feeling in my heavy hands when a beautiful marble hand reached between me and the floor. I grabbed it and used it to stand.

Artemis, puppet strings cut and moving independently, smiled down at me. She stood me upright in an embrace.

"Finally, my little fawn."

The voice was bright, crisp, clear...and real. The heavy arms wrapped around me suddenly became light, and in a flash of moonlight, she was gone. In my chest, I felt her absence. There was a grief so concrete and certain that I was positive I'd lost her forever. Tears flooded my vision, fogging my glasses. I heard a shutter sound snapping me back to reality. Xóchi lifted her phone and pointed it at me from her spot on the ground below.

Apex had his foot on the statue and was trying to dislodge the arrow pinning his cape. Čapek had reassembled enough to display again. The words "I Have Proof" scrolled across his cracked face. I readied myself to jump the railing, taking off my jacket to use as padding to lift myself over the broken glass. When I did, I was impossibly light. I realized I was not even touching the ground when I kicked off and flew up and outward, then fell slowly, as though diving in water. I kicked off again, and my feet felt an invisible ledge from which to jump.

I am flying!

I landed on the ground in front of Xóchi.

"Are you okay?" I asked. She was grinning like she had lost her last bit of sanity.

"You're glowing," she responded, and I could see it on her face and on the metallic back of her phone. I saw a reflection wholly mine but glowing like the moon: glasses cracked, nose bleeding, hair wind-whipped and messy...and utterly beautiful.

I turned my attention to Apex, who had finally dislodged himself from the statue by ripping off his cape, leaving it pinned to the chest of his bronze likeness. I readied myself for a proper fight.

The man lunged toward the robot and scooped him off the ground. He flew up toward the tower. I started to chase after him when a voice cut through the noise of the sirens and screams. It was a thick New York accent reminiscent of an old movie character, and it played through a megaphone.

"Don't you think you oughta go on home?"

A woman with olive skin, black hair neatly tucked in a bun, and a perfectly tailored suit stared at me from the ground below. She smiled and mouthed the word "home," and I heard it echo in my mind again. All the other noises became muffled, distant things, and the word "home" echoed again. I felt myself fly off without my own consent. Below me in the square, everyone else left. People moved as if pulled away on invisible strings, all scattering in different directions.

"No, they need me. Wait, stop."

I couldn't even hear my own voice, just the word "home." I tried to resist, but my body moved like a train on a track. I felt my feet kick off the air, again and again, twisting and turning between skyscrapers, until I found myself outside the window to my apartment, on the balcony, out of breath and bewildered. I was home. Apollo barked from inside the door, spinning and howling and trying to climb up the door to get at me.

How!?

I collapsed from exhaustion and saw myself in the reflection of the window, the glow now gone. My glasses fell off my face as I tried to kick off the ground again and uselessly jumped only feet off the floor, with no resistance to kick off again and fly. Grounded, I ran through my apartment and out the door.

I got to the elevator and felt a twinge of fear. I started dialing Xóchi.

She answered immediately. Before I even got to speak, she interjected, sobbing, "I can't stop walking—help. My body won't listen to me. Everyone left. *Everyone*—the square, we are all pushing past each other."

"Where are you? I'm on my way."

I ran as fast as I could. A block from my home, my powers returned, and I could fly again. I tried to keep Xóchi on the phone but found multitasking difficult. It was probably twenty more minutes before I caught up to her, just a half block from the Cactus Café food truck. Leo waved happily at us from the window between guests. Xóchi kept stepping forward in an unnatural robotic way.

"I can't stop. Make it stop. My foot hurts!"

I looked down to see that she had lost a shoe at some point, and her left foot was trailing blood. I picked her up and carried her to the food truck. Leo, realizing something was wrong, flipped his sign to read *Closed* and rushed to help. Xóchi regained control over herself just as she leaned against the café door. She lifted her foot up to inspect it and plopped down on the curb. Leo came out of the back of the truck with a first-aid kit. it was worn, both snaps were broken, and the front was cracked. He used tweezers and picked glass and rocks from the sole of her foot and bandaged it up.

Xóchi took some kind of pill and then plopped backward onto the sidewalk.

"What the—what was that? I...I couldn't...I couldn't stop. Not for cars, not for glass, not for my shoe. I couldn't stop."

She was panting between words. I thought about the woman with her meticulous suit and hair. She seemed familiar but hard to place. I felt like I had seen her in the Zephyr Building but couldn't pinpoint any memory specifically.

"I think it was a power," I said.

I could see the woman clear as a bell a moment ago, but now her face was blurred in my memory. I knew time passed because Xóchi's foot was entirely bandaged, but there was a hole in my memory as to what happened after that. When I regained my thoughts, I seemed to be in the middle of a conversation with no idea how I got there.

"How do we fight mind control?" Xóchi said.

"What's this about mind control?" I asked.

Xóchi looked concerned. "You said you thought it was a power. That woman told us to go home, so we had to."

"What woman?" I responded. I couldn't remember what we were talking about.

Xóchi looked more distressed than before. She dug in her pocket and pulled out her phone. She scrolled back through photo after photo until she found what she was looking for. In a somewhat blurred picture, there was a woman with a megaphone. Her hair was in a bun, and she looked serene and calm, though she was surrounded by debris and broken glass, as if she had been somehow edited into the scene. She was looking directly at the camera with her sharp, golden eyes, and it looked like she had been saying something. The woman seemed familiar, but once again it seemed I couldn't place where I knew her.

"I'm sorry, I don't think I saw her during the chaos of the fight," I said, though somehow my words felt untrue. Leo stopped assisting Xóchi and put a palm on my forehead, his hand warm to the touch but rough and calloused from his work. He looked concerned for me. His eyes were kind despite the worry, and though I had met him several times, I don't think I'd ever seen him this close. My cheeks flushed.

"She doesn't have a fever, so the forgetfulness might be part of the mind control power. Do you remember anything, Xóchi?" Leo asked.

"Oh my god, who are you? Where am I?" Xóchi answered in an overacted performance.

Leo looked at her, rolling his eyes, and threw a dish rag from his apron at her.

"Be serious for two seconds," he said before turning his attention back to me.

He sighed, then shone a flashlight in my eyes and away.

"Did you hit your head?"

I shook my head no, and they both looked even more concerned.

"Do you have any other holes in your memory?"

I thought back, and there were a few, usually surrounding Apex. It was like I could barely recall small moments. Most of them were blurry or gone, including times I teleported home, unsure how I got there. I thought I was just overly tired.

"Maybe a few," I admitted, afraid of the deeper implications.

"Why don't I take you home, Dianna," Leo said softly.

I agreed before Leo stood up and pointed down at Xóchi.

"You, *go lay down!*" he scolded and pointed toward the truck. There was the sound of paper tearing, and the inside shifted behind the open window.

Xóchi got off the curb and said, "Yes, *Dad*," before hopping on one foot into the truck and plopping onto the lower bunk.

"I dread to see what a mess the café is when I get back," he said with a sigh, leaning the A-frame sign with their specials against the side of the building.

"Sorry," I answered, wondering how often that happened, or how much he paused his life for his sister. "I can get home on my own, really."

"What? Absolutely not! At least I got through the morning rush. Afternoons are slow anyway. Besides, if you have a concussion, I don't want you passing out on the street somewhere. It's the least I can do—you probably saved her life...again."

He reached his hand out to help me up, and I was reminded of the marble hand this morning. Once I was on my feet again, I found myself staring at his face. Our eyes met, and I watched his face flush red before he turned away.

"You live this way, right?" he asked. He pointed down toward my apartment. "Or would you rather see Dr. Siu? Are you up for walking?"

I nodded, and we headed down the crowded sidewalk. It was close to sunset at this point. shadows were long, and the sky sported a hint of pink to the clouds, like spun sugar. I looked up and wondered how I flew before.

What's next? Do I get a job or look for a different agent? Do I get a new name?

I didn't know how long I had been silent before Leo piped up. "You were amazing today. I knew you were Artemis, but I couldn't believe what I saw when you flew by over the truck. Really, I can't stop thinking about it."

"I flew over the truck?"

I tried to remember my flight from Zephyr Square to my apartment, but it was all a blur.

Why did I leave like that in such a hurry?

"Yeah, I was lucky I was handing a drink out the window or I would have missed you! You seemed almost like you were dancing, jumping through the air. You were so graceful."

I felt the heat rise in my cheeks, thinking about the concept of me dancing. Grace wasn't really my strong suit.

"I'm sorry if we, uh, interrupted your business."

Leo started laughing. The walk home suddenly felt very short.

"You brought Xóchi home, and the truck doesn't need more repairs. Today was a victory."

"How long has she been like this?"

The sheer amount of injuries the poor girl had in the last two months would make even the most seasoned heroes want to retire. He scratched the back of his head and looked up at the pastel sunset between the skyscrapers. He pulled his beanie off his head, and black hair fell to his jawline.

"It got worse about two years ago, but she never showed fear. She used to jump from her fire escape to mine across an alley when she was eight. We both lived on the fifth floor of buildings that were next to each other. We used to send paper airplanes across the gap or throw a ball back and forth. Then one day, she just jumped. Gave her poor mom a panic attack. It's just who she is."

I pictured her doing it now, even years after the fact, her grin just as wide. "So y'all go way back?"

"Did you just say *y'all*?"

I immediately shrunk back.

"Yeah, you know, *you all*," I meeped out, and Leo let out his familiar, easy laugh again.

"Aren't you from Queens? What's with the Texas bit?"

"I'll have you know y'all is used everywhere now, old man."

I thought of Olive's thick southern drawl and wondered if it had rubbed off on me. Leo started walking like a cowboy, still giggling, before he threw his arm over my shoulder and squeezed me in a half hug.

"I'm sorry, I'm not trying to pick on you. It's cute."

He let go of the hug after just a second and pointed at the building in front of us.

"This is you, right, cowgirl?"

I felt frozen in place. I didn't want to go in, afraid that if I walked away, the bond would shatter like glass. I lingered just outside the doorway to the big old building.

Our eyes met for a moment, and then he broke the silence.

"See you tomorrow?" he asked. I nodded and squeaked a little in an embarrassed response before running inside the lobby. I took the elevator up to my apartment and was greeted by Apollo. A note from the dog walker said he got out into the hallway and that my balcony door was left open. I tried to remember landing in my apartment, but it was still a blur. I petted Apollo between his ears.

"Go on a little adventure, did we?"

I pulled up my phone to tip the dog walker extra for her trouble and saw about fifteen missed messages from Xóchi. Most of them were images. In one of them, Artemis embraced me on the broken remains of an elevator, her normally dense stone giving way to ethereal iridescence as she vanished in my arms. There was another one of me flying, glowing—weightless and strong. The next was a blurry photo of the woman she and Leo kept asking me about—pretty, mid-thirties, olive skin, black hair in a bun. I still couldn't place her. And then there was an image of Leo and me walking away from her on a street, the sky pink and blue, and the two of us silhouetted against it. My cheeks flushed.

I flopped on my couch, staring at the vaulted ceiling. I supposed it now belonged to Zephyr. I wasn't sure I owned anything anymore. I looked around at my apartment and realized just how much of it was branded, floor to ceiling. This was Artemis's home, and she was gone.

I texted Xóchi back: "I want to tell the world what happened today. Tell the world who I am."

A small word bubble with three dots hovered at the bottom of my screen. The ellipsis rose and fell in a wave, stopping and starting again.

Eventually, after what felt like an eternity, I got a message back that read, "Please meet me at 6 am at the food truck. I can get us a spot on the news."

I let the phone drop on my chest and felt myself drift off to sleep on the couch with Apollo curled up beside me.

It was five in the morning when my phone vibrating on my pillow woke me up. Half asleep, I answered the call.

"WHAT ARE YOU DOING? WE TALKED ABOUT THIS!"

The southern drawl pinned the loud voice on Olive.

"Good morning, Olive. What?"

I sat up and pulled the phone a few inches from my ear, waiting for a loud response.

"Your friend *So*-Che just published your secret identity and a bunch of photos. DIDN'T EVEN SHOP AROUND! I DON'T LIKE BEIN' SURPRISED, DIANNA!"

Yesterday was still swimming through the fog of sleep.

"Olive, is there a-a, um, well…someone with powers that makes people do things?" I asked, trying to hold the blurry photo in my mind, losing the details by the minute.

"Dianna, you are *way* out of line."

"Dark hair, well-dressed, New York accent?"

"Dianna, drop it. We can make this go away. We can just say you're her daughter and *So*-Chu got it wrong." Her accent seemed to thicken as her temper rose.

"Why won't you answer? Black hair, dark eyes, was at the

square yesterday?"

Olive abruptly hung up the phone.

I pulled up Google and saw the article Xóchi must have written through the night.

I swear she doesn't sleep.

I clicked through to the photo of Artemis hugging me, then the one of me flying, the impossible glow of moonlight radiating from me. I knew I would read the article hundreds of times, but I only skimmed it this time as I made my morning coffee. Xóchi stated this was the true face of Artemis, gave my first name, and stated that there was a conflict in Zephyr Square.

I felt a smile cross my face before I processed the emotion. I was about to lose everything: my contracts, my cut of the action figure sales, and possibly even my apartment. And somehow it didn't even bother me. For the first time in my adult life, I was free, honest, and fully myself.

CHAPTER 17
IN SICKNESS AND IN STEALTH
"I WOULD MAKE THEM ANSWER."

POX | SEPTEMBER 20

I had been represented by Zephyr since I was sixteen. They'd paid me reasonably, and I had good benefits. They'd always supported me in my vision of what it meant to be a hero. I never realized quite how much they did for me. My apartment, my medical care, my phone, my contract with the PPD, the costumes, the TV appearances—their logo was even on my Powered registration ID.

As I entered the building for what must have been the thousandth time, I looked around carefully. The woman at the desk flashed a forced smile as I walked up before buzzing me into the elevator room. Despite the events of last week, the building seemed pristine, aside from the "Out of order" sign on the leftmost elevator door. I scanned my key card and stepped into the adjacent elevator. Ascending to eighty-four, the highest floor my key card grants access to, I stepped out at the top floor of Powered Second-Class Security. Wishing I had Dianna's previous clearance, I set my mind on nabbing a card that could get me up the remaining sixteen floors of the building.

I had opted to wear my civilian clothes, hoping to get through this without throwing my career down the toilet. The medical mask turned a few heads, but in a world where masked heroes were common, no one really lingered long. I was here, so I simply must have belonged. I walked down the center aisle of cubicles, the felt walls obscuring the workers within. They were only as high as my chin, allowing me to see others strolling around. Swiftly and with purpose, I circled the office until I noticed someone get up to go to the bathroom. I sat in their chair with caution as soon as they were out of sight. I lowered my mask and exhaled.

Mononucleosis. The fatigue—just the fatigue symptom. Even I could feel my eyes losing focus as the fatigue settled over the room like a fog. Soon I heard a yawn behind me, then to the left, slowly checking off cube by cube. People shifted and chairs squeaked as people settled, trying their best to fight the ever-increasing weight of their heads and eyes.

It took nearly twenty minutes for the entire office to drift to sleep. I waited until the phones rang endlessly with no answer before I decided to stand. I looked around for the biggest office and was pleasantly surprised to find a corner one with two glass walls and a stunning view, belonging to one Ray Ritcat. Mr. Ritcat was the agent of the new and upcoming speedster hero, Mercurial. She had just been promoted to First-Class Hero, to replace Artemis.

The office was all boxed up, ready to move upstairs. The salt-and-pepper man, snoring face down on the table, had the name badge I was looking for in his hand.

I was bending down to take it from him when the world began to spin. I felt my limbs become heavy and weighted. Each finger movement creaked as I grabbed the badge and swiftly made my way to the elevator. I waited for the doors to open before I inhaled deeply, taking the fatigue with me. I faltered and leaned against the glass wall of the elevator. The view out the window from this high up increased my vertigo as I watched the light tick up the remaining floors.

Floor 100 was reserved for the top six heroes during crises or for meetups. Dianna said Floor 99 was her best guess as to where Čapek would be, so that's what I pressed.

I got a phone call. Once in the elevator, I glanced at the screen and saw Apricity's face, sticking out her tongue. I shook my head no, and she pouted and leaned back into the phone. The door to Floor 99 opened as I leaned back against the buttons on the only steel portion of the elevator.

Beyond the opening doors I heard, "State your name and purpose for visitation."

Not having enough time to spread fatigue, I settled for a less subtle approach. I inhaled and caught the air in my throat momentarily, then let out a soft, muffled cough. The person started coughing and sputtering as I walked in, and I saw two guards incapacitated by coughing fits as well. Their guns hung limply to their sides as they struggled on all fours and emptied their lungs of air and their stomachs of their contents. A third guard, sitting at a desk with a computer, was choking as well.

I ran past, grabbing one of the guard's cards. As I went, it snagged on the cord attached to it, but with a forceful pull it snapped off. My breath was still caught in my throat, my head getting lighter. As I ran, an alarm blared. The lights dimmed, then began flashing red.

This floor looked more like a prison than an office. Felt walls were replaced with concrete, and narrow halls and steel bars took the place of an airy glass floor plan. The key card scanned and unlocked a steel-barred door, which I slammed behind me before exhaling fully, my coughing and retching giving way to ragged, desperate breaths as my lungs cleared up. I knew the guards would come to soon as well. But I couldn't hold my breath longer than I did.

The hallway beyond the metal door was divided every twenty feet by more steel doors.

"Čapek!" I croaked down the hall, hoping for an answer. I eventually saw a single, rolling bolt on the floor, bouncing and sputtering, about four hallway dividers in front of me. I started running, coughing and clearing my throat.

By now, the guards had recovered and started pursuit. They cleared the first door as I passed through the third. I chased the tiny bolt as it bounced and twirled down the hallway and into a door slat. Tapping the key card, the door opened, and inside I found Čapek in disrepair, his parts spread across three separate plexiglass cages.

I slammed the door behind me. Swiping the card to lock the door resulted in a startlingly loud buzz and the words "enter pin" flashing across the security panel. App tapped the glass of my phone and gestured at the card reader. I let her out of my phone, praying the art of stealth was a miraculous, long-withheld skill of hers. She only half-materialized before vanishing into a gold light on the keypad.

My apprentice had a sordid past with crime. I was able to piece together some of it, but despite her being one of the most vocal people I knew, she had never elaborated on it. The pin flashed cyan, pink, and white a few times as I heard the guards in the hall shouting and clearing rooms one at a time. Eventually, she reappeared, confidently typed in the pin, 0628, and the fish-tank-looking prison popped open with a hiss. As she opened the other tanks, the hair on my neck stood on end. Something was wrong. The blaring alarm had given way to an eerie silence.

"App, get in the phone," I said.

She let out a snicker.

"Oh, come on, I'm actually being useful."

"Now." I tried to sound authoritative as I heard a beep. The door in front of me clicked, and the latch unlocked. I saw light, and my sidekick vanished just as the third cage opened. Čapek started reassembling.

As the door opened, I was taken aback by the golden glow around the man on the other side. I had seen him a number of times, but up close he seemed larger, his lines sharper. Looming in silhouette, he ducked to clear the doorframe, a smile full of teeth flashing. Apex stepped into the room.

"Hello, little rat. How did you scurry in? No matter, I have been looking forward to letting off some steam."

I heard the metallic scraping and clicking of Čapek still reassembling himself behind me, but at the moment I was alone in the room, face to face against the strongest man in the world.

I ripped off my mask and jumped up, hand going for his face. I knew I only had one shot. I felt my hand cover his mouth and thought hard about hemorrhagic fevers. I felt something warm hit my hand, and simultaneously, my nose started bleeding. He coughed and spit, but somehow still managed to grab the top of my head, throwing me like a rag doll across the room into Čapek, who was still only large bits of metal instead of the heavy-hitting backup I required.

I felt my bones break as I spit out more blood. The impact was shattering, but I felt my fever rise as I got back to my feet and put my fists between him and me. He wobbled, his balance shifting as his fever spiked and he, too, spit out blood.

"What did you do to me, you little freak?" he shouted. He gripped at his chest, a glow starting to form. I noticed another glow forming on my side. A dismembered robotic hand hit my phone and released App. She leveled a gun against Apex just as he released a laser from his chest. Searing pain sliced through me as the laser made contact with my shoulder, cutting into the bone of my bicep before the gun went off. The bullet knocked him back, but rather than doing damage, it just ricocheted off of him. His laser, still active, twisted, cutting through the wall instead of the rest of me. He kept coughing and sputtering blood.

App screamed as I saw a flash of light, and she vanished. The robot stood tall beside me and charged. As it swung at Apex, I saw Apricity encased in the screen of its face. She was still ducking, covering her head, and holding the gun in her hand. The text on the screen, layered over App, said, "RUN!" I didn't hesitate. I heard the metal man's feet charge after me. As I sprinted back through the lobby, I spotted scattered corpses of men burned by lasers all over the silent lobby—no alarm, no red flashing lights, just piles of dead people. I ran into the staircase beside the elevator and started my descent.

My head spun. The toll of the various illnesses was compounding, and the exhaustion was unbearable. The staircase seemed to become a rubber band, my perspective shifting closer and farther as I lost my balance and fell. I toppled head over heels until the staircase turned and I hit a wall and saw a small puddle of blood below me. My arm was spurting a grotesque shower into the ever-expanding pool of blood below me and dangling from tissue I couldn't identify, the white of bone visible through the cut on my coat.

I called *them* on my phone.

"Andy, hey...I, uh, overdid it. I'm at Zephyr, in the stairwell. I can't walk...can you get me? They don't seem to be chasing me. I don't know why."

I didn't know how much time passed. It felt like mere seconds before I smelled peppermint and saw a wheelchair. Well-tailored white trousers and oxfords interrupted my steady image of a red puddle on tile. The pain faded, and I wrapped my arms around them. Red ruined their white collar where my face gently rested on their shoulder.

"I'm sorry for your clothes."

"Shh, Vincent. Sleep."

I fell heavily into their arms. I was aware of a wheelchair under me, but I didn't remember sitting.

They wheeled me into the lobby. It was bright—blindingly, glaringly bright and far too loud.

Guards tried to stop us, but they faltered at Andy's cutting tone.

"They need a doctor. I am their doctor," they insisted. Their conviction granted us street access.

The world was suddenly dark, and I was so very tired.

In the apartment, my eyes opened, and I wondered how I ended up across the city. Andy was covered in blood. I hoped they were okay. I went to reach my hand to their face, but my arm wouldn't move, so instead, I spoke.

"I'm so sorry, there's so much blood."

"Shh, shh, shh."

"I can't move my arm." The words rasped in my throat.

"Shh, shh. I know. Shh."

They seemed so worried. I didn't think anything worried them.

"I messed everything up," I whimpered. The pain was gone, but the weakness made it so hard to talk. My tongue was thick, my lips heavy and clumsy, and my voice barely sounded like my own.

"Shh, sleep. You're gonna be okay, everything's okay. Shh."

I thought they were crying. I didn't think they cried.

"I still love you." Were I a coward, I would blame the blood loss, but I knew the words as I said them. I meant them and always would.

"Shh, shh. I know. Shh."

CHAPTER 18
ANDY'S AILMENT

"NO. I WILL MAKE THEM SUFFER."

ANDY SIU | JUNE 28, 1946

It was warm and muggy, but the sun was shining, and the sky had the perfect amount of white clouds. It looked like a cartoon or a drawn advertisement. It was early enough in summer that people weren't yet angry with the heat, and instead crowded to the beaches and parks for cute nights out. The air had a sense of celebration to it, and the hospital had been so slow and was as peaceful as ever. I was working in the emergency room, and not to sound ungrateful, I found myself with a lack of work.

I took a sip of coffee and gazed at the door to the quiet waiting room. I knew to stay on guard for the mood to shift, as it often did in the emergency room. It was calm—that is, until suddenly it wasn't. I got up fast enough that my coffee splashed all over my desk.

He was being half-carried by a cab driver, and although the cabbie was a big man with no shortage of strength, he nearly dropped the guy writhing in his arms. He screamed and jerked left and right in a seizure of some kind and appeared to have an infected wound on his chest. Blackness oozed out alongside crimson blood, all down his white T-shirt.

"Help! Someone help us!" the orange-haired cab driver yelled, trying to deposit the injured man in a wheelchair and having a rough time of it. There was a girl following behind them, small, well-dressed, shaking a little. Her brown eyes released a steady stream of tears as she walked after them like a duckling. She held a small silver box, beautiful and intricate. I couldn't tell if it was a music box or held jewelry or other such treasures inside.

Dr. Čapek seemed to be missing in action. I thought of all the times I found him smoking, flirting, or napping on shift, but I chased the irritation away with a sense of duty.

"Help me move him to a bed," I said, and the burly, bearded driver nodded. "One, two, three, lift."

As we lifted him, the man vomited over my shoulder, and black ichor streamed from his mouth. Gold and black tendrils moved in impossible ways, defying gravity while hitting me and the helpful citizen. They felt cold against the cloth of my shirt and seemed to wriggle and slither like snakes or worms rather than liquid. The two of us struggled to heave the man, still thrashing, onto the bed.

"You ever seen anything like this before?"

There was fear in my impromptu assistant's voice.

"I can't say I have."

I tried to feign confidence as he shook his head, agreeing to the strangeness of it.

"Help me get that strap," I said as I gestured to the restraints opposite the bed. We eventually secured the man, even though he was still thrashing, screaming, and whimpering.

"Aren't you a nurse? Can't you help him?" someone said.

I heard the thick city-accented voice come from behind me. It belonged to a woman I had seen following them in.

"Something jumped out at him from inside this box," she continued. "Some kinda weapon or creature?"

She handed me the box with shaking hands. It smelled powerfully of the sea.

The man lurched and broke the strap on top of him. I jumped

away, terrified. Those straps should be enough to hold four men down, let alone one who's lost so much blood.

The man screamed, "It hurts! Dear god, make it stop!"

The woman started sobbing.

"Aren't you a nurse!? MAKE HIS PAIN STOP NOW!"

Her words echoed in my mind, drowning out all other thoughts.

I rushed toward the medication cabinet to grab something to sedate the man, wondering where the fuck Dr. Čapek was all the while.

I finally saw him through the sheer curtain standing beside my coworker, both of their clothes askew, lipstick still on his collar. I grabbed the needle with anxious haste and turned toward the man to sedate him.

There was a sound like a wave hitting the shore, and I felt suddenly numb. A haze clouded my vision. I barely felt my own feet on the ground. The room became calm. The man said a few thank yous through labored breaths. I placed the still-unused needle on the cart.

It was the last time I saw the pain in someone's eyes up close.

The man fell asleep as Dr. Čapek walked into the room. The girl with the box set it down on the table next to her partner.

"You have to help him! You have to cure him," she pleaded to Čapek, who seemed just as lost as I was.

The patient, whose name I later learned was Maxwell, lay peacefully, a hole burned in his shirt, the straps smoldering at his side. It seemed the acidic wound had snapped them in mere moments. We treated him for infection, though both of us were unsure of what was actually wrong. Anytime I left the room, he screamed, so I stayed with Maxwell and his girlfriend for three days straight until men with guns and suits came and took them both away. They tried to take the box too, but it had taken root. Gold and black tendrils affixed it to the table, the table to the floor and the wall. Several men sawed at tendrils only to break saw teeth on the acidic roots. That room became inaccessible. The men with suits and guns sealed the room shut, a number of them falling ill after the exposure. Eventually, they bricked over the door, the glass, and the windows, sealing it in place.

We signed paperwork promising never to talk about that day or what we had seen, but inside a year, the entire world knew Maxwell's face, though the name was Apex.

I often thought they would have closed the hospital if it weren't for the impending shortage of hospital staff. The emergency room became very busy in that first year as more and more Powered folk showed up with newfound dangerous abilities. Their victims, whether accidental or intentional, piled up. It was less than three years until a new branch of medicine was being taught to keep up with them. Within five years, the Powered Police Department was formed, then talent agencies like Zephyr followed suit. Apex eventually became a household name, and that face was on lunchboxes and trading cards. Honestly, at the time I thought, *Good for him.*

The years went by in a haze, and time bent and stretched as most of a century passed. The useless Dr. Čapek retired to the island. The hospital closed and was bought by Apex, probably as a sentimental keepsake of some kind. My family died, and I felt numb, as did all of them. Decades passed, but none of it felt real, as though someone had turned the radio down to its lowest setting until only the suggestion of music was left, like the softest whisper of emotion. It was as if my heart had been sedated by both time and my power. Only the strongest emotions bled through the numbness—love and grief.

First for a woman, the voice of an angel whose talent shined brighter than time. She never got the chance to grow old and passed before the world knew her name. I felt pain again, in her absence, but only fleetingly.

Then many years later, I loved again, this time a man. The man was thin and sick but noble, with a beautiful optimism I thought had left the world.

I was killing him.

Simply being near me was much akin to being on morphine, and like morphine, he became attached and obsessed. Every kiss, every touch, every time he so much as held my hand was a hit for his addiction. But even in his intoxicated moments, he was always gentle and polite. I knew I would rot that goodness out. I knew. Eventually, my powers would end him, so I let him go. I chose to grieve his absence instead of his death.

The numbness came back not long after. Days seemed to be short again, and time seemed to run on too long. I took away the pain of many people, mostly those whom hospitals couldn't help. And then, after an eternity of monotonous gray days, I felt hope. That useless Dr. Čapek was less dull than I thought. He proved I could cure people. I could even heal myself and take my love's pain away.

I was hurt when Vincent didn't suggest using the cure over champagne and dinner, so I didn't suggest it either. He always took his duty so seriously. Perhaps when he was done and victorious, we could rest together in comfort. There was no need to rush. I could be patient.

Though little more than two weeks later, he lay crumpled at the bottom of the stairs, bleeding, suffering, and broken. I numbed his pain and stabilized him. Once I reattached his arm and he was sedated, he rested. I poured myself a tall drink and fell into the cup.

Some nebulous amount of time later, a knock on my door shook me sober enough to stand, though just barely. Xóchitl was waiting. She looked frustrated and tired. She was why Vincent had been hurt. She was why I had been elbow-deep in his blood. It was her fault, and she had the nerve, the FUCKING nerve to ask, dripping in my doorway like some stray dog, if she could come in.

"No."

She looked shocked, but I was still covered in blood, so she didn't press.

"Do you know who this is?" she asked, trying to switch subjects. Her phone showed a ghost I could never forget. I had looked for her and had assumed she was dead. For eighty years, I had not seen her once, not on the news, not on the street, nowhere. The girl with the box was a ghost dredged up from my past to haunt me.

Maxwell's girlfriend, whom I had met the day the world broke, was photographed clear as day—apparently, less than a week ago.

"No," I lied, but my face must have given me away.

"I knew you'd know her. We think she has mind control. She made me and Dianna leave in the middle of a fight—just said the words, and we had to."

I remembered the girl whose name I still couldn't recall, her words echoing in my mind. The night I saw the strange, metallic box.

Make his pain stop.

Realization dawned on me. I needed time now that my past had been abruptly dredged up. I slammed the door on the drowned rat on my doorstep without another word.

I stood there in shock with my back against the door.

That's it. That's what caused…all of this.

That woman in the photograph…her singular command had robbed me of my life for eighty years. It was her fault this was the power I was given. All this time, I had been nothing more than a vessel for fulfilling her wishes.

CHAPTER 19
WANTED AND WANING

"BUT WHEN I FINALLY WASHED ASHORE, THEY WERE GONE."

XÓCHITL | SEPTEMBER 19

My blog was *everywhere*. Zephyr tried to suppress the news at first, but Dianna's conflict on the day of her unmasking, and then her unexpected exit from Zephyr, led most people to believe it was just a super Powered contract dispute. Dianna had to pay a hefty ticket, but she managed to walk away with her reputation largely unscathed. The public was so taken by her true identity and the bravery she showed to be the most honest version of herself. Nobody else had ever stood up to any Super company, let alone Zephyr. It was my story first, and this…well, it changed *everything*. If I was going to take down Apex, it had to be with this momentum. My voice was finally grabbing ears, so it would be best to have them listen to the real story. I texted Mason. He said he was done, but I hoped I could be convincing.

"Can you pull a file for me? It's life or death."

The dots on the screen flickered in and out with the indecision of his response until eventually he texted back: "the café 4 pm."

Leo's food truck had been the popular place to be that day. I was surprised at how busy it was. There were people lined up around the block. It took until I was right beside it for me to realize why. Sitting neatly perched on top of the truck was Dianna in her new costume: silver laurels on her copper hair and an iced latte with the Cactus Café logo in her hand. She didn't have an agent or any assignments at the moment, and I had noticed she tended to stay near the café. She had been around nearly as much as me.

This meeting spot won't be as discreet as Mason needs.

Dianna waved as I approached. She seemed excited to see me, and I tried to muster up the same enthusiasm in spite of her presence ruining my plan. I forced a grin, waved back, and looked around. I scanned the faces in the crowd for Mason, my eyes pausing on men with dark hair and stubbled chins, hoping to spot my favorite under-caffeinated hipster in the sea of strangers. Dianna floated down to me, looking graceful with her hair and her costume fluttering in the breeze. The crowd parted for her, New Yorkers and tourists alike trying to pretend they weren't interested, even while casting glances or gawking.

"Xóchi!" Dianna exclaimed. She gave me a pleasant, soft hug. For a moment I felt lighter, as though her weightlessness and peace had somehow transferred to me.

"Hey, I'm meeting someone, it's supposed to be discreet. Could you take the light show for a walk around the block?" I asked. I tried not to let the irritation show through.

Not her fault — she's been nothing but helpful.

"Oh, uh, I guess there is a bit of a crowd. I was just talking to Leo, but yeah…yeah, I can go." I saw the glow around her flicker and dampen slightly, and the guilt panged in my stomach as the hug broke off. The weight returned to my sore limbs.

"Thanks, Di."

She smiled, and the light flickered brighter again as she bounded off, a trail of moonlight following behind her. A quick bounce, and she was floating in the window of Leo's truck. The two of them whispered something, lingering a moment. Then she flew down the street, leaving Leo to stick his head out of the café window to watch Dianna leave. He stared so intently and leaned at such an angle, it was a wonder he didn't fall out.

It was mere minutes until the crowd dispersed entirely. I lounged against a nearby light pole and gazed at my brother. He was humming as he made his drinks. It was a hypnotic sight that made me feel as though all was well. I snapped out of it when I was alerted to the presence of a man next to me, slurping loudly from their drink before making a sharp sound as it scalded them. The cup had a certain green mermaid belonging to a large chain on it, and he looked a bit disappointed as he blew through the lid.

"I said last time was the last time. I adore you, but it could be the end of my career if I get caught talking to you," Mason said. It seemed he had aged a year in the short months since I'd last seen him. His eyes were more sunken, his hairline was rising to reveal a steeper widow's peak instead of the loose suggestion it had been before, and salt now peppered his stubbled chin.

"I'm sorry, I don't know who else to trust. I know you will always do the right thing," I said.

"I try," he responded. He chuckled into his cup and took another sip.

"Do you know anything about Frisson?"

"Yeah, he was my favorite as a kid. Sounded like Motley Crüe but saved the world. What's not to like?"

For a second he was back, my hopeful friend from freshman year, a gleam in the eye of the now rough-around-the-edges detective.

"I know for a fact Apex killed him. I need help proving it."

There was a pause in the air, the muggy afternoon heat seeming to weigh on the silence.

"What good does that do?"

"What? What do you mean? The truth is everything."

"He's dead. He's gone. There's no fixing it, and if you already know for a fact, then what do you need to prove it for?" Mason said, sounding agitated.

"To show the world...to tell the world. If Apex is dangerous, then people need to know. He needs—" I was interrupted as a hand cut me off with a dismissive wave.

"We all *know*, Xóchi. We all know he's dangerous. Hell, it says on his action figure, 'Strongest Man Alive.' You won't prove anything, you will simply die. Apex'll kill you." I heard a hint of his partner's voice, an accent he never really had starting to creep into the vowels as he talked. My heart sank. He suddenly felt so far away.

"Can you just…pull the investigation file on his death? For me? I've got to see it even if it says nothing. I just need to know."

"Why? It won't bring him back."

"It's not about that. He needs justice, people need to hear the truth."

"Why? It won't bring them peace."

"Because without accountability, there are no heroes."

"There are no heroes. There never were," he said, his voice bitter.

His words sat in a pit in my stomach.

"What happened, Mason? You're off."

"Long day, lots of problems, another Powered conflict. Dozens dead, some of them were my men," he said after a moment. He seemed withdrawn as he spoke.

"Jesus, I'm sorry, Mason. You know I'm here for you if you need a different job or to talk about…that."

"You're not even here for me now, you just want something," he quipped, sounding hurt. The words rang too true for me, a valid sting.

"I just want to help," I protested.

"No, you just want a file. And I'll give it to you," Mason conceded. He turned to walk away, groaning as he did. "Oh, and Ramirez?"

"Hm?"

"Stay low profile. Don't make me work your case."

Once he was gone, I sat on the sidewalk, my back against the truck. I started typing everything I could remember. I was going to be an anonymous source credited with seeing all Dianna witnessed —the jealousy, the threats, the broken table, the collapsed building.

I tried to keep the tone from sounding like a bad op-ed about celebrity gossip or some kind of conspiracy nut job. The article was only around a thousand words, but I rewrote it over and over until it was dark out. I didn't notice the change from sunset to streetlights until the temperature dropped. With the air no longer stagnant and hot, its chill bit into me, and it felt as though autumn had finally started to creep in. Soon, but not yet, the leaves on the gingkoes were going to be gold and poor Leo would be selling pumpkin spice lattes to lines of people too long for him to manage. I heard the café window shutter roll down and the door open to the back of the truck. Leo jumped down and stretched before walking around to me, herding me into the cab to drive to our parking spot.

"When were you gonna tell me about Dianna?" I asked.

"When there's something to tell. It's nothing...yet," he responded with a shrug, but I saw the smirk growing as he spoke. The interior of the truck shifted with the familiar paper-tearing sound.

"Did I do something wrong? Everyone's been so weird today," I asked.

"Nothing. Well, nothing new anyway."

My phone chimed. There was a text from Mason, and he had sent an attachment. When the file finally opened, it contained a series of photos. Each one showed documents with redacted text and barely any visible words other than the date. It was over twenty pages of mostly black rectangles. Instead of answers, I had been sent a frustrating puzzle with intentionally missing pieces. I closed my eyes and rested my head against the side of the truck with an audible thump.

"Not my day, Cactus," I said absentmindedly to the logo above me. Opening my eyes, the streetlight above looked too bright. I shuffled into the truck and plopped on my bed. I heard Leo texting on his phone above me, followed by the vibration of a new message, a pattern that repeated until I drifted to sleep. Was that how it was supposed to go when you felt something for someone?

I thought about messaging her, but what would I even say? I turned to face the wall and forced myself to sleep.

My dreams were fuzzy, incoherent journeys through a city devoid of people. Buildings that should have been familiar felt looming and hollow. The streets that would normally be filled with cars got narrower with each step forward. It was like a force I couldn't fight. I couldn't stop myself from walking into its inevitable grip.

Soon the sidewalk was gone and there was no street to speak of —just a small patch of concrete between suffocating storefronts. Gold lights in the windows entangled with each other to form a web of golden strings. I felt the spider's silk break as I moved through them, ever forward. My feet hurt, and my shoulders were crunched between the half-familiar walls. I turned sideways to shimmy onward, still moving forward outside my own volition. My chest compressed, and it hurt to breathe. Still, I squeezed through as far as I could go.

I could see it now, Hero Square, golden light shining over the large statue and fountain. People were laughing and kids were throwing coins just a few feet away. I reached my hand out ahead of me. The space between the towering vise of buildings was only inches apart now. My hand could barely reach beyond the crack. I was twisted and crushed, incapable of inching onward. Only my hand could still feel the open air as I was consumed by the buildings like teeth in the maw of the city. I saw Leo in the square and tried to scream, but my chest was too compressed, and instead I wheezed, "Help…"

"Xóchi, you're having a nightmare. Did you forget to take your meds?" a voice said.

A hand on my shoulder shook me awake. Leo stood over me. I felt tears on my cheeks, and I coughed out a wheeze, my laptop on my chest aggravating some of the bruises I'd acquired. I sat up, laptop falling to my side on my bunk as I hugged my brother tight enough to hurt my bruises again. I heard the medication rattle in its container. How long had it been since I'd stopped taking them?

"This has to end," I said, crying on his shoulder. He nodded and hummed comforting words into my hair and let me stay like that for a while. A clock over his shoulder said 2:33 a.m. I broke the hug and said I was okay. He asked twice if I was sure before climbing back into his bunk. He fell asleep fast, exhausted.

I couldn't go back to sleep at all. I pulled my laptop back onto my lap and started typing. I wrote about my mom, about Čapek, and I talked about Frisson. I was careful to protect my sources. I didn't mention Pox or Dianna or even Čapek by name. I didn't mention the cure, just the wreckage of the explosion at the lab, just an anonymous witness's account of Frisson and Apex.

When I was done with draft one, it was five in the morning on a Monday. That meant the city was starting to come to life. Other trucks were fixing to leave, carts on the edge of the building were shifting around too—the normal chaos of mornings. Leo stayed in bed later than normal. It was nearly six before he was off his bunk, making coffee and brushing his teeth.

I should have had him read it. I should have made sure it was safe, but knowing I'd lose my nerve, I exhaled and clicked submit. It took a few minutes to upload and another half hour before traffic ticked up. I started getting messages, and the analytics monitoring visitors skyrocketed.

Then it stopped.

Just under five thousand views in less than an hour, then at five thousand forty-two, it froze. I hit refresh...and nothing. I clicked "view the article" and was greeted with the PPD logo.

This website has been seized due to illegal activity.

"Hey, Leo, take a look at this," I said with a little apprehension. He came over from the shower stall and stared at the screen.

"Wh—Xóchi, what did you do?" he asked, startled. The sharpness in his voice was mounting toward a lecture, but it was cut short by a knock on the back of the truck.

"PPD, open up."

Leo sighed.

"Stay still," he said. He got out of the truck and shut the door behind him, then I heard a click and that sound of paper tearing. There was a pressure change, and I tried to pop my ears while standing up from my bunk. I could see out of the windshield, but the world was empty, just a deep cold blue as if at the bottom of the ocean. I was alone. I pulled my phone out of my pocket, zero bars, no Wi-Fi. Completely alone.

The electricity didn't even work, and for a moment I wondered if I had enough air. I started pacing. I'd never hidden in Leo's pocket dimension before. It was colder than I expected, cold enough I could see my breath. I grabbed a blanket, wrapped it around my shoulders, and plopped down at the desk. I pored over the photos and articles I had saved on my laptop, the document of redacted lines from Mason, all the pieces I could.

"Fuck, I can't do anything in here," I said to no one. I spun in my chair and leaned my elbows on the table, fingers getting tangled in my hair. I thought of all the times Leo had bailed me out —metaphorically or literally—and I worried for him.

Is he being arrested? Are they searching the truck? Is he safe?

I hoped Mason was the investigator. At least Mason would know it wasn't him. It had never been him. It had always been me acting like a selfish child. It had always been him swooping in to take all the accountability for my actions.

My laptop ran out of power. I had no idea how much time had passed. I fell asleep again, my stomach sore from screaming and crying into the nothingness around me.

I woke up when a loud tearing sound ripped the green surroundings from the van. I jumped up from the desk and stared out of the cab. I appeared to be in a police impound lot, or maybe a dump. My laptop chimed with a loud *bing*, and I quickly slammed it shut, listening carefully. Now reconnected, the clock on the wall said 11:00 p.m. I'd spent most of a day in the safe pocket of the void Leo had made for me.

Hearing people outside walking around and seeing a flashlight shine down the garage in front of the truck, I sat still, hoping the threat was nearly past. I looked at my phone. The *Storm Chaser* blog was gone. Its Twitter, Facebook, hell, even its Tumblr and Paypal were gone as well. All the pages were replaced with a banner from the PPD marking it as a threat to Homeland Security.

My life's work was gone. My family was…imprisoned? Gone? Who knew where? I waited a while longer. I snuck out of the cab as soon as the coast was clear. It was pouring rain. It took me nearly an hour to find my way out of the lot. Maybe it was luck, maybe it was the rain, but the security guard was nowhere to be seen. Out of discreet options, I headed to Dr. Siu's apartment. As the door opened, a wave of warmth and comfort washed over me. I asked for help and was met with disgust.

The door had been slammed in my face, taking with it the comforting, Newport-scented numbness. I couldn't get ahold of Apricity or Pox. Dianna was headlining every paper and too busy dodging paparazzi to be of any actual use as an ally. Čapek had been captured, and now Andy had shut me out. It was back to the beginning, six months ago, when it was just me and Leo. Except this time, no Leo. I was on my own for now. I didn't know how to feel about that.

I walked down the long ornate hallway until I arrived at the elevator and pressed the button. I caught my reflection in the mirrored wall. I was dripping wet, and I realized I was still in yesterday's clothes. Catching my own eye, it dawned on me I had nowhere to go.

Maybe I should just go and turn myself in. I jumped the gun. I hurt Leo, and now I need to pay the piper.

I stepped into the elevator and hit G, already planning the best route to the PPD station, when a hand in a latex glove shoved its way in between the closing doors.

Vincent was standing there, wearing only pants, his shoulder covered in blood-soaked bandages and his arm strapped to his chest.

"Wait," he rasped as the doors reopened. "They have Apricity. I need your help."

He almost collapsed in the doorway, and I tried to get myself under his arm. The man was even thinner than he looked. Jagged bits of bone pressed through my clothes into me. I started shuffling him back to the door.

"Vincent, you don't look so good," I said. He coughed and shook his head no.

"I feel fine, don't even worry."

He smiled behind the surgical mask. I could see it in his eyes. Maybe I did still have some family on my side after all.

The door was still open to Dr. Siu's apartment, and he seemed to catch his own weight under him as soon as the aura of pain relief hit. Siu was, for all the world, pouting into a glass of whisky at the bar.

"Fine," they said in an exasperated tone and shut the door behind us.

We sat at the table and deliberated. We had so few assets between us and even fewer leads. App and Čapek were cut off from Wi-Fi, incapable of communicating with us. Though no one had yet pointed a finger at Pox for his escapades that morning, it wouldn't be long until they matched the powers that had been used to him. Dianna no longer had a contract or access to the building they were kept in. Leo was…in jail as far as anyone could tell.

I asked to borrow Pox's phone and dialed the number on the black and red card I'd received months ago. The phone rang only once before someone picked up.

"Ramirez, glad to hear they haven't caught you yet," Tafari's smooth voice answered. "I saw your article. Doing what I can to get it in as many hands as possible. I have kids handing it out at street corners." I grinned, despite everything he and I had been through recently. I didn't know if it was worth anything, but at least we were in good standing.

"Thanks for that. Think you can help me with another side project that's a bit more your speed than mine?"

"Are you finally going to kill someone, Xóch?" he asked. The familiarity and casualness of his tone was as unsettling as it was comforting.

"No! No, still not murdering anyone. But I got some friends stuck in Zephyr Tower, and I think I need the anti-heroes' help," I explained. I heard a cackle on the other end of the phone. I watched the eyes in the room widen.

"Eh? The place is a fortress. But I have people inside, might be doable…if they are sufficiently distracted."

"We are having a meeting. If I give you directions, will you—"

I paused.

How do I say this without sounding like a prick?

"I'll play nice, even come alone," he said, finding the words before me. "You took a swing at the Big Man himself this morning, Ramirez! Let me be in the ring for round two!"

"Texting you the address."

I grinned as I hung up and did so. The smile faltered as I made eye contact with Pox and Dr. Siu, who seemed much less pleased.

"He cannot know about the cure," Andy warned.

"But—"

"NO!" they both shouted in near unison.

"You may be able to forgive and forget, but some of us are less forgiving when it comes to murder," Dr. Siu said, putting their palm to their face as they talked. "Also remember, this is a rescue mission. The last time Apricity saw this man, she nearly died."

"I *know* that. I nearly died too, but that doesn't change the fact he's our best shot," I answered icily.

I shot messages to Dianna, writing the address and the time with "please be discreet" and five praying hands emojis. She responded with a thumbs-up.

I thought about contacting Mason. Maybe we could see about getting Leo out.

I mean, what could they possibly have on him? I'm the only one who broke any laws. Hiding a fugitive maybe? Am I a fugitive? Shit, what is the etiquette on this? A thank you card? Maybe an apology card? Does

Hallmark have a "Sorry I got you arrested and got your business impounded" card?

I shifted in my seat. I couldn't physically feel uncomfortable in Dr. Siu's presence, but the glare they shot over their glass still unnerved me.

Dianna arrived first, her copper hair tucked into a baseball cap with her own logo on the front, large sunglasses replacing her normal round spectacles, and in lieu of her normal athleisure attire she was wearing a sundress and cardigan. Standing in the door, I did my best not to laugh.

"This looks like a disguise a child would pick out."

"What? Uh, I don't know. I thought I did well."

"You're wearing sunglasses at night, and your hat literally has your logo on it."

"Lots of people wear my clothes," she said, her cheeks flaring up a little.

I let her in and looked up and down the hall. No one seemed to have followed her, even if her disguise was insane. It was the middle of the night in the most populous city in the U.S. Maybe she didn't need to do much.

As she walked in, she looked around sheepishly before putting her regular glasses on and taking her hat off.

"Where's Leo?" she asked.

"Oh, uh...well, the PPD picked him up." I answered. I felt uncomfortable again. She didn't know, and there had been no way to get a discreet message to her about it before. She paused and looked mournfully at her own feet.

"Is that why we are here? OH! What happened to you?" she asked, suddenly realizing Pox was lying in a heap of bandages on the couch.

"Apex," he rasped out. Dianna nodded and sat carefully on an accent chair.

"Before we get into it, we are expecting more company, and there are things I want only this room to know. As far as our incoming guests are concerned, there is no cure for powers, and we would like to keep it that way," interjected Dr. Siu. They leaned forward as they talked, swirling their drink in a crystal cup and watching the light dance through it to cast small flecks on the floor and walls.

"But I do want to try to cure Apex," I said. "I think we need to. It's only luck that we aren't all dead, and the looming threat of a vengeful superhe—" I stopped, interrupting myself.

He's not a hero. Dianna is, Pox is, hell, Leo is. He doesn't get that reverence anymore.

"The threat of a looming Super-Powered individual is too great," I started again. "I suspect the only reason he didn't just throw the food truck in the East River with me and Leo in it is that the PPD got there first."

"Who else is coming? I can't imagine keeping the cure from someone being more important than the mission succeeding. I mean, Apex is going to try to kill you. I don't think I can protect you forever," Dianna said.

"Tafari," I answered, with guilt panging in my stomach. "I think he's the best shot at this working."

But this is not a conversation that feels comfortable.

"Who's Tafari?"

"The current leader of the anti-heroes. The one who almost killed us," I said.

Pox and Dianna stared at me for a moment.

Pox already knew. Why does he seem shocked?

"I hadn't realized you were on a first name basis with him," Pox said. I shifted uncomfortably again. Maybe Andy wasn't using their powers after all.

"We don't talk regularly, but we have spoken, yes."

"Does the PPD know this?" Pox asked.

How can anyone so battered manage to seem so judgmental? He just broke a bunch of laws, and yet somehow, I feel guilty.

"No. I rarely tell the PPD anything—this isn't the point," I jumbled out.

"I agree. He of all people can't know there's a cure," Dianna interrupted. "But having fought him, I think his odds are best against Apex in short-range combat. Pox is clearly not up for it, and...well, I fight best from a distance. On top of that, I'm unsure if I can fire the cure or anything like that from my bow. I don't even fire a real bow, it's only semi-corporeal. I'm not even sure we could, like, dip an arrow in the vaccine or something. Realistically, he's our best shot at actually hitting Apex with it."

"What if we told him it only ruined Apex's power?" I suggested. It sat in the air for a moment.

"That's a lot to hang on a lie, and there would be too many possibilities to make a mistake. What if he pockets some just in case and figures it out? There are a lot of powerless scientists and doctors who might be able to reverse-engineer it. And *if* he somehow gets the cure, do you really trust him to use it responsibly?" Pox said, talking through his own hand.

"Okay then, I'll do it. I'll get Apex," I said, surprised at my own words.

Dr. Siu burst out laughing in the corner. Between hearty chuckles, they managed, "You really wanna die, huh?"

Dianna sighed but seemed to agree.

"Okay then, I'll get Tafari," I said. The words left my mouth before my brain fully caught up. It worked, but it felt wrong. "After he cures Apex, I'll cure him. He trusts me."

But not for long, I guess.

The room fell silent, but there was a round of nods.

Eventually, Andy spoke up, "Yeaaaaah, okay. That works for me. You're probably gonna die, but no skin off my back." They stretched as they walked toward their office. "I have to get to work then." They shut the door behind them with purpose. Pox looked at me apologetically.

"They're not really that bad. They just...don't have your optimism anymore, Ms. Ramirez. It has been difficult for them, I'm afraid."

I nodded, still unsure about Andy's allegiance.

"So just to be clear, we say the cure only works on Apex, and for safety's sake, we try to eliminate Tafari's power as well," I confirmed. There was a round of nods. My stomach turned. I didn't even disagree with him. Heroes needed to be regulated. Powers needed to be controlled better where people got hurt. Betraying him would be...wrong. I tried not to let the doubt register on my face.

If it has to happen, it has to happen. We need to save Apricity. We need to get the proof from Čapek, and we need Tafari's help. We can do this. I CAN DO THIS.

We sat in uncomfortable silence for a while. Pox stashed his uniform and tried to sit in a way that made his injuries look less severe.

There was a knock on the door.

Pox sat upright, struggling to maintain balance for a moment. He looked like a frail, injured man instead of his normal self. Dianna had replaced her hat and sunglasses with her laurels and was glowing lightly, perhaps as a threat, perhaps just to be ready for the potential of a fight.

No one got up to answer the door.

Eventually, I stood and walked over. Looking through the peephole, I saw him there, red canvas jacket and all, hands up to show he wouldn't be a threat. The handle was cold in my hand. As I opened the door, he walked in, and a moment later I saw his shoulders drop as a wave of calm washed over him.

"You didn't tell me you were rich, Xóchitl," he said with a smirk, looking around the lavish apartment.

"I'm not. My home got impounded this morning."

He chuckled softly, voice warm and strangely casual.

"Right, the food truck. Heard about that."

He strolled with easy confidence to the chair Andy had been in recently and sat comfortably, waving at Dianna as he did.

How is he so relaxed? Maybe it's because he's not used to Dr. Siu's aura?

"So, Imma guess this has to do with the break-in at the tower?" he said, nodding a head over to Pox. "Was that you?" Pox shot him a venomous look. "Clever hitting them with the article and making your move for the robot the same day. They live off PR. It's all they really care about."

"It wasn't enough," Pox said, and Tafari nodded, appraising the state of the man before him.

"Eh, but I think it was. The Big Man in the cape hasn't come down from his tower since the article. No one's heard a peep out of him. I think they're waiting to see if enough people know about the article to address it or if they can spin it as a theory for the tinfoil hats. That's why we've been distributing it left and right."

Pox nodded, then turned to me.

"I guess I owe you my life. He didn't follow me. He didn't want anyone to know I broke in because of you," he said with sincerity.

I stared wide-eyed and started smiling.

"Not just that, it's better still. They're moving your friend. You spooked them, and in order to keep everything under wraps, they basically wrecked all their own defenses. It's one in the morning now, and at six they're moving your robot in pieces on a convoy to a secure compound in the Hudson Valley."

We all turned our heads toward the newest member of our crew.

"How can you be sure your info is good?" I asked, apprehensive.

"Guy on the inside. We had more but, uh...they stopped talking this morning. The guy in charge of data recovery for your robot's one of ours. Says he's transferring operations to the compound upstate."

"What compound?" Pox asked.

"Don't know, but it doesn't matter. We're going to catch them on the road," he said before patting me on the shoulders, already speaking as though we were all old friends and teammates.

CHAPTER 20
FAREWELL FARADAY

"AFTER YEARS OF PLOTTING
VENGEANCE AGAINST THE GODS,
CUT OFF FROM THE WORLD, I
BROKE FREE TO FIND THE AGE OF
HEROES WAS OVER."

APRICITY | SEPTEMBER 20

I was grateful for many things about my tiny new world. I was in the part of the robot that had a camera, so I could see the hacker trying to find me and watch his frustration mount as I avoided his attempts to isolate or even locate me in the code. I was also grateful that I had access to a clock from this camera angle.

It had been six hours since they marched this man up here past the corpses in the hall, and five hours since he was informed there was "malware" on the bot and that he had to remove it. Four and a half hours ago, he plugged into the bot with a clean computer.

In this world of data, I found myself at home. Unless I chose to open a video, the world was made of light. Each file was a star. Each program was a constellation I could float between. The new computer was an unfamiliar, barren sky.

I took a quick stroll through the laptop, examining its green field background. I had hoped to find access to the internet or any way to send myself home safely with the video. Unfortunately, the machine was not online. After the brief stroll, I returned to my friend's memory. The robot was occupied by a galaxy of information, the complexity of which I'd never seen. At its core was one like me, a person made of light and stars—Čapek. The man's form was clearly defined in a cloud of his own information. Nebulas flared with connections between them, and the two of us watched out through the camera lens at the frustrated man, now six or so hours deep into a hack that defied all he knew about computers.

"Almost feel bad for him," Čapek said in an even voice cracked with time.

"He works for the enemy. He's not worth your pity."

"So did you, once, I'll remind you. It's best not to be blind to the people across the battlefield."

"How many bodies do you think he had to step over to get into this room?" I asked.

"He may not know who killed them, he might think he's a hero. Even Apex, as you call him, used to be just a sick man. He's gotten lost. The power eats at you, whether you know it or not. Even I lost my way for a moment," Čapek said.

I fidgeted and thought about what I believed about Apex even a month ago, and what I knew about all heroes less than a year ago.

Čapek has a point. There's no easy way to know what this computer man really feels.

I grabbed some files—the videos from this morning and the one from the nineties—the proof I was trying to get out. I copied them, pulling apart the stars into two and whispering, "Watch me, please." I threw them down the long tunnel cable and looked after them as they went.

As the files emerged on the man's computer, I could see the confusion knotted on his face. He looked at the files named WatchMe.mp5 and Please.mp5 that appeared on his desktop and checked over his shoulder. I held my breath.

Maybe he'd watch. Maybe he'd be a good person. Maybe he'd help.

He watched the first video. I heard the sounds of Apex killing all the men out in the hall. The last one begged, promising he wouldn't say anything, swearing on his life and the lives of his wife and kids. Apex stated they would be compensated, but his voice was followed by a flash and then silence. The man looked over his shoulders again with fear on his face and deleted the videos.

"...or he's a coward," Čapek said next to me, an admittance of defeat.

"What the hell was that?" the computer man asked, staring into the robot again. "Can it edit videos?"

He must have been talking to himself. We hadn't seen or heard anyone else. Both of us were still in the black-out box of a room, cut off from the rest of the robot's body. There was no internet and there were no windows, just lead-lined walls and this one terrified man who was scratching at his hairline.

I grabbed one of the lights, pulled it apart to copy it, and whispered, "No, this was this morning. Help us," and sent the file down the tube. The man started visibly sweating as the screen popped up with the video of Apex and Vincent fighting. Vincent started running off, and Apex laughed, swearing, "I CAN'T CHASE HIM? WHAT DO YOU MEAN? I CAN'T LOSE! I DON'T LOSE!"

Apex screamed, kicking a dent into the steel-lined doorframe in the video. The man turned to see the dent behind him. The video kept playing.

"Sir, I'm sorry...orders from up top say we are to stay on this floor," some PPD guard in the video said.

"I didn't ask you," Apex answered, voice menacing. Then there was a blast, and the man was cut in half. Apex began mocking the dead man.

"Orders from up top? I AM THE TOP!" he said and pushed the severed half of the guard over, kicking the man's other side out of his way. The data retriever, an ordinary man in his mid-thirties with a gentle face, looked visibly sick. He deleted the video.

"I'm out," he declared. He stood and walked into the hallway, flagging someone down. We could hear the second person walk toward him, but the sound was obscured by the wall.

"Hello? Oh, yes ma'am, hi. I am terribly sorry, but I can't get anything off of the computer. I tried a tempest attack, and I was able to display some information. But only a live feed of what it wants me to see," the computer man said, still standing in the doorway. "It's not like any tech I've seen. You'd need a whole team to figure it out. Oh, and I wouldn't let it online. It seems to be able to corrupt information. A really nasty bit of work. We can move it to the Hudson complex and get more tech guys on it."

There was the sound of a foot tapping, then someone said, "Alright then, that's what we have to do, I suppose. I'll get Maximus and Mercurial to move them. Be ready for a driver in the morning. I want you to front this project, Mr. Triddi. Pack for a long stay."

The woman's voice was high and nasal. She sounded how I thought New Yorkers did before I ever lived here. The man shot one more nervous look at the dented steel he had seen Apex kick in before leaving.

"I have obligations in the city—a dog," he said.

She clicked her tongue and repeated, "Go pack." The man left without coming back for his laptop.

Čapek had chosen to represent himself as a man in his thirties in a lab coat with an old-fashioned, almost rockabilly look.

"You are an interesting little one," he said, still looking out of the large screen window to the real world. Only the empty, battered room was in view. "I spent the majority of my life looking for a way to do what you do as easily as breathing."

"You want to make yourself into nothing?" I asked.

"Dear girl, you are thinking too small! You are not nothing. You are data, and data can be anything."

"I don't follow."

"I knew I was dying for a long time. Death didn't miss me like it did Siu, Maximus, or Ginerva. I knew my time was limited, so I wished to prolong it by turning my mind into data. But you can do so much more," he said. A nostalgic look crossed his face.

"I only manifest if someone observes me. I wind up trapped

and alone so easily. My powers don't make me strong. They just strand me again and again in a box somewhere only I can see. I can't really help those around me," I said, feeling sorrow set in.

"You are thinking so small, as I said. You can transmit yourself. That means you could be immortal! You could be a time capsule and outlive us all. You could be the Linear B Tablet of our age, or even go into a quantum computer lab. Then you could move faster than light! Data can be anything. You could be a pile of paper or titanium. You could send yourself anywhere—maybe even any time. You might just be the most powerful person in this world," Čapek said with enthusiasm and sincerity.

I laughed so loud, I wondered if they could hear it outside of the robot. But Čapek looked serious. He reminded me of my father, the thin line of his lip impossibly straight, not a glimpse of a frown or a smile.

"You'll have to tell me more once we get out of this hunk of junk," I managed to say. I thought I could take a shot at optimism if someone believed in me.

"If," he corrected.

"Yeah…if we get out of this hunk of junk."

"I spent most of my life making this body for myself. Try to have some respect," he said. His voice sounded distant as he thought. Then he literally disappeared, and I was alone. Again.

I started humming a lullaby from my childhood, picturing the green hills covered in prairie flowers and my father's horse.

"Sleep, baby, sleep. Your daddy's tending sheep. Away, sleep, baby, sleep. Your mother's taken the cows away…schloof, bobbeli, schloof," I sang softly to myself, until I drifted to sleep in the comfortable clouds around me.

A few hours passed before someone put us in a metal-lined box. I could tell we were moving but not how or where. I could tell we were being jostled by the sound of the metal robot frame hitting the interior of our cage. We still couldn't connect to the internet.

No service, no outside sound, nothing.

Čapek broke the hours of solitude, finally, after I spent too much time alone. He corporealized out of nowhere beside me.

"Something is happening," he said, sounding worried.

I squinted at the screen and cupped my hand around my ear, trying to make sense of the commotion outside. The box was torn in half, and suddenly, light filled the room. I shaded my eyes from the brightness while I struggled to make sense of my surroundings.

We appeared to be on a wooded road. There was a truck on fire in front of us and other scattered debris visible. The man who fought Artemis the day Xóchi got thrown off the fire escape was laughing as he ripped apart the box containing us. I had thought for a moment I was being kidnapped. Then the shambling robot pieces around him start to assemble.

"I FOUND THE HEAD," he shouted with obvious joy.

I heard a familiar voice call from somewhere behind the man.

"Tafari! Let me see! APP, ARE YOU IN THERE?" Xóchi yelled, crying and turning the screen this way and that in her hands. A wave of relief came over me, and I went to leap into her arms before a hand grabbed me in the digital space.

"Wait, take this," Čapek said and handed me two points of data. With the videos of Apex nestled firmly in my grip, I jumped out of the screen and into Xóchi's phone. The alert didn't even finish chiming before my feet were on solid ground, finally. I stood next to her, and she hugged me.

"We have proof! It's in your phone," I said, delighted to be holding onto her. The embrace was so tight, it felt as though she worried I was an illusion.

I heard an explosion in the distance and saw a light arrow go shooting past us, only inches away.

"INCOMING!" Dianna screamed as some kind of metallic blur ran past us, so fast I couldn't process what it was.

Less than a hundred feet from where we sat on the street, there was a black SUV and the hacker from earlier was getting ushered into it by men in uniform red chore jackets. Mr. Triddi was bruised and bleeding, but he was smiling, his kind eyes looking back at us triumphant. For whatever part he played in our freedom, I was grateful. I started to say thank you when the blur collided with him and the car, ripping through it like the ribbon at the end of a foot race.

The SUV screeched as metal scraped against concrete and smoke started billowing up. Mr. Triddi was thrown from the area into the nearby treetops, where he hung in the branches. His lifeless face was still smiling, almost as if it didn't have time to process the change before he breathed his last breath.

Tafari cursed and got up, standing between the wreckage and us. His form fractured and crystallized into something onyx black, with sharp facets. His hands glowed red, and the silver blur was running back toward us. It was Mercurial, the new leading female for Zephyr. That explosive sound hit us again, and I realized it was her making all that racket. She was running so fast, it boomed out around her as she broke the sound barrier.

There was no time to react. I just continued to hold onto Xóchi and waited for the end. But it didn't come. I opened my eyes after the explosion of sound and wind whooshing around me.

Tafari had crouched low and launched Mercurial over us. The silver-clad woman tumbled down the road, creating sizable cracks and dents in the concrete as she bounced away.

Overhead, flashing lights zipped this way and that as Dianna and Apex traded arrows and lasers. She narrowly missed him, and he made contact with her, the sound of the beam exploding in front of her. Dianna lost her balance and went shooting off, tumbling through the air and treetops until she was lost from sight.

Apex landed next to us, denting the concrete. I jumped quickly into Čapek's screen, disappearing with a flash.

"Come on, Xóchi, run," I muttered under my breath, full of hope as I stared through the robot's eyes.

She didn't run.

Instead, she jumped up and tried to hit Apex with something.

He batted her to the side and swatted the robot, who was still only partially assembled. Čapek crumbled into computer bits and fragments along the road. The looming man turned his attention to Tafari, who wound his fist up toward him. The blow was cut short.

Another sonic boom and Mercurial impacted with the glistening crystallized form of Tafari. A horrific shattering sound rang through the air. Blood began pouring out of Tafari between cracked crystallized skin. They kept colliding again and again. Tafari had his arms up in a defensive position, trying to block each blow as they came. Apex loomed over Xóchi and picked her up by her face, hand squeezing. He lifted her up over his head.

He was laughing.

"What did you think you could do, you cockroach? Did you really think you could hurt me? You? You're nothing, NOTHING! I AM A GOD!" he declared, lifting her entirely off the ground. She looked over at the cracked screen I was hiding in. Tears were pouring down my face. Then I saw it—something glistening on the ground in front of the screen. It was a needle.

I jumped, grabbing for the needle so fast and hard as I ran past that I scraped every knuckle on the concrete. I plunged it into Apex's neck, injecting its contents into him.

A god. Okay, sure, whatever.

He screamed and dropped Xóchi, whipping around toward me. All my smug bravery was gone in an instant. I wanted to jump away again, but I was frozen in place.

The spark in his chest charged up and flickered. His iconic laser shot over my shoulder.

If this is it, at least maybe I saved her.

In that prolonged, painful second, I thought about confessing to Xóchi, telling her what she meant to me and that this was worth it, but I barely made a peep as the light lined up with my center. I felt a searing hot laser connect with my chest. It faltered and shone harmlessly across my body, warm and benign as a flashlight. Then, it flickered out.

"WHAT DID YOU DO TO ME!?" Apex wailed, and the giant of

a man wound a fist back toward me before screaming again, wobbling and falling to the ground with a grunt. Behind me, the cracks of contact between the crystalline defender and his assailant stopped. Both were stuck in a pose, a fist in contact with a bloodied forearm while they stared in awe as the man everyone thought was unkillable hit the ground. Dianna returned and lined up a shot to end everything. The silver-clad speedster swore under her breath, breaking the eerie silence.

"Later, gator," she said. The silver blur rolled her shoulders over the much larger Apex, picking him up in a fireman's carry before running down the road. She wasn't fast enough to break the sound barrier that time, but she was still gone before I could even blink.

Xóchi lay on the ground near me, and I fell to her side. She was coughing and wheezing, and I felt the spot in the center of my chest burning, as though I had been branded by an iron.

Somehow, through her raggedy breaths, she said, "Is this real? Am I alive?"

I felt the burn start to a blister just below my collarbone. Even though the pain stung my skin, I laughed.

"It is. We are," I said softly, then I sprawled next to her on the cold concrete. It started to rain, fat drops cascading all around us. I reached for her hand, and she took mine. Too tired to stand, we stayed beside each other for what seemed an eternity.

CHAPTER 21
SETBACKS AND SALUTATIONS

"I WILL BRING THEM BACK. I WILL
MAKE THEM ANSWER."

XÓCHITL | SEPTEMBER 21

I was starting to get used to defeat. The bittersweet feeling was growing on me, the way coffee did when I was younger. Sitting in Dr. Siu's apartment, surrounded by the ones who got me off of that wet, cold concrete, I couldn't help but smile. Apricity bundled herself in my coat and leaned her head against my shoulder as we sat side by side.

The bruises on my face were starting to show. Five quarter-sized marks had bloomed where fingertips dug in when Apex lifted me.

Was this even a defeat? Sure, my blog was gone, Leo was in jail, and my home was impounded—but we made Apex *mortal.*

This may actually be a win.

Tafari seemed to be chewing on mixed feelings more than I had been. His eyes were fixed on his hands as he picked at his nailbeds. He lost more than the rest of us—at least four men and his informant all passed before we could get them out of the trees. His arms had already healed to a smooth brown where the skin had been crackled black and bloody. I had plenty of time to use the cure on him on the ride home, but it still hung heavy in my pocket.

I couldn't bring myself to do it. He had brought Apricity back to me, and in my mind, that outweighed any evil he could have done. If the rest of the crew disagreed with my choice, they were too tired to argue it. App kept touching her burn on the two-hour drive back downstate, but she appeared physically fine, and the moment she saw her mentor alive and well, she lit up and started recounting her heroism from earlier that day.

Siu was off sulking somewhere. They seemed to be unhappy with the number of people in their home.

Dianna came back into the room after stepping into the hallway a moment, hanging up her phone with a smile.

"Leo should be home in the morning. They didn't actually charge him with anything, and my lawyer seems to think the worst thing they can get on him is sleeping in a private lot," she assured us.

I got up and hugged Dianna before I could even process the information. Tafari excused himself, saying he had to talk to some families. He ducked out of the apartment, winking at me on his way out.

"Call me if you need anything," he said, before shutting the door behind him. Tafari's departure seemed to relax everyone, and the rest of the night was filled with laughter and drinking. Even Siu smiled to themself when Vincent started praising Apricity for her two amazing rescues. I didn't remember falling asleep or even having found a place to lie down. Still, before I knew it, morning came.

When I woke up, the room was still dark, deep eggplant-colored curtains only allowing in a thin, gold light, which slipped faintly through the edges. A TV in the corner of the kitchen was on, and Siu, Vincent, and Čapek were watching it. Apricity slept on the other side of the L-shaped sofa from me, and we were sharing a large pillow in the corner. Her hand was resting on mine. When I got up, I carefully slipped my hand out from under hers, trying not to wake her. I placed my coat over her like a blanket before heading to see what the others were watching.

I walked in gentle silence to the kitchen to sit with my friends. I couldn't remember when I last had time to watch TV like this. On this one, Apex was talking to a reporter about the anti-hero attack and how they stole valuable equipment after they had killed a top scientist. He called it a terrorist attack and urged anyone who knew anything about the whereabouts of the terrorists to come forward. A bright yellow message appeared on the screen with a hotline number. A small box with Tafari, Dianna, and Apricity's faces each appeared in rotation, which then flashed to mine.

"These suspected terrorists are still at large," he said. "Now if you'll excuse me, I have to find them myself."

And then he jumped up...and flew offscreen.

"Did...did he just fly?" App asked. Her voice was raspy from just waking up, but standing behind me, she seemed more alert than I was. Rage twisted her face.

"DID HE JUST FUCKING FLY!?" she yelled.

I nodded in quiet, solemn fury, and Vincent spoke up next.

"It could have been a camera trick," he said, disbelief obvious in his voice.

Apricity looked at him and rolled her eyes before storming back to the other room.

"FUCK THIS! Do you know how close I was to dying?" she said, furious. She tore at the neckline of her shirt, revealing the line of blisters that sliced through her torso. She said, "If it kicked in half a second later, I WOULD HAVE DIED for this. And for what, to be a criminal? I STARTED THERE."

"Apricity, wait. Just listen for a second," Vincent started.

App started loading up a backpack as he trailed after her, trying to get her to calm down.

"I don't need all of you to get myself killed as a...as a villain," she said, ripping open the door. She paused for half a second and then was gone. The door slammed so hard, I thought it was going to break the frame. It slowly opened back up.

I chased after her.

"Apricity, wait!" I yelled, but there was a flash of light and my phone and coat hit the ground. The screen cracked in an intricate web. I walked over and picked up the discarded phone and coat.

On the home screen were two new video files, watch.mp4 and please.mp4. I pressed play. The first video was retro. It was short and choppy, but I could tell it was Apex caught on a security camera. He was flying into a penthouse apartment. The film quality was old, but the camera was set up to see the large man fly onto the balcony of the double glass door penthouse. It occurred to me that this apartment building looked just like Dianna's, and I shivered to think it may have even been her unit. In the bed there was a sleeping man and woman. Even with the old film, the voice of the man was undeniably Frisson. He screamed as Apex sliced him and his partner in two.

The second one was crystal clear and modern. In this one, Apex killed a guard who mouthed off. This was the proof Čapek had. This was it, and it was meaningful. Out of habit, I went to upload it and found my blog was gone. I was reminded of the wanted screen on TV. Though my face didn't pass by again in the news cycle, I was already being hunted before the incident even began. I looked up and down the hallway. There were no other people. I returned to the apartment, heavy and tired. The room was tense with questions in everyone's eyes. Vincent, Dianna, and Siu all stood around the kitchen, avoiding asking anything.

"Maybe it's because...well he's...ya know, *the* hero? Maybe it wasn't enough, what we did," Dianna mumbled, leaning on the kitchen island. Dr. Siu reached into the cupboard and pulled out a bottle of whisky and a glass. They poured a drink silently, and time seemed to stand still.

"We tested it on his blood specifically, and we confirmed that it, in fact, worked. On him, specifically," Vincent answered. He looked over at Siu, who only sipped their drink. After a moment, he continued, "And the effects were permanent on the sample. And they were permanent on the few of Dr. Siu's patients who opted for their own cure."

Dianna nodded and considered the information carefully. Siu

finished their drink and poured themself another. Their shoulders tensed while their jaw clenched.

"Maybe there's another factor. I always felt stronger when more people were around—spectators, you know? Like somehow, their hope made me more powerful," Pox said.

Thinking about this made sense, as if it was some kind of prayer. Powered people all seemed like gods in their own way. *Maybe every little child who watches these heroes with star-struck eyes gives them power.*

"I...I realize it doesn't sound scientific. Not to mention that if this were the case, I...I think I'd be much weaker," Pox said, interrupting my thoughts with an embarrassed-sounding stammer.

"It's the fucking box. *They have the box,*" Andy growled. Their voice cut through the air like lightning. Loud and sharp, it crackled through the tension in the room. Tears streamed down their face into their whisky. They half-laughed as they noticed this. "It tastes better with a few drops of water anyway."

They sunk heavily onto their leather and gold chair. The three of us shared nervous looks.

"What box?" I asked, trying not to sound angry. Čapek made a noise that sounded like a slide changing on an old school flip reel, and his shattered TV screen of a face displayed an image of a silver-lidded container. It was a photo taken of a drawing, sketched in a shaky hand. "The box that it all came from. They must have the stupid thing," Siu said. They were laughing in a miserable sort of way.

"When you say *it*, what do you mean?" I asked.

"The parasite that powers the plague that affects all of us."

As they swirled their whisky, they spoke as if this was obvious, even though the information had never been shared.

"Are you saying this box affects whether or not someone develops powers?" I asked, apprehensive.

"No. They have the *source*. We could cure them a thousand times, and *bam*—they can just start again. Or worse...they could make more," Siu explained. They sat forward in their chair, their smile shifting to fury. "This was all a waste of time."

We sat in silence, stuck in our thoughts and filled with dread.

Our silver bullet didn't work. They have no real weakness.

Another *click* and Čapek showed the Zephyr Building, abandoned, with green vines weaving throughout.

Orange text read, "The box's last known location is my old hospital. It had taken root there."

Click, and a sketch of the box rooted into a room with golden tendrils sprawling from it showed on Čapek's face. Siu stared hard, downing the rest of their drink without blinking.

"So we take it?" I asked, feeling lighter as hope returned to me.

"And do what with it? We can't move it, so hypothetically if we managed to get to it in spite of every powerful agent with the PPD and Zephyr in the way, then what?" Siu asked, anger in their voice. "What's your next grand plan?"

There was a knock on the door.

A familiar voice called out, "Have you seen Xóchi?"

Leo's voice cracked a little. He must have been tired.

"Come in," our exasperated host called before muttering, "Is this actually a shelter for lost pets?"

I didn't remember my feet hitting the floor or walking over to the door. I was simply in my brother's arms as soon as he crossed the threshold.

"You're okay! Thank god you're okay," he said, holding me tight.

"Right back at you," I managed between tears. I closed the door behind us, and we waddled, still hugging, into the apartment. I accidentally stepped on Dianna's foot on the way in. She exclaimed with a laugh and then pulled him into a gentle hug.

"Glad you're back," she said. His face flushed red, and I wished I had my camera ready for the opportunity to tease him later about his strawberry cheeks.

"I'm glad everyone's safe, for now," Leo managed to say.

"I'm shocked they let you out! I imagine Carol must have

gotten quite busy when the warrant for my arrest was issued," Dianna said, looking guilty.

"Actually, it was Mason who got me out. He said something about botched paperwork and told me to give Xóchi this," Leo said. He handed me a paper. I took it and noticed he was still holding onto Dianna. I opened my camera app before even looking at my phone. In one of the first genuine moments of bravery in my brother's life, he turned his attention back to Dianna, pulled her chin to him, and kissed her. They stood perfectly interlocked for a moment—just long enough for me to pull up my shattered phone to take an out-of-focus, blurry mess of a shot. But I got it. One *great* photo.

CHAPTER 22
HOPES AND HESITATION

"NO. IT WILL NOT END LIKE THIS."

XÓCHITL | SEPTEMBER 22

Dear X,

I hope this finds you well. I always loved you—never thought I'd get the courage to say it, but I think we both knew in college. I promise this is not me being pessimistic. We were ordered to shoot you on sight. Run. Do not use your phone and do not use your cards. This is my debit card. Buy a burner and RUN. Do not tell me where you go. Just live to old age for me, would you? Please? – M

I stared at the letter and folded it in my hands over and over, the creases worn heavy from reading it again and again, weighing its content.

I guess I knew.

I felt a pang of guilt. I didn't want to use him. I didn't mean to abuse his feelings, but I *had* needed his help and maybe purposely missed the signs. I had hoped I could ignore it forever so I could keep my friend with no resentment or rejection between us. I folded the letter again. I didn't know how this would change things.

I used the debit card to pull out a bit of cash, no more than I needed. I resigned to leave all my things behind: my camera, laptop, phone—everything. I kept only my memory card with the photos I'd taken for *Storm Chaser* and the video files from App. I kept my sunglasses on, even in the darkness, and left my hood up. I hoped it would be enough to keep me anonymous. I walked back to the apartment and tried to throw together some sort of plan.

I called the number App sent herself to and a wispy cackle answered. There was a lot of laughter and music in the background.

"Hahaha! What can I do for you, X-O? Oh, EX OH!! Hugs and kisses! Your nickname is even cute, but I bet you knew that," Apricity said. She sounded off. It was probably some new level of intoxication for her. "Did you know I can DO SO MANY things!? In just one day I made...I don't know, like fifty thousand or something?? Haha! It's so easy!! Why didn't I think of it before? X-O, thank *Cap-ich* for me."

My brows furrowed as I stepped into the empty entrance to Dr. Siu's apartment. It seemed obvious now that they owned the whole building and chose to occupy only one unit. The building was always empty now that I paid attention.

Why have I never thought of that?

"I wanted to ask a favor, actually. Do you think you could send those videos to every phone in the city if you used an emergency alert system?" I asked, ignoring the chaos.

There was a crackle. The line had a lot of static, and I heard a click when App hung up. I stared at the phone for a moment until I got a text. I opened it, and flashing light filled the hall. She appeared in front of me in an intricately bodiced designer dress, the kind you see on red carpets. Her cheeks were flushed, and her hair looked unkempt, but she was glowing brighter than she had in months.

"Xóchi, hun...I get it. I almost let the job consume me too. But ya gotta stop and just…live. Look at how well I'm doing," she said, gesturing at herself. She was sparkling, and her smile was genuine, which was rare. I was wearing an oversized shirt and hoodie. I smelled like dirty cloth, and by comparison, I felt made of dirt. I noticed that her eyes were hazy though.

"Do you think you could do it? If you got into an emergency alert server, could you send it to all the folks in the city?" I asked.

She considered it again, and then her face grew somber.

"I don't send or magically transmit information—I carry it. I can barely send myself safely. I need someone else to read me so I can reform from data. If anyone didn't see me, that piece of me would not reappear. If they did, only that piece of me would reappear. The only way to send it to that many people is to slice me up itty bitty, and since I don't feel like being split into a few million pieces…nah," she said, making the motion of cutting with her hand, fingers wiggling and separating. She watched her own hands, transfixed as they moved to represent her being sprinkled onto a million phones. "Just post it on YouTube or something! Aren't you overthinking this?"

"I tried that already. It gets taken down instantly, no matter where I post it," I answered, feeling defeated.

She looked lost in thought, her hand over her lips as if to keep a secret. Then she moved to hold mine, a smile spread wide across her face in an almost manic expression.

"Then just join me, X6. YOU WOULD LOOK SO GOOD in Gucci!" App exclaimed. She threw a heavy arm over my shoulder in half an embrace. Her eyes lingered on me as she continued to talk. "We could go anywhere in the world. We could even walk into the royal vault and steal the Crown of England. We could go to Paris, for something more simple. Whatever you want. It's easy! Come on, just stop this obsession and live free. Ya tried, ya failed. Let's move on."

"It's past revenge, App. This is my purpose. It's what I'm meant to do. I have to show the truth to everyone, and you can help me! Please help. We are making plans. You'd be perfect."

"I'm not going to die for your revenge or for your obsession. I have lived my whole life as a possession—my dad's, then Greg's, then...even Pox's. No more. I'm gonna live on my own for myself. You should try it, Xóchi. Really. No purpose, no destiny, and definitely no revenge. Just *freedom*. Join me." Apricity seemed sincere as she held my hands in hers and stared into my eyes.

I wanted to. At that moment, I could have easily gone with her, lived a wild and free life with no more broken bones and trauma... but something inside me pulled me in another direction.

"I can't, App. I have to do this." I could feel the threat of tears as I cherished the warmth of her hand and the comfort of the possibility of real freedom. She bridged the tiny gap between us, her hand on the nape of my neck, and pressed her lips to mine. She smelled and tasted of gin. Her tongue traced my lips and slid between them as I fell deeper into the kiss. My hands lifted from my sides to wrap around her as I melted into her embrace. I remembered that first hug in the van, how she disappeared right in my arms and pressed against me, afraid to lose her warmth for light. She broke the kiss, and I felt her absence as a pang in my chest, a fear that she would leave. But she stayed so close, her lips grazed mine as she spoke.

"Please." She went to kiss me again, but I backed up.

God, why did I pull away? I could have just gone with her or stayed tangled with her in the hallway. I looked down, afraid that if I met her gaze, I would abandon it all and follow her to the ends of the earth in selfish bliss. I was looking at our feet when the flash of light and cold came. I watched my phone fall to the ground. I was alone.

I wished I had begged, I wished we had talked about the night we spent together, or about us or about how perfect she was, or how none of this mattered. How only she mattered. But by the time I found the words, she was gone. That would have to be okay. She was safe. I had time; I could tell her how I felt once it was all over. She would know then that it was true, not a manipulation. I had to respect her choice.

And so what if the world can't know the truth? We can still fight. We just have to do the rest of the plan.

"Here. Just in case you think of any way to tell the world without dying," I texted her, attaching the videos in case she thought of another solution. After a moment, I added, "Let's go to Paris on the 4th."

OCTOBER 3

My eyes lingered on the time. It was two in the morning. Tafari would be here in a moment. I decided I would send one more text to App. At first, I considered begging for her to come back again, but after typing and deleting four long messages, I eventually sent "Tomorrow, Paris?"

There was no response as I paced around the hall outside Dr. Siu's apartment. I became restless, and I left to wait on the first floor.

My family came down via the slow, old elevator. The first load had Dr. Siu and Pox. Pox was suited up and walking straight, but his once partly severed arm was still fixed to his body with braces and slings. Čapek came down next on his own, for fear of the elevator's weight limit. We waited a moment longer for Dianna and Leo, and then we all sat in the calm, beautiful entrance. Too afraid to talk, too afraid to laugh or sing or anything, we just waited.

"Any luck with Apricity?" Pox asked. He sounded less than hopeful. I shook my head.

We sat in solemn silence until the door slammed open. Tafari, grinning ear to ear, strutted in with a sense of eagerness.

"I BROUGHT YOU A PRESENT! We have a guy in the PPD," he said, thumbing over his shoulder at a slightly dented version of my once-home. Its logo was still smiling back at me, the words "Cactus Café" in its typewriter font. It was half-parked on the curb, barely illuminated by the streetlight. Tafari was dangling the keys in front of me.

I grabbed them and turned to the group. I knew it was time to inspire the troops, but in my stomach, I felt dread.

I'm sending this room filled with my family to die for what? For my mom? For revenge?

This felt stupid and childish, and as I faltered, Tafari spoke up.

"This room is full of the most amazing people in this city, people stronger than steel," he said. He flexed and shined a bright flash of teeth.

I stopped for a second and listened.

"Smarter than death," Tafari continued, gesturing at Čapek, "who solved *unsolvable* problems." He gestured at Dr. Siu right as they took a drag of their cigarette.

"I don't know about *solved*, entirely, but yeah," Andy said, waving their other hand at the comment. Tafari flashed that grin of his again before he continued his speech.

"And what about the people who had everything and gave it up for what's right?" he asked, gesturing at Pox and Dianna. "And maybe most impressively, managed to keep Xóchitl Ramirez alive despite herself."

Tafari gestured at Leo, who chuckled. He beamed again.

"And speaking of, here's the woman herself—brave enough to go against the big man with nothing but a camera! We wouldn't be here without you," Tafari said. He clasped a strong hand on my shoulder.

"You've got this," he whispered. Tears welled up in my eyes as I stood facing my family.

"I always knew the world was cold and careless," I started, my voice already thick with emotion. "The small and powerless people lived in the shadow and under the feet of those with power. Ever since I could remember, I wanted to show the truth. I wanted the world to see how the powerful use that power for selfishness and cruelty.

"However, in my journey to prove to the world that heroes

aren't real, I met people who were able to change my mind. Heroes do exist. They're just rare, and they are here in this room using power to do what's right. They're not doing it for themselves alone, but for love, for truth...for the benefit of everyone.

"You all here are the real deal and...and if I do die today...I...I'm just glad I learned how wrong I was."

CHAPTER 23
SHUTTING PANDORA
"I WILL HAVE MY REVENGE."

XÓCHITL I OCTOBER 3

The sun was still down when Dianna spotted the first traffic copter on our way. She flew close enough to the camera that it couldn't miss her and waved, signing "You should follow us," before pointing at the truck. It hovered in the air like a big bug, unsure as she flew back and landed on our roof. It did not follow us. We needed an audience to have any chance; we hoped it might slow them down.

Ten minutes from our destination and that was the first clear news copter we had seen. Tension rose inside our sparse truck. Eight minutes out, we went over the plan one more time.

"Gather as much attention as possible. Dianna will fly ahead a bit. Tafari and Pox will get out first to engage any big hitters. They will jump out the back of the truck and make a lot of noise. Meanwhile, Andy, Leo, and I will sneak out through the front doors of the cab and run into the hospital. Everyone, headphones on!"

We went around doing thumbs-ups. Five minutes from the hospital, Čapek handed out a round of syringes. Tafari studied the newest iteration of the cure. He was fixated on the liquid in the premeasured amount. He almost looked afraid of it.

It wasn't until two minutes to our destination that we noticed another large shape against the sky following us. Only moments later, a second and a third arrived. It was still dark as the headlights illuminated an empty exit ramp that led to the long, curved road and a tall, brick building with a central spiral. Everyone but Leo, Siu, and I turned on shoulder-mounted flashlights, hoping that would make us less noticeable. The idea was to keep the attention on Tafari, Dianna, and Pox, who would do better in a stand-up fight. Dianna literally glowed, after all.

Dianna jumped out in front of the car, and we screeched to a halt. She turned her back to us, her bow drawn. She shot an arrow toward the large, brick building, and it sunk into the ground as something blurred past it. Tafari exhaled heavily, but grinned wide before he shouted in excitement and threw open the two back doors. He jumped down just as the blur came into view. It bounced off him hard, and as he crashed back against the bumper, a woman fell backward. She was all too recognizable with her silver clothes and shoes with wings. The blur had been Mercurial.

Tafari raised his foot and went to stomp on the woman while she was prone, but he was too slow. Before he could blink, she was gone. Pox was next on his feet. His hand lingered on Dr. Siu's for a moment before he hopped out of the back of the van. A moment later, there was a rush of flame from the left of the van, and Tafari shifted his attention to blocking the wave of fire with his rapidly crystallizing skin.

We snuck out of the truck while the fighting ensued. We disabled the internal lights, quietly opened the passenger side door, and slipped into the night. We ran as fast as we could through the field toward the looming fortress of a building. Dianna peppered the ground with her arrows, each one a beacon of glowing silver that illuminated our path.

At first, I thought she was guiding us. It wasn't until Mercurial passed within three feet of me, followed by one of the massive glowing arrows, that I realized she was just trying to hit her. The roar of flame, the drum of the helicopters, and the impact of the arrows drowned out her footsteps.

I put on my noise-canceling headphones as I ran, realizing I was the last to do so. We were thirty feet from the emergency exit of the hospital when I caught the reflection of an explosion behind us. I turned just in time to see a familiar caped figure cutting the truck in half with a chest laser before flying down to investigate the debris.

Leo froze at the hospital door, looking at the wreckage, and seemed for a moment incapable of moving. I pushed past him and had to pull with all my strength to get him to follow me into the building. Once inside, Dr. Siu took point. As we wandered the dark, labyrinthine halls of the hospital, I noticed that vines were growing through what were once tall, ornate windows. The place appeared not of this earth or time. It might have been impressive, once.

The first passage we took led through a waiting room. Chairs were knocked this way and that, and graffiti covered the walls. On the other side of the room, rotting plants and vines covered a door. As we walked toward it, our feet crunched over broken glass. Andy turned and leaned over the shrapnel of a receptionist's window and pulled a lever, then circled back to open the door. I held Leo's hand as we walked. I should have been terrified, but the doctor's soothing aura wouldn't let me panic. Still, I gripped Leo's hand tighter as we walked into the even-darker emergency room.

APRICITY I SOMEWHERE IN NEW YORK

It's 5:00 a.m. and I still can't fucking sleep.

The conversation with Xóchi mixed with the dull throbbing of my head into a cocktail of regret. I put out my cigarette. Normally, it would have been a comfort, but the smoke and the hangover twisted my stomach.

I went up the brownstone steps through the large doors and walked past a woman puking on the arch around the doorway. The house party was long over—most folks still here were half-dressed and asleep. Those few awake seemed to regret that they were. A man in a thousand-dollar suit sat on a beautiful chesterfield chair, drinking cheap whisky and flipping through channels.

"It's on every one, man," he complained. On the screen, an aerial view of some Supers played. I rolled my eyes and snatched the man's whisky. I went to take a swig but paused the bottle against my lips.

Pox.

My Pox was fighting someone—that speedster, probably. Dianna and Tafari were there too. I could see them clearly.

The crawler at the bottom said, "The infamous Artemis and anti-hero terrorists are currently fighting Apex, Mercurial, and Spitfire. Stay tuned for the showdown."

"Who the *fuck* is Spitfire?" I said to the bottle more than to the half-conscious couch-dweller.

"Oh, he's awesome! He breathes fire. He's new but so strong. He's been all over the news," the man said.

I walked closer to the large flat-screen television to see this *Spitfire.* He had blond hair, tan skin, was pretty short, and had a pox scar on his cheek. He was targeting Vincent, whose normal trench coat had been lost to the fire already.

"The...bank robber! That-that's the bank robber," I stammered.

I dropped the whisky, and it shattered against my foot. I felt a bit of glass hit my shin.

This is the man who burned me, the one we locked up. Now he's... HE'S SUPPOSED TO BE THE HERO? I did one good thing...only one, and this is how the world repaid me.

I leaned on their entertainment stand, my heart racing.

A still-drunk man behind me shouted, "Yeah! Fuck him up, Spitfire!"

I whipped around fast enough that my balance was compromised, and I shoved my finger in the man's face.

"You don't know what you're talking about! POX IS A HERO," I said, my voice severe. I heard a reporter mention that the feared and deadly Pox was down, and I spun to look at the TV. I grabbed my phone.

"No one knows what they are talking about!" I yelled.

I'll show them. Someone has to show them.

I googled the Powered Incident alert system and hit the phone number. This time, I didn't hesitate. I jumped, and while I did, I held the two files containing the irrefutable proof I had handed to Xóchi for her to do nothing with. It was up to me.

I sent myself through the full alert system's range. It didn't hurt. I was sure it would hurt. I sent myself out to every connected phone. Twenty-three million pieces of me holding forty-six million copies of those videos went to every person in the tri-state area. Maybe this time my *one heroic deed* would stick.

DIANNA |SOMEWHERE OVER THE OLD HOSPITAL

A vibration in my pocket and a discordant chime distracted me, and I heard a robot voice say out loud, "The National Powered Protection Department has issued a severe warning for this area. Please shelter in place."

All this was followed by the audio of an old video auto-playing. I heard a man snoring and then an explosion.

I was floating above the battlefield. I didn't check the video itself, but I removed my headphones for a moment. I recognized what I was hearing immediately. It was the Frisson video. Mercurial held still, head tilted like a dog at the sound of her own phone alert. I exhaled and loosed an arrow, catching her in her left foot.

"Sorry," I muttered, mostly to myself. As she got pinned to the ground, she screamed. Apex turned his attention to me, a blast charging in his chest. I dropped from my invisible platform, plummeting to the ground just as he fired his laser. It blasted between my head and my shoulder, singing my hair and burning the top of my shoulder. The beam shot into the distance behind me, briefly illuminating the sky.

I hit the ground between Spitfire and Pox. Pox had lost his coat and part of his mask, and the shoulder of his shirt had burned away. I felt the fatigue emanating from him and was sluggish to jump back into my heavenly perch. Spitfire inhaled deep enough for me to hear him.

I turned in time to see fire crackle at his lips and a red-hot metal hand clasp over his mouth on the exhale. The fire slipped through the cracks between Čapek's fingers. He screamed as he lit a portion of his own hair and face on fire.

I pulled Pox up to his feet, then launched back up, bow pointing toward Apex, who was about thirty feet away. I tried to aim at him, but his attention was on Tafari. The two of them were trading blow for blow, each punch cracking louder than thunder. I trained my arrow, bowstring pulled taut, and waited for a clean shot. From my pocket, a man begged for his life as the video on my phone kept playing.

Apex screamed, "I AM A GOD," just as Tafari tackled him to the ground.

"NO!" I shouted, panicked. I'd seen this play out before.

The laser whistled, buzzed, then cracked against Tafari, sending him flying off, toppling head over heels down the field. He lay limp fifty feet away from me.

Spitfire was trying to pull Čapek off of him to no avail. Čapek injected Spitfire with the cure. With Mercurial still pinned, my only priority was Apex. I shot another arrow, but he rolled out of the way. He got to his feet again, and the way he was looking up at me sent a shiver down my spine.

He launched himself at me. I tried to get out of the way, but I was too slow. His fist hit my shoulder with a crack, and I toppled off-balance to the ground. I didn't even register the pain from the first impact by the time the second one came. My body crumpled into the dirt. Apex loomed over me.

"I never did like you, but at least you used to be hot," he said, stomping a foot on my stomach. The pressure of the man's weight on me was unbearable. My ribs cracked, and I heard a popping sound as he increased pressure. I wanted to cough but couldn't. With his weight on me, I couldn't even scream.

Then, just as the edges of my vision were blurring, Pox jumped over me with all his might. He clasped his hand around the much larger man's neck, skin exposed and blistering. The disease spread to the chiseled jaw of the tyrant.

Apex stepped off me and thrashed at the hand on his face, fighting it until he was able to get a grip on Pox's wrist. He used all his strength to throw Pox to the side. I gasped for air and tried to sit up. I felt my mouth fill with blood and coughed out a chunk of something.

As Apex fought to get away, I drew the moonlight bow and fired an arrow. My vision blurred and I blinked, unable to see straight. The darkness was eventually replaced with the image of Apex with a lance through his shoulder, his face marked with blisters. I started to feel woozy and lost the ability to sit up. As I lay back, Čapek jumped over me with another syringe in his metal hand. I could feel my vision fading again, but I could hear Apex panicking and screaming.

"You can't kill me! I'm immortal! I'm a *fucking god!*" he yelled, losing his balance. He fell to his knees first, then toppled forward. The glowing lance caught the ground next to me, and the bulk of the man went limp around it. I heard a haggard, raspy breath exhale, followed by a long silence as the false god fell slowly down the spear to the dirt. The last thing I heard was his body hitting the ground.

XÓCHITL I INSIDE THE OLD HOSPITAL

My phone vibrated against my leg. Leo jumped in reaction to the same thing. Dr. Siu was frozen at the nurse's station, glancing at their phone with their brow furrowed. They took off their headphones, eyes locked on the phone. As soon as their headphones were off, they seemed to lose their balance. In the span of a second, Andy collapsed to the ground. I rushed over and grabbed their wrist and felt for their pulse. A gentle drum beat against my fingers. I was grateful that they had not dropped dead and that I could still see their chest rise and fall in a steady rhythm. They were asleep.

Leo and I laid them out flat, and I took off my coat to cover them and keep them warm. Their phone had fallen next to them on the ground, and the screen had cracked. A severe Powered Incident warning was showing, but above the text a glitching video of Apex killing a guard in Zephyr Tower replaced the widget where the time and details should have been.

"She got the video out! She did it!" I said out loud, even though Leo couldn't hear me. The conversation with the drunk, belligerent App replayed in my head as I reached for the phone.

She must have figured out how to do it safely. She's amazing.

As the video stopped, returning the phone to its default wallpaper, I noticed a single, long cyan hair next to it. The sting in my eyes was dulled by the throbbing in my heart as I realized what she'd done—what *I* told her to do.

She's gone and it's my fault.

I wanted to lie down next to Andy on the cool linoleum and just exist there as I had next to Apricity only a few weeks earlier. I wanted to let the storm pass. I was so, so tired. I saw drops hit the ground before I realized I was crying. Leo put his hand on my shoulder. He looked down, appearing worried, and pointed at Siu before pulling a finger across his neck. I shook my head and stood.

We have to keep going. We have to make this count.

At first, I was worried we had lost our guide, as the doctor was apparently in some kind of slumber. But once I stood up, I noticed something. Thin, gold threads stretched across the room like spiderwebs. In the corner of the hall, the threads snaked down the passage, eventually intertwining with others. They created gold rivers of pulsing light, leading to a hole in the wall. I followed the river, running my fingers against the plaster, and noticed how the tendrils shifted to avoid me. A few reached out to Leo, who was walking behind me. They tangled with his coat but seemed to offer no physical resistance. They were as harmless as beams of light brushing against skin. I wished I could ask him how they felt. Every attempt I made to touch a tendril was dodged as if I were a same-sided magnet repulsing them.

The rivers all merged into a sea of gold. They seemed to have created a tunnel here, and I could see into the bright room beyond. Bricks and drywall were scattered around. I stepped over it all as I approached, pausing outside the room filled with pulsing, golden light to inhale. Then, I stepped through the door.

There was a pressure in the room, as though the light was trying to force my eyes shut and push me backward. Pulsating, kinetic energy pressed on my skin and clothes, but I stepped forward.

I couldn't see—it was too bright. I couldn't hear with my headphones on either. It almost felt as though I had disintegrated, like the version of me I was a moment ago had been absorbed. It wasn't until the impact on my left shoulder from someone tackling me and grabbing for my headphones that I felt real again.

I hit the ground hard, the ache of familiar injuries setting in. I grabbed and pushed at my assailant, able to open my eyes for only a fraction of a second because of the bright light. I tried to push them off of me with my left hand, getting it between me and their chest, putting all the force I could muster into my elbow.

Still they pressed down on me, thrashing and grabbing at my face and hair. I rolled my right shoulder and arm out from under me, and it found purchase at my waist. Grabbing the small pistol Apricity had handed me months ago, I struggled with the holster while it was pinned between me and the ground. My assailant kept scratching at my hair and head with all their might, finally succeeding in ripping off my headphones.

"STOP!"

The voice echoed and reverberated in my mind, and I became limp, my arms heavy at my side. The woman from before—the one in my photo—stood up next to me, straightening out her suit.

As my eyes adjusted to the room, I studied her. Her once-raven hair was still twisted in a knot on her head, but now it was laced with pulsing threads of gold instead of the white streaks it used to have. Her smug face was still that of a young woman, but her dark eyes were replaced with a vibrant gold that emitted pulsating light in sync with the room around us.

"Stand," she said, and my body, bruised and battered as it was, obeyed. She rubbed the back of her neck and rolled her head, tossing my headphones to one side. They clattered to the ground and were quickly knotted over by the tendrils of light, until they vanished, ensnared by the power of the room.

"You caused so much of a headache," she said, sighing and clicking her teeth. "Apex is going to have to be retired. He had such a good run. Do you have any *idea* what a PR nightmare that little stunt with the emergency broadcast system will cause? You have cost me billions, little bug."

The gold threads rippled out from her as she stepped slowly around me.

"And I recognize my voice in you. I hear the echo to go home from that day with Artemis, so that's two of my pantheon you lost me," she said and clicked her tongue again. "What am I supposed to do, huh? Start over? I, of course, could kill you, but you seem too useful an asset for me to just toss away."

My hand was on my holster, and I had been trying to unclasp the simple snap over my gun while maintaining eye contact. The snap made an audible sound. The woman looked me up and down and then laughed.

"No, no. GIVE ME THAT!" she commanded, in a tone one might have used to scold a child. In spite of myself, I handed her the gun, betrayed by my own hands. She was now waving the gun as she thought.

"Hmm. I think I want you on my side. I would rather you obey me, *so*...yes. That's why I took you here at the source, where my voice rings the clearest."

She placed a hand on my shoulder as though we were old friends. Behind her, Leo was shuffling along the perimeter of the room, his back against the wall, waves of gold washing over him. He was inching toward the opposite side, and I hoped the woman hadn't noticed him. I locked eyes on the woman, who was now only inches from my face.

"You want me to obey you? Wouldn't it be better for me to adore you or trust you? Wouldn't you rather I follow you forever out of my own devotion? After all, it was my own orders that got me this far," I said. She turned to look at something I couldn't quite make out on the wall opposite the door and gestured.

"No, no, no, little bug, you don't understand...that's *the* source, the one where it all comes from. It's what I speak for. I am its voice, that little silver box. You're going to open it, and then you're going to gain the power of a god. And you will worship *me*, the proper owner, the person who found it all those years ago and opened it first."

My eyes were transfixed on the wall, and I could see where the pulses of bright light had been coming from. There was a square at the center, so bright it was almost too hard to distinguish against the light behind it.

I looked back at her, pleading, "It won't work for me."

I gestured at my feet where the rivers of the light parted to avoid me. She clicked her teeth in that annoying way and shook her head.

"Look, you're going to *walk to that box and open it* whether it eats you or blesses you. I will not worry about you again," she declared.

My footsteps through the room were difficult. The waves of energy pushed me back and made it feel as though I was walking up a roaring river. My host grew restless. In her odd tone, she said, *"Faster."*

My legs moved faster, and my muscles ached. My cuts reopened and my bruises deepened, but I took another step. It was only five paces across the room, yet each one took seconds that dragged into what felt like hours. I went to put my hand on the lid of the box to lift it, but darkness spread out of the crack, emanating black rays of anti-light that shot out and scattered the gold in the room.

The void washed over me like ink, and I felt a twist in my stomach. I wanted to crumple to the ground. Every touch of the rays felt cold and acidic. My hand cramped up, and every injured part of my body felt like it was being twisted, but the order in my ear kept ringing.

"Open it" echoed through my core. I tried opening the lid, but my finger snapped back, broken as a tendril shot at it. Then another tendril took another finger. My whole hand snapped back, twisted and deformed. I screamed, but still I pushed forward, trying to use my other hand.

I heard laughing from behind me as the darkness continued to consume me, but the lid slammed shut as a familiar hand on top of mine pressed firmly. I heard the tearing sound of paper.

The gold in the room dissipated to dust. Relief washed over me, and I fell to the ground. As the gold light and black ichor disintegrated, the cold light of dawn washed in through a large window. The now-empty box clattered down beside me.

I heard a loud pop and another and then a third. In front of me,

Leo crumpled, a spattering of bullet holes through his leg and stomach. I turned to look at the woman with the magic voice. She was leveling my gun at Leo. Leo stared up at her, his face smirking in what looked like a mirror of my smile, and then he plunged a syringe into his own leg.

The cure.

The woman's eyes widened, and she charged across the room to the box. She opened it and held it upside down, shaking it, but nothing happened. She ripped Leo's headphones off of him, and in an impossibly loud reverberating shriek, she screamed, "WHAT DID YOU DO?"

"I put it in my pocket. Then I sewed it shut permanently," he said with practiced calm. The woman looked past the box at something out the window, her eyes wide with terror, and then she turned and ran.

I scooted toward Leo. There was nothing but blood everywhere. All the gold had evaporated in an instant. I looked out the window and saw Apex impaled on a spear, unmoving. I helped Leo sit up against the wall and tried to put pressure on the bullet wound in his side.

"Xóchi...I did it," he said with a small laugh. His head slumped forward a bit. Out the window, Čapek was holding a limp Pox and marching toward us, Dianna and Tafari shambling after them. I waved, trying to flag them down, but before they got to me, they were backlit with sirens and lights from every kind of emergency vehicle. A megaphone was blaring "HANDS UP," and all the silhouettes stopped to assume the pose of tuning forks.

I opened the window and screamed, "HERE, HELP IN HERE!"

I waited, feeling the blood seep through my fingers and hearing Leo's raspy breath stagger and sputter. I screamed out the window again. I wasn't even sure I formed real words, just screams and sobs.

"PUT YOUR HANDS UP!" a voice shouted. The sound of boots crushing glass came from the doorway as a light blared in my face, and a PPD officer pointed a gun at me.

"He's shot! I'm putting pressure on it," I snapped back. I heard the order repeated, but I just leaned on the wound, blood pooling enough that it was difficult to see my own hands. Then, I heard a pop and a click as something bit into the flesh on my side. Next, there was repeated clicking and the electrical pops of a taser, all sounding so far away as I convulsed and curled up on the ground. I knew my head had hit the steel leg of the table, but I couldn't feel it over the cramping of all my muscles. I locked up tight in a small ball, my vision fading as I was tugged out of position. I was thrown in cuffs and dragged out of the room. EMTs ran past me as I was tossed into the back of a police car.

First responders dragged multiple stretchers past. Dr. Siu was still asleep as another EMT pulled them along. Pox was more of a showcase with five people hurriedly buzzing around the stretcher, performing various medical treatments and tests. As Andy was moved near them, the tempo changed, and they all went about their business in a lackadaisical sort of way. The car I was in started moving before I saw Leo come out of the once-hospital. I saw people in white and blue scrubs run toward him. Everyone moved with frantic energy, and we pulled over to let the ambulance scream past.

"Hold on, please," I whispered to the window. My voice sounded alien to my ears, and speaking felt like coughing up thorns.

They drove me toward the city. My vision blurred, and I slipped into a deep sleep. My heart was heavy as the last scraps of consciousness fell from me.

I expected to wake up in the police station or jail, but found myself in a hospital bed. A nurse was adjusting some medication in the bags of my IV. I jolted to sit up, but I still felt heavy, and my muscles didn't answer as requested.

"Leo," I rasped out as the nurse placed a hand on my shoulder and called out. I felt the cold steel of a handcuff on my wrist.

"She's awake! You're okay, you're okay. If I can get a doctor in here, you're gonna be just fine, honey," she said and smiled at me.

"Leo?" I asked again, wishing my voice could be louder.

"He's okay, you're okay, shh," the woman answered. I felt my face pull into a smile. It was strangely hard to emote. Every movement felt like running a marathon. My eyes closed again, my body weak and numb.

I heard who I thought was Mason say, "PPD, we need to talk to her."

At first, I didn't open my eyes. There were footsteps, and I heard the nurse say from a bit farther away, "She needs a doctor. You all can wait."

I like this nurse.

I made a noise that was supposed to be a laugh, but it came out as a groan from a sharp pain the effort caused in my stomach. I heard some rustling, and then the door slammed. Heavy footsteps drummed toward me. I forced my eyes open, and Mason was standing over me. He looked anxious.

"You never listen," he said, leaning down to take my hand. "For what it's worth, you won every prize but death in this suicide mission. Apex videos were released to everyone within a hundred miles of the city. Someone hacked the PPD alert system.

"Once they were out, people started coming forward—hundreds of victims and survivors who had been hushed or thought they were the only ones. Zephyr's likely to be shut down. Apex is in critical condition and will most likely not live to see a trial. It appears he was responsible for thousands of unauthorized deaths. There's talk of criminalizing vigilantes, mandatory training, and conflict resolution, but who knows if that will stick…

"Which brings me to you. You should be tried with a good dozen felonies, but the average citizen thinks you're the pinnacle of justice."

His words flowed out like water, and it took all my concentration to keep up. I didn't have the energy to respond to it all just yet. Something else was weighing on me.

"Leo? Pox?" I asked hopefully. Mason sighed and sat down in the visitor's chair next to me.

"They're both stable, though your doctor friend hasn't woken up. They seem to only be in a heavy sleep. Everyone seems to have avoided the morgue," he answered. He looked haggard, a frown creasing his face. I could only think of the single blue hair in the background of Siu's phone.

"Mason, would you…would you do me a favor?" I asked. He laughed and put the heel of his hand to his forehead. My face flushed, but I persisted. "Can I talk to Leo?"

I asked him again in a whisper, knowing the answer would be negative, knowing he'd be risking everything to say yes, knowing I already asked too much.

"If you sign this," he said after a long sigh. He pulled a clipboard from his bag. He held it for me as I looked it over.

It was an immunity contract. The PPD would drop all jail sentences and criminal records if, and only if, I become an informant for them.

"What is this for? Why?" I asked.

"You need to sign it, and you need to get Tafari to sign. Leo has already signed. Dianna and Pox have as well. They…they don't know what to do with you yet. This gets you your website back and makes you an independent contractor. Let the politicians sort out what Powered individuals can and cannot do legally, and I think it's a fair deal," Mason explained.

I thought I should have read it more closely, but I didn't. He braced the clipboard for me as I signed a scratchy version of my signature. Even this small action hurt. Mason smiled, took the clipboard, and uncuffed me.

"Your first task is to get Tafari to sign that," he said. I raised an eyebrow as he handed a similar piece of paperwork in a folder to me.

"So, what are you? My handler?" I asked.

He shrugged and squeezed my shoulder.

"Yeah, but I think turnover will be pretty high."

CHAPTER 24
A WARM LIGHT

"SHE TOOK IT FROM ME."

XÓCHITL I ONE YEAR LATER

"After everything I've done for you? You were just going to leave me there?" Apricity's voice called to me from the memory of the day we met. I startled awake, clutching my phone and missing the one who once occupied it.

"Did you say something back there?" Tafari called from the cab.

"In a quarter mile, take Exit 6. Merge on-to I-270 west to-war-ds Bould-er," the GPS said. It called out the directions in jumbled jolts as it connected and disconnected from service.

"May need a navigator if you're awake," Tafari said.

I swung my feet over the edge of the bunk and stood in the aisle. In three short steps, I poured burnt black coffee from a discount machine into my cup. I glanced up at the fridge magnet with Dianna's and my brother's faces on it. A photo they paid someone other than me to take, it seemed stiff and forced. He was holding her from behind, chin resting on her shoulder. Along the bottom, it read "Save the Date" in an elegant script and "6-22-24." It had been a few weeks since he'd called, and even last I was in the city he didn't have time for me. He was focusing on rebuilding his business as a brick-and-mortar café and planning the wedding, but I recognized that the coldness between us was my fault. I had his last café blown up by an evil Super villain, and he got so hurt that his new café needed to be built with his wheelchair in mind. I took a sip of the bitter burnt coffee. It tasted how I felt, and I considered giving up on coffee altogether.

A bump in the road knocked me slightly off-balance, and the coffee sloshed over my hand, splattering on the ground. I stumbled toward the cab of the truck. The GPS put us twenty minutes or so from our destination in Colorado, and the view out over the dashboard did not disappoint.

Snowy fields leading to white-capped mountains looked like something out of any Christmas special.

"For purple mountains majesty," I sang and giggled.

"Those are the Rockies, and they look more blue and white to me," Tafari retorted.

"It's an expression! You know…the song?"

I laughed, taking a sip from the coffee, then plopped in the passenger side bucket seat. I pulled out my phone from my pocket, and a man's file filled the screen.

"So this guy in Boulder, he's dangerous?" Tafari asked.

"Take exit si—" the GPS started to say, cutting off halfway through. I skimmed the notes on the phone. Pox had written the case report and sent the note, "Please get this one for me. I don't want to leave Andy for that long."

Though there had been no changes in the doctor's sleep, Pox had visited them daily regardless of his own obligations and increasing fame. On several occasions, despite direct orders, he could be found by their side during the brief visitation window allowed by the hospital.

"Pox seems to think this will take a while," I said. "Think he'll take the cure? Willingly, I mean."

"Eh, no, not exactly…but he's hurting people, so we have to change his mind on the matter," Tafari said. There was an audible crunch as his hand crackled and morphed into a metallic version of itself.

"Don't get too excited. I don't want to replace the steering wheel…again."

He threw an empty gum packet at me in response, grinning as it bounced off my cheek and into my coffee nesting in the cup holder.

"Continue on to US-thirty-six-we—"

"—Xóchi!?"

The GPS's cold, familiar, robot voice cut out and was replaced by a voice, warped slightly by interference crackling through the speakers. The screen glitched and fragmented into crystallized rectangles of cyan and magenta. A black silhouette of a girl with long hair, heavily artifacted and crystallized in large, pixelated blocks, appeared for a moment.

"I found you, I finally found you," the GPS said in the voice of Apricity.

Startled, Tafari swerved and pulled to the shoulder of the road.

"What the hell was that!?"

"You heard it too? APP!! Can you hear me, Apricity!? I'm here! I'm right here!" I screamed. I slammed on the screen in the dashboard, turning the volume all the way up. Squinting into the glowing screen, her form solidified.

"I will be there soon," her voice said, sweet and hopeful.

Tears streamed down my face. She wasn't gone. I hadn't lost her. And just as the thought appeared, she was gone.

The GPS screen flickered from cyan to black, then restored the map.

"GPS signal lost. Reconnecting…"

Thank you for reading! Did you enjoy? Please add your review because nothing helps an author more and encourages readers to take a chance on a book than a review.

Don't miss more from Ariel Dominelli coming soon, and see her drawings of the characters on the next page.

And then read <u>CINDERS OF YESTERDAY</u> by City Owl Author, Jen Karner. Keep going for a sneak peek!

You can also sign up for the City Owl Press newsletter to receive notice of all book releases!

Leo

Xochi

Apricity

Dr. Andy
Sui

Daianna

Pox

Taatari

SNEAK PEEK OF CINDERS OF YESTERDAY

For some people, comfort came from a hot cup of coffee and a warm blanket wrapped tight against the cold. For the hunter, it had always been adrenaline, the thrill of a fight, a blade in her hand, and a smile that promised death to the wicked.

Anyone else would have turned back two miles ago when the sun still hung low in the sky and they could see the trails ahead clearly. In the misty rain and fading light the deep furrows in the ground were almost invisible, almost. Dani stopped at a tree torn in half and looked for tracks. For months a monster had been slicing its way through hikers, and she was here to stop it.

Exhilaration pulsed through her. She hadn't felt this alive in a long time, not since Alabama and the fire and everything that followed. She was doing her job, not looking back over her shoulder for signs she was being followed.

Most hunters didn't tussle with the talented, humans with unique abilities and internal reservoirs of power and magic. The problem being that when they went bad, they turned into something else and evolved into monsters. Like the one that had murdered her partner, Graham, in front of her.

She'd needed a run-of-the-mill job, and tracking down a talented gone wrong was right up her alley. Dani chuckled darkly. Hunting a monster in the rainy woods—totally normal way to decompress from too much stress.

An inhuman screech cracked through the air, and she stopped short. Dani looked like Mortimer's type: young, dark haired, and alone. Then again, the shotgun probably ruined the look. She licked at her lips, trying not to let the grin threatening at the edge of her mouth take over. He wanted her alone and afraid, and off the beaten path in the woods. She'd give him that to look him in the eye and be sure everything that had been human in him had burned away. Then she could blow him away and leave his bones for whatever animals were living up here. Talented this far gone had a habit of more less dissolving when you killed them, proving they were more monster than human.

As she slinked through the trees, her thoughts drifted to the monster who had ripped the life from Graham. Spectre. He was as old and as nasty as they came. Far as she could tell, far as every hunter she knew could tell, Spectre's ass just couldn't be killed. But Mortimer? Him, she could put down, keep someone else from feeling what she endured each morning when she woke up and her partner was still dead.

"Little girl get lost?" a hoarse voice croaked from behind her.

Dani stopped in her tracks. Every muscle quivered, the moment between action and inaction. The rain coated her skin in a cool blanket. She counted her heartbeats. One. She held the shotgun steady in her hands, and she shifted her weight to her back foot. Two. She pivoted, swinging the barrel up so she could look right down the sight. Three. Stock braced against her shoulder, she looked into the dark eyes of Mortimer Byrant as he growled at her. Where irises should have been, only dark pools of cold fire remained. There was nothing human left inside them. Her finger curled over the trigger, and she bared her teeth in a vicious smile.

"Oh, sugar. I'm not lost."

The modified shotgun with its riot magazine of ten rounds kicked like a mule. She racked it as his chest exploded in a spray of crimson. He snarled as the impact threw him back. One of his clenched fists transformed into a deadly blade of bone as he lurched back to his feet. He charged at her, but Dani was waiting. She fired again, racking another round into the chamber as he was thrown backwards again.

Dani stepped forward with every shot as the slugs tore his body apart and forced him back, step by step. That was the way she wanted it—keep him at a distance, far enough away he couldn't touch her, close enough that each slug tore him more to pieces. Five rounds in and he hit the dirt. Six and the light went out of his eyes. But some lessons got learned early. You always kill them a little bit more. She kept firing until the shotgun clicked empty and nothing remained but a mass of flesh and bone sinking into the mud.

The thing that had been his arm, or a weapon, or both, didn't shift back as he died. Happened that way sometimes if a talented was corrupted enough. Dani smiled, a predator's smile, more to warn things off than to invite them in. It took a few minutes, but as his body cooled, the power inside him ate away at the flesh. She spat on the ground next to it as it smoked away, leaving a bed of grey ash.

Trekking back down the path took forever, the dark and the rain combining to make a treacherous hike back to the truck. She ducked inside and settled the shotgun onto the rack behind the empty passenger seat. Graham's seat. Memories of his eyes going dark surrounded by fire washed over her, and she forced them away. While killing Mortimer had felt good, it hadn't been enough. Each monster she felled only reminded her of the one she couldn't kill, the one whose blood she ached for. She couldn't will Graham alive again, or erase his murder, but she could hunt down the son of a bitch that had done the deed.

She had to stop filling the void with the death of other monsters. It was time to stop running from Spectre.

But how do I kill a necromancer? Dani had worked every lead, talked to anyone who claimed to have any information, everyone, except for the one man she needed to speak to. A single name kept coming back up who might have details on something to help. Just so happened it was the same person she didn't want to face.

Joe's Grill, the last hunter hub she hadn't checked in with, was three hundred miles away, and his name the final one on her list.

At least she hadn't done so since before Alabama when Spectre had murdered Graham in front of Dani's eyes while she was helpless to do anything. But there were no more options. He might have the intel on Spectre she needed, like how to kill him for good.

She had to talk to Joe.

It was time to go home.

Don't stop now. Keep reading with your copy of <u>CINDERS OF YESTERDAY</u> available now.

Don't more from Ariel Dominelli coming soon! Until then, discover CINDERS OF YESTERDAY, by City Owl Author, Jen Karner!

Paranormal Hunter Dani Black wants nothing more than revenge. Until she meets Emilie.

A year ago, the rogue Necromancer Spectre murdered her partner during a hunt gone wrong. She's been looking for a way to kill him —and keep him dead—ever since.

When rumors of a weapon capable of killing anything surfaces in Dawson, Maryland, she sets out on a mission to get her hands on it. While unraveling a web of clues about her own past, Dani runs into the alluring Emilie Lockgrove, eldest daughter of a magical family inexplicably tied to Spectre.

Emilie Lockgrove survived the catastrophic fire that killed her mother and hospitalized both her and her sister.

Ten years later, she has returned to Dawson, expecting to confront the trauma of her past. Instead, she discovers magic is real, encountering actual ghosts like the necromancer hunting her family for 200 years.

Dani intends to kill Spectre…or die trying. Emilie wants to reclaim her life. To survive, they'll need to work together to confront their pasts, break the spell capturing Emilie's magic, and destroy Spectre once and for all.

Please sign up for the City Owl Press newsletter for chances to win special subscriber-only contests and giveaways as well as receiving information on upcoming releases and special excerpts.

All reviews are **welcome** and **appreciated**. Please consider leaving one on your favorite social media and book buying sites.

Escape Your World. Get Lost in Ours! City Owl Press at www.cityowlpress.com.

ACKNOWLEDGMENTS

I am Dyslexic. As a young child, I wanted to be a writer, but it never seemed possible. I learned to draw, hoping to make it in comics to be at least a part of fiction. In 2022 I had an identity crisis; I was a broke, queer, single mom working as a barista, and I decided enough was enough--I'll just write. Maybe it will be bad, Maybe no one will read it, but I have to try. To my delight and surprise, Lisa Green, my fantastic editor, read and liked my manuscript. Her hard work and dedication turned my idea into a readable form, and I will always be grateful for her.

Thank you to the folks at Owl City for taking a chance on a new author. I'll do my best to make it worth your time. It's my first book. Wait till you see the next one!

Thank you, Maya Kern, for employing me and treating me as a peer even though, by all rights, you have more experience and talent in your pinky toe than I have in my whole body. I will catch up one day and earn all that respect you have given me.

And thank you, Ollin. You're too young to read this, but you being the best kid in the world, has made waking up every day a joy instead of a chore.

To the rest of my family, skip chapter 13 if you want a mild experience.

Thanks to everyone who reads. I can not believe this is real. Thank you.

ABOUT THE AUTHOR

 ARIEL DOMINELLI lives in Troy, N.Y., with her two dogs, Totoro (large) And Pippin (small), and her son Ollin. She writes Fantasy, sci-fi, and romance and draws as much as she writes, but mostly she drinks coffee and daydreams. Other hobbies include sword fighting and making weird medieval things. *Storm Chaser* is her debut novel.

 twitter.com/NotOkayGuys
instagram.com/NotOkayGuys

ABOUT THE PUBLISHER

City Owl Press is a cutting edge indie publishing company, bringing the world of romance and speculative fiction to discerning readers.

Escape Your World. Get Lost in Ours!

www.cityowlpress.com

facebook.com / CityOwlPress
twitter.com / cityowlpress
instagram.com / cityowlbooks
pinterest.com / cityowlpress
tiktok.com / @cityowlpress